U0039195

聊齋誌異一百段

100 PASSAGES FROM STRANGE STORIES OF LIAOZHAI

一百叢書 ㉛

漢英對照Chinese-English

王娟 編譯

100

PASSAGES FROM

STRANGE STORIES

OF LIAOZHAI

聊齋誌異一百段

臺灣商務印書館發行

《一百叢書》總序

　　本館出版英漢(或漢英)對照《一百叢書》的目的,是希望憑藉着英、漢兩種語言的對譯,把中國和世界各類著名作品的精華部分介紹給中外讀者。

　　本叢書的涉及面很廣。題材包括了寓言、詩歌、散文、短篇小說、書信、演說、語錄、神話故事、聖經故事、成語故事、名著選段等等。

　　顧名思義,《一百叢書》中的每一種都由一百個單元組成。以一百為單位,主要是讓編譯者在浩瀚的名著的海洋中作挑選時有一個取捨的最低和最高限額。至於取捨的標準,則是見仁見智,各有心得。

　　由於各種書中被選用的篇章節段,都是以原文或已被認定的範本作藍本,而譯文又經專家學者們精雕細琢,千錘百煉,故本叢書除可作為各種題材的精選讀本外,也是研習英漢兩種語言對譯的理想參考書,部分更可用作朗誦教材。外國學者如要研習漢語,本書亦不失為理想工具。

商務印書館(香港)有限公司

編輯部

前　言

　　《聊齋誌異》成書於清代初年，是中國古代文言短篇小説的傑出代表。自成書至今，風行兩百多年，被稱為文言短篇小説的"空前絕後之作"。由此可見此書在中國文學史上的地位。

一

　　蒲松齡出生於明代崇禎十三年（1640），卒於清代康熙五十四年（1715）年，字留仙，號劍臣，別號柳泉居士。山東省淄川縣蒲家莊人。蒲松齡排行第三，自幼隨其父研讀詩書，由於天性穎慧，經史子集均能過目不忘，因而深得父親鍾愛（蒲箬〈柳泉公行述〉）。順治八年，蒲松齡十二歲時，其父亡故。十八歲時，娶妻劉氏。劉氏性情溫謹，樸訥寡言。過門後，不僅夫妻感情篤厚，而且婆媳關係也十分融洽。但是婆婆對劉氏的喜愛卻招來了其他媳婦的嫉妒，不得已，蒲松齡只好分家獨過。身居簡陋，薄產也不足自給，只得"賣文為活"（蒲松齡〈述劉氏行錄〉）。

　　蒲松齡十九歲"初應童子試，即以縣、府、道三第一，補博士弟子員"（張元〈柳泉蒲先生墓表〉）。受知於學使施愚山，文名籍甚。施愚山是當時的一位名士。他對蒲松齡非常賞識。在《聊齋誌異·胭脂》一篇中，蒲松齡對施愚山的評價很高，表現了他對施愚山的仰慕之情。入泮的

第二年，他便和同鄉李希梅、張歷友等摰友建立了郢中詩
社。把盞吟詩，寄興風雅。此後，蒲松齡曾多次參加科
考，但都以失敗而告終。在他三十一歲的時候，曾應同邑
進士孫蕙之邀協辦文案，辭家遠遊。兩年之後，蒲松齡對
乏味無聊的幕賓生活非常厭倦，也無意繼續那種寄人籬
下、仰人鼻息的生活，再加上對故鄉的思念，因此辭官返
回家鄉。為了謀生，他來到同邑名人西鋪畢際有家設館，
在那裏度過了三十年的教學生活。《聊齋誌異》的作品大部
分都是在此時寫成的。

　　四十八歲時，蒲松齡又一次參加了鄉試，但由於答卷
不符合八股文的規定格式而被黜。三年後，蒲松齡又再次
應試，雖然主司已經打算取他為第一名，但由於健康的緣
故，未能參加二場，主司深為惋惜。命運不濟使蒲松齡心
灰意懶，完全放棄了繼續參加科考的念頭。康熙四十八年
(1710)蒲松齡結束了他的教書生涯，撤帳回家。雖然簡居
素食，卻也自得其樂。兩年之後，七十二歲高齡的蒲松齡
補了一個歲貢生。康熙五十二年(1713)，夫人劉氏去世，
這對蒲松齡的打擊非常之大。因為妻子不僅是一位安貧守
賤、勤儉持家、相夫教子的賢內助，她可以説又是蒲松齡
的一位知己。在一種淒楚悲涼的心境下，兩年之後，也就
是1715年，蒲松齡去世，享年七十六歲。

　　蒲松齡一生著作頗豐，除了《聊齋誌異》之外，還包括
文、詩、詞、戲曲、俚曲、鼓詞、韻曲和雜著等。如《聊齋
文集》、《聊齋詞集》、《聊齋詩集》、《婚嫁全書》、《日

用俗字》、《農桑經》等等。《聊齋誌異》傾注了蒲松齡一生的心血，是他的代表作。

<h2 style="text-align:center">二</h2>

蒲松齡是一位非常有責任感的知識分子，滿懷報國治世的政治願望，並希望通過科舉進仕，實現兼濟天下的志向。但他的仕途卻被八股的格套無情地封鎖了。因此，他把自己的失望、鬱悶、悲憤和感慨，以及滿懷的志向都寄託在創作之中。留下了這部"孤憤之書"（蒲松齡〈聊齋自誌〉）。

蒲松齡是一位傳統道德倫理觀念的維護者，"提倡良知、悟徹，贊成天人合一，主張道德的自我完善，也就是說要使儒、釋、道三教在他所幻想的、純美的、理想化的思想、道德、精神境界上，得到統一"（李厚基、韓海明《人鬼狐妖的藝術世界》）。蒲松齡的這種思想一方面來源於他對社會的觀察。面對百姓困苦的生活，社會道德的淪喪，官府的腐敗，和暴吏的肆虐，蒲松齡在他的《聊齋誌異》中大膽地提出了許多發人深省的社會問題，而且還試圖運用道德的手段如"因果報應"、"人做孽，天報應"等來解決這些問題。另一方面，這種思想可能和他幾乎一生從事教書有關。教書育人，不僅要傳授知識，而且要宣揚道德，傳授做人的道理。因此，"勸善懲惡"便成為蒲松齡思想的中心。

既然不能通過以科取仕來實現自己以"仁心德政"教化民心的願望，蒲松齡轉而尋找其他途徑來實現自己的抱負，完成自己的責任。於是他借助"憤抑無聊"之筆，"警發薄俗，扶樹道教"，發揮道德勇氣，以盡知識分子對人類應盡的責任，其成果便是《聊齋誌異》一書（羅敬文《蒲松齡及其聊齋誌異》）。蒲箬在他的〈祭父文〉中也談到，《聊齋誌異》"大抵皆憤抑無聊，借以抒勸善懲惡之心，非為談諧調笑已也"。民間故事傳說，作為口頭民俗學的一個重要類型，其主要內容之一，便是借助於"天、仙、神、鬼"的或獎或懲來"勸善懲惡"。民間故事傳說是民間大眾以口耳相傳的途徑，傳授道德倫理觀念、信仰，推廣修心立性知識和分辨善惡美醜能力，確立社會行為規範，在民眾的生活之中佔有重要的地位。民間故事傳說短小精悍，生動活潑，通俗易懂，是文化傳統得以傳播、保存和功能得以實現的一個重要載體。在民間故事傳說裏，蒲松齡似乎找到了自己不僅可以做，而且還大有可為的天地。因此，他開始廣泛地搜集民間故事傳說。關於蒲松齡的寫作目的，劉東侯曾談到：

> 鄙則以為柳泉之志，實在提倡道德。……蓋徑言道德，人或目為陳腐而不加意。故多為寓言，凡鳥獸蟲魚木石花草，胥納之於父子兄弟夫婦朋友倫常之中。目前之事情，恒幻而為空中之樓閣，遂使人賞其新奇而殺於瀏覽。觀其自序云："寄託如此，亦足悲矣！"則柳泉之志，其果在搜神談鬼也乎？（劉東侯〈聊齋誌異仁人傳序〉）

《聊齋誌異》的創作正是來源於作者對民間故事傳說的

喜愛,以及對民間故事傳說的地位、功能和意義的認識,蒲松齡曾談到:

才非干寶,雅愛搜神;情類黃州,喜人談鬼。聞則命筆,遂以成編。久之,四方同人,又以郵筒相寄,因而物以好聚,所積益夥(〈聊齋誌異自序〉)。

據鄒弢的〈三借廬筆談〉所記:

相傳先生居鄉里,落拓無偶,性尤怪僻,為村中童子師,食貧自給,不求於人。作此書時,每臨晨,攜一大瓷甖,中貯苦茗,具淡巴菰一包,置行人大道旁,下陳蘆襯,坐於上,煙茗置身畔。見行道者過,必強執與語,搜奇說異,隨人所知。渴則飲以茗,或奉以煙,必令暢談乃已。偶聞一事,歸而粉飾之。如是二十餘寒暑,此書方告蕆,故筆法超絕。

真公氏所撰〈蒲留仙與聊齋誌異〉也有如下的記載:

他搜集材料的方法,夏天選擇涼爽的地方,如豆棚瓜架,物背樹陰之下;冬天則在簷下曝太陽的處所。備有茶煙;招待那些過路的村夫野老,行旅小販,以及三教九流,評書賣唱的各色人等,從容休憩。一面談天,他一一記下來,加以剪裁潤飾,寫成了一篇篇的故事。

蒲松齡為民間故事傳說加工、潤飾、改編和再創作,完成了這部膾炙人口的傑作。

三

《聊齋誌異》的主旨是宣揚道德倫理。蒲松齡認為，"政莫急於民命，化莫先於倫常"，"蓋倫常者，生民之大命也"（〈為許邑侯募修明倫堂疏〉）。因此，《聊齋誌異》"諸多篇目，顯示出家庭以至倫理的可貴。故事中若無這些倫理道德的充實，則必然缺乏中心主題，其內容也必然乏善可陳，甚至索然無味。因而《誌異》的所以能傳頌古今，流播中外，即是其深且雄厚的道德力量"（羅敬文〈蒲松齡及其聊齋誌異〉）。如〈孝子〉，〈席方平〉，〈商三官〉，〈于江〉等篇中的主人公有以利刃割肉為母治病的周順亭；有遍遊冥界，嘗盡各種酷刑，誓死為父伸冤的席方平；有喬裝改扮，怒殺殺父仇人的"俠女"商三官，這些人物的行為不僅受到了世人的肯定，而且還感天動地，並由此而獲得了超自然力量的佑護。蒲松齡在他的《聊齋誌異》中充分肯定了這些人物。相反，對那些不孝的人及其行為，作者予以強烈的抨擊。〈杜小雷〉中的那位虐待婆婆的婦人最終就化為了"豕"，遭了報應。

除了宣揚"孝"以外，蒲松齡還推崇忠、義、仁、誠、信。忠、義、仁、誠、信是中國社會人際交往關係的準則，也是每一位正人君子必須具備的品性。《聊齋誌異》讚美和肯定了〈張不量〉的"仁"、〈喬女〉的"忠"、〈斫蟒〉的"德義"。不僅人類需要這些美德，就是動物也不例外，相反，它們往往比人做得更好。如〈義犬〉、〈義鼠〉、〈趙城虎〉、〈鴻〉、〈毛大福〉中的“狼”等。一旦人們喪失了這些品德，他們的行為就會受到懲罰，遭到報應。如〈罵鴨〉中盜食鄰人鴨子的某君，渾身長滿了鴨毛；〈瞳人語〉中好色的方棟變成了瞎子；〈種梨〉中吝嗇的賣梨人最終失去了所有的梨子。另外，始亂終棄的“南三复”（〈竇氏〉），嫌貧愛富的“姐姐”（〈姊妹易嫁〉），荒淫無度的“和尚”（〈僧孽〉），喜新厭舊的“景星”（〈阿霞〉）等人都受到了他們應得的報應。

對官府的腐敗，貪官污吏暴戾行徑的揭露和諷刺也是《聊齋誌異》的主要內容之一。〈席方平〉中的冥府，上至冥王，下至郡司、城隍、乃至衙役相互勾結，殘害百姓，製造了一起又一起的冤案。在〈潞令〉、〈放蝶〉、〈鳥語〉、〈祿數〉、〈王者〉等篇中，蒲松齡借助於超自然的力量使得這些魚肉百姓的邪惡行為受到了嚴厲的懲罰。

歌頌愛情和友情是《聊齋誌異》的重頭戲。這裏有人與人之間的感情，如〈姊妹易嫁〉、〈胭脂〉、〈喬女〉等；有人與狐之間的感情，如〈青鳳〉、〈嬰寧〉等；有人與鬼之間的感情，如〈聶小倩〉、〈陸判〉等；還有人與其他異類之間的戀情，如〈綠衣女〉中的人與蜜蜂等。這些作品大都以女性作為主角和頌揚的對象，在蒲松齡的筆下，這些女主人公雖然都是些非人的鬼、狐、仙、妖，但她們美麗、多情、善良、堅強、正直、勇敢。對愛情忠貞不渝，對朋友重情重義。成功地塑造了一大批女性形象是《聊齋誌異》得以廣泛流傳的又一重要因素。

另外，《聊齋誌異》還有一些關於明清時期的民風、民俗、民間信仰和觀念的記錄。如〈鏡聽〉、〈龍〉、〈餺飥媼〉、〈雷公〉、〈鹿銜草〉、〈四十千〉、〈某公〉等。還有一些趣聞軼事，如〈蘇仙〉、〈小官人〉、〈鴝鵒〉、〈狼〉等。這些都對我們了解明清社會生活具有一定的意義。

本書在對《聊齋誌異》篇目的選擇上，主要是從"宣揚道德倫理"、"表現人與人、與鬼、與狐、與仙和與其他異類的愛情和友情"、"揭露和諷刺貪官污吏的殘暴"、"表現民間風俗、信仰和奇聞趣事"、"動物故事"等幾個方面中，選出了一些譯者認為比較有代表意義的篇目。尤其是那些以往經常被人們忽視的有關風俗信仰的短篇，譯者也選了一些。《聊齋誌異》中還有一些反映歷史事件，自然災害等內容的篇章，限於篇幅，譯者沒有收入。另外，由於《聊齋誌異》中的一些精品如〈勞山道士〉、〈瑞雲〉、〈石清虛〉、〈促織〉等已收入《一百叢書》中的其他書籍之內，這裏就不再選錄了。在古文注釋和英文翻譯方面，如有不妥之處，懇望讀者不吝賜教。

王　娟

一九九八年七月

PREFACE

Strange Stories of Liaozhai was written during the beginning of the Qing Dynasty. It is a representative collection of Chinese classical short stories. For more than two hundred years, it has been regarded as an "unprecedented and ultimate work" in Chinese literary history.

I

Pu Songling, its author, was born in 1640 and died in 1715. He was a native of Pujia Village, Zichuan County, Shandong Province, and the third son of the Pu family. He began to study the Confucian classics with his father when he was still a child. Being talented and intelligent, he could learn the works by heart after reading them once. As a result, his father was very fond of him. When he was 12 years old, his father died. Pu married Miss Liu at the age of 18. Liu was gentle, kind, simple and taciturn. After the marriage, the couple had a deep affection for each other. At the same time, Liu also had a good relationship with her mother-in-law. However, other daughters-in-law of the Pu family were jealous of their mother-in-law's fondness of Liu. Finally, the Pu family broke up and lived apart. Pu Songling and his family resided in a humble house. Since the land allotted to him was infertile and unable to produce enough food for the family, Pu spent almost his lifetime to make a living as a teacher.

At the age of 19, Pu took the imperial examination at the county level, came first and made his name. Shi Yushan, a famous scholar at that time, admired Pu's talent. Pu also highly appraised Shi and expressed his respect for him in the tale of "A Girl Called Rouge". The next year, Pu and his good friends founded a poet's society. They often met in the club, drinking and composing poems together. Later, Pu took the imperial examination at a higher level several times , but all attempts failed. At the age of 31, at the invitation of his friend, Sun Hui, a successful candidate in the highest imperial examination, Pu left home and assisted Sun in his public office. Two years later, he was tired of being an assistant and living under someone else's roof. Besides he was also homesick. So he quitted the job and went back home. In order to support his family, he worked as a teacher in the family of a celebrity named Bi Jiyou. Pu spent thirty years there, and most of his works were written during that period.

When Pu was 48, he took the imperial examination again. However, he was disqualified merely because his answers to the exam paper did not accord with the standard form of the "eight-part essay". Three years later, he took the exam once more. Though the chief examiner had decided to put him in the first position, he was unable to take the second round of the exam for health reasons. Pu was dispirited by his bad luck and finally gave up the idea of taking the imperial examination continually. In 1710, Pu retired, returned home, and really began to enjoy a simple life. Two years later, he was conferred the title of *gongsheng*[1] at the age of 72. In 1713, his wife died, which broke his heart as she was a very good wife who was content with poverty, industrious and thrifty in housekeeping, and who looked after her husband and children very well and thoroughly understood her husband. Another two years later in 1715, Pu died at the age of 76, with a sad and dreary heart.

During his lifetime, Pu Songling wrote many works besides *Strange Stories of Liaozhai*, such as many articles, poems, dramas, popular music, lyrics and miscellaneous essays. Better known works include *Collected Works of Liaozhai, Collected Poems of Liaozhai, Collected Ci of Liaozhai, A Book of Marraige, Colloquial Expressions in Daily Use,* etc. *Strange Stories of Liaozhai* is the result of his lifetime effort and his representative work.

II

Pu Songling was a scholar with a great sense of

---

1. *gongsheng* : the successful candidate who passed the imperial examination at the county level and was recommended to enter the imperial college.

responsibility. He was imbued with the political wish of dedicating himself to the service of his country and the people. He hoped to pursue an official career through taking imperial examinations, so that he could do good to society. However, his hopes were shattered only because of the old rigid form of the "eight-part essay". So he placed his disappointment, depression, grief, indignation and aspirations in his writings and left us his great work.

Pu was a guardian of traditional moral principles. He advocated the ideas of conscience and enlightenment, unity of man and nature and self-improvement in morality. In other words, he looked for the fusion of Confucian, Buddhist and Taoist ideals on conceptual, moral and spiritual planes. On the one hand, his ideas came from his own life experiences. He understood common people's difficulties and hardships. He saw the decay of social morals, government corruption and the bureaucrats' inhumanity. In his *Strange Stories of Liaozhai*, he revealed many social problems which called for deep thought. He saw morality as a means to solve these problems and believed in such ideas as retribution and "heaven will punish bad people". On the other hand, his thoughts could possibly be related to his lifetime career as a teacher. He believed that a teacher should not only impart knowledge but also inculcate morality and teach people how to behave themselves. Hence, "encouraging people to do good and punishing the evil-doer" became the centre of his thoughts.

Since there was no way that Pu could obtain an official position, he was unable to realize his ambition of educating people through benevolent rule. So he began to seek other ways to fulfil his wishes. *Strange Stories of Liaozhai* was the result of that purpose. Pu used his pen as his weapon to promote healthy tendencies and combat unhealthy ones. Pu's son once said that his father's work was not just for people's entertainment, but to put over his idea of "encouraging people to do good and punishing the evil-doer" by means of stories. Folk tales and legends are important forms of folklore by word of mouth, and their themes are often related to how heaven, the gods, ghosts and spirits "reward the good and punish the evil". Hence they have the function of promoting moral principles, beliefs and various kinds of knowledge, and establishing social norms. They occupy a significant place in people's lives and are important carriers of cultural traditions. These stories are short and pithy, terse and forceful, vivid and vigorous, popular and easy to understand. Pu saw in them the right forms that he could employ for his own purposes, and so he began to collect folk tales and legends extensively.

Regarding Pu's intention of writing *Strange Stories of Liaozhai*, Liu Donghou once said he believed that Pu meant to advocate morality. If one talked about morality directly, people would see it as clichéd and pedantic. So Pu employed allegory, incorporating morality among parents, sons, brothers, friends, and husband and wives into stories of animals, plants and things of nature. People would be educated while they were reading those fascinating stories. In the foreword to his work, Pu remarked that it was really sad that he had to carry out his wishes this way. Obviously, Pu did not just collect and write stories of gods and ghosts for their own sake.

Pu liked folk tales and legends and realized their function and significance in society. He once said, "I do not have the talents of Ganbo[2]. But I like to collect tales of mystery and the supernatural. Like Su Dongpo[3], I love listening to ghost stories and whenever I hear them, I will write them down. In the lapse of time, learning that I have this habit, friends of all kinds send me a lot of tales. So my collection grows very fast."

Zou Tao described how Pu collected tales and legends in the following words: "It was said that Pu lived in a village.

---

2. Ganbo: a famous writer in the Northern and Southern Dynasties. His famous book, *Story of Mysteries and the Supernatural*, is one of the works that marked the beginning of the Chinese novel.

3. Su Dongpo: a famous poet in the Song Dynasty.

He was eccentric and had no friends. He was the teacher of the village children. Though he was poor, he never asked others for help. While he was writing *Strange Stories of Liaozhai*, he would sit by the roadside, bringing with him a big pot of tea and some tobacco. Whenever he saw a passer-by, he would talk to him and gather strange tales from him. He would provide tea and tobacco for the person and encourage him to talk freely. Occasionally when Pu heard an interesting story, he would return home and rewrite it. For twenty years, Pu kept on collecting tales like this and finally finished this great work."

Zhen Gong also had a similar record. He wrote as follows: "The way Pu collected materials for his work was first to select nice and cool places in summer, such as the shade of trees or trellises, and warm places in winter, such as places exposed to the sun. He would supply tea and tobacco to passers-by that included villagers, travellers, pedlars, entertainers and people of all sorts. Through chatting with them, he wrote down what he had heard and created many stories."

Pu wrote, rewrote and re-created the folk tales and legends, and finished this widely loved work of *Strange Stories of Liaozhai*.

III

The purpose of *Strange Stories of Liaozhai* then is to

promote morals and ethics, which Pu believed were the foundation of society. Hence, many stories in the book highly value the family, morals and ethics. Without such themes, the book would be flat and insipid, devoid of a central subject. The reason why the book becomes so popular lies in its moral force. In stories such as "A Filial Son", "Xi Fangping", "A Brave Girl Named Shang Sanguan" and "Yu Jiang", there are Zhou Shunting, who cuts a piece of his own flesh to cure his mother's sickness; Xi Fangping, who travels the underworld and suffers all kinds of cruel tortures in order to redress the injustices done to his father; Shang Sanguan, a brave girl who disguises herself as a man and kills the murderer of her father. The acts of these characters not only win the approval of the public, but also move the gods and spirits and gain their support and protection. On the contrary, unfilial people and behaviour are attacked. For example, the unfilial daughter-in-law in "A Man Named Du Xiaolei" is punished and turned into a pig.

Besides filial piety, Pu also highly praised qualities like loyalty, righteousness, benevolence, sincerity and trustworthiness which served as the yardstick for all human relationships and were the essential qualities of the gentleman. In *Strange Stories of Liaozhai*, Pu praises characters such as Zhang Buliang, who is benevolent to his village neighbours; Qiao's daughter, who is loyal to her friend; the younger brother in "Fighting Off a Python", who shows his moral courage. Animals in this book also possess these virtues, and they even do better than humans, as seen in "A Loyal Dog", "The Tiger of Zhao City", "A Faithful Rat", "Doctor Mao Dafu" and "A Wild Goose". People who have lost these qualities are punished. For instance, the person who has stolen and eaten his neighbour's duck is penalized with duck down growing on his skin ("The Man Who Stole a Duck"). Fang Dong, who followed beautiful girls at their heels, is punished with blindness ("The Talking Pupils"). The stingy pear vendor has all his pears taken away and shared as a punishment ("Planting a Pear Tree"). Other bad people including Nan Sanfu, who seduces a girl and abandons her ("A Girl Named Dou"); the snobbish elder sister ("Two Sisters"); the dissolute monk ("A Sinful Monk"), and Jing Xing, who loves the new and loathes the old and divorces his wife ("A Girl Named A'xia"), all get the punishment they deserve.

In *Strange Stories of Liaozhai*, Pu exposes the corruption of the government and satirizes the brutality of the corrupt officials. In "Xi Fangping", the government of the nether world is utterly rotten. From the king of the nether world and the provincial and town gods to the runners, they collude with one another and tyrannize the people. So unjust cases are created one after another. Corrupt officials who ride roughshod over the people in "The Prefect of Lu City", "The Butterfly's Revenge", "The Message of Birds", "The Allotted Life Span" and "The King of Judgement" are all punished by supernatural forces.

Singing the praises of friendship and love is another main theme of *Strange Stories of Liaozhai*. There is affection among humans, as in "Two Sisters", "Qiao's Daughter" and "A Girl Called Rouge"; between humans and fox fairies, as in "Qing Feng" and "A Laughing Girl Named Yingning"; between humans and ghosts, as in "Nie Xiaoqian" and "Judge Lu"; between humans and other beings, as in "A Girl in a Green Dress". In stories of this kind, females are always the protagonists and positive characters. Though these female characters are not human but ghosts, fox fairies and goblins, they are beautiful, affectionate, kind, honest, strong and brave, and are unswervingly faithful to their friends and lovers. The positive image of women in the book constitutes another factor in its popularity.

Besides, *Strange Stories of Liaozhai* also records interesting aspects of folk life, customs and beliefs of the Ming and Qing Dynasties, such as in "Listen with a Mirror", "A Dragon", "The Dumpling Woman", "The Thunder God", "Deer Grass", "Forty Strings of Coins" and "A Man Who Remembered His Previous Life". The book also features some interesting episodes and anecdotes as in "Su Xian",

"A Wolf" and "A Myna". They are valuable information for us to learn about the social life of the Ming and Qing Dynasties.

The stories selected for this collection are arranged according to the following themes: "morals and ethics", "friendship and love between humans and ghosts, fox fairies, immortals and other things of nature", "corrupt officials", "folk customs, beliefs and anecdotes" and "animal stories". Most of the selected stories are popular and representative of the original work, while some are about folk customs and beliefs which are often neglected. However, a few stories about historical events and natural disasters are not included owing to limited space. Some great stories in the original work have also been excluded since they can be found in other books of this *One Hundred Bilingual Series*.

Wang Juan
July, 1998

目　錄
CONTENTS

種染

任教惺惺奉福人家天道原未
達好遠頃初花開頃討貴
神仙心赦譽貪碩

一　種梨

　　有鄉人貨梨於市，頗甘芳，價騰貴。有道士破巾絮衣，丐於車前，鄉人咄之，亦不去；鄉人怒，加以叱罵。道士曰：“一車數百顆，老衲止丐其一，於居士亦無大損，何怒為？”觀者勸置劣者一枚，令去，鄉人執不肯。

　　肆中傭保者，見喋聒不堪，遂出錢市一枚，付道士。道士拜謝，謂眾曰：“出家人不解吝惜。我有佳梨，請出供客。”或曰：“既有之，何不自食？”曰：“吾特需此核作種。”於是掬梨大啗。且盡，把核於手，解肩上鑱[1]，坎地深數寸，納之而覆以土。向市人索湯沃灌。好事者於臨路店索得沸瀋[2]，道士接浸坎處。萬目攢視，見有勾萌[3]

---

1. 鑱（chán）：掘土的工具。
2. 沸瀋：開水。
3. 勾萌：植物的幼芽。

1   Planting a Pear Tree

Once upon a time, there was a peasant selling pears at the market. His pears were very sweet and fragrant, but extremely expensive. A Taoist priest in a worn-out Taoist hood and ragged clothes begged for a pear in front of the cart. The peasant scolded the priest and wanted him to leave, but he would not listen. The peasant started to shout abusively at the priest. The priest said, "You have hundreds of pears in your cart. I only want one, and it will not be a great loss to you. Why are you angry at me?" The bystanders all tried to persuade the peasant to give a bruised pear to the priest and let him go, but he insisted on not giving one.

A servant of a store could no longer stand the endless bickering, and he took out a coin, bought a pear and gave it to the priest. The priest bowed to thank him and said to the crowd, "We priests do not know what stinginess is, I have some wonderful pears and I hope you all will enjoy them." Someone said, "If you have pears, why don't you eat your own?" The priest replied, "Because I need this one for its seed." Then he took the pear in both hands and ate it in big bites. After finishing, he held the pit in his hand, unfastened a shovel from his shoulder, and dug a hole in the ground several inches deep. Finally, he placed the pit in the hole and covered it with earth. After doing this, he asked the crowd for some hot water. Among the bystanders, a busybody got some boiling water from a nearby shop. The priest took the hot water and used it to water the place where he had planted the pit. Thousands of eyes gazed at the spot, and a shoot suddenly sprang up from the ground and rapidly grew bigger and bigger. It did not take long for it to

出，漸大；俄成樹，枝葉扶蘇；候而花，候而實，碩大芳馥，纍纍滿樹。道士乃即樹頭摘賜觀者，頃刻向盡。已，乃以鑱伐樹，丁丁[4]良久，方斷；帶葉荷肩頭，從容徐步而去。

初，道士作法時，鄉人亦雜立眾中，引領注目，竟忘其業。道士既去，始顧車中，則梨已空矣。方悟適所俵散[5]，皆己物也。又細視車上一靶亡，是新鑿斷者。心大憤恨。急跡之，轉過牆隅，則斷靶棄垣下，始知所伐梨木，即是物也。道士不知所在。一市粲然[6]。

---

4. 丁丁（zhēng zhēng）：伐木的聲音。
5. 俵（biào）散：分發。
6. 粲然：大笑。

become a tree thick with leaves. Soon, flowers bloomed, and in an instant, it fruited. Large and fragrant pears were hanging all over the tree. The priest picked pears from the tree and handed them to the crowd. In no time, the pears were all gone. After this, the priest began chopping the tree down with his shovel, and everyone heard the chopping sound. Finally, the tree fell, and the priest walked away at leisure, carrying it over his shoulder with its leaves still intact.

When the priest began doing his magic, the peasant had been in the crowd, craning his neck to see what was happening, and he had completely forgotten about his business. When the priest left, the peasant turned around and noticed that all of his pears were gone. Only then did he realize that the pears given away by the priest were his pears. Looking closely at his cart, he noticed that one of its handles was gone, and it seemed that it was freshly broken. The peasant was very angry, and he hurriedly chased after the priest. Turning the corner of a wall, he saw that the missing handle from his cart had been discarded under the wall. He suddenly realized that this was the pear tree which had been cut down by the priest, but no trace of the priest remained. All the people at the market burst out laughing.

二 斫蟒

　　胡田村胡姓者，兄弟采樵，深入幽谷。遇巨蟒，兄在前，為所吞；弟初駭欲奔，見兄被噬，遂憤怒出樵斧，斫蛇首。首傷而吞不已。然頭雖已沒，幸肩際不能下。弟急極無計，乃兩手持兄足，力與蟒爭，竟曳兄出。蟒亦負痛去。視兄，則鼻耳俱化[1]，奄[2]將氣盡。肩負以行，途中凡十餘息，始至家。

　　醫養半年，方愈。至今面目皆瘢痕，鼻耳處惟孔存焉。噫！農人中，乃有弟弟如此者哉！或言：「蟒不為害，乃德義所感。」信然。

---

1. 化：沒有了。
2. 奄：氣息奄奄。

6

2   Fighting Off a Python

In Hutian Village, there was a family named Hu. One day, two brothers of the Hu family went out to chop wood. When they were deep inside a secluded valley, they met a python. The elder brother, who was walking in front, was bitten by the python. At first, the younger brother was terrified and was about to run away. However, when he realized that his elder brother would be swallowed, he was furious. Taking out his axe, he hacked at the head of the python. The python was injured and stopped trying to swallow the elder brother. The elder brother's head was completely inside the python, but fortunately, his shoulders remained outside. The younger brother was extremely worried about his brother's life. Having no choice, he struggled and succeeded in pulling his brother out by holding onto his feet. The python went away in pain. He found that his elder brother had lost his nose and ears and was breathing feebly. So he carried him all the way home. On their way back, he was so tired that he had to rest a dozen times before he could get home.

After six months of medical treatment, the elder brother recovered. However, there were still many scars on his face. He had only holes where his nose and ears had been. It is surprising to imagine that there was such a good brother among the peasants. Someone said, "The python did not hurt the elder brother because it was moved by the virtuous deed of the younger brother," and one can easily believe this.

三　僧孽

　　張姓暴卒，隨鬼使去，見冥王。王稽簿，怒鬼使誤捉，責令送歸。張下，私浼[1]鬼使，求觀冥獄。鬼導歷九幽[2]，刀山、劍樹，一一指點。末至一處，有一僧，扎骨穿繩而倒懸之，號痛欲絕。近視，則其兄也。張見之驚哀，問："何罪至此？"鬼曰："是為僧，廣募金錢，悉供淫賭，故罰之。欲脫此厄，須其自懺。"

---

1. 浼（měi）：請求。
2. 九幽：九泉之下的地獄。

3 A Sinful Monk

When a man named Zhang died suddenly, his soul followed a ghost messenger to see the king of the nether world. After checking the life-and-death register[1], the king reprimanded the ghost messenger for having taken the wrong person and ordered him to bring Zhang back to life. When they walked out of the king's courtroom, Zhang begged the ghost messenger to show him the prison cells of the nether world. The ghost messenger led the way for him, travelling the length and breadth of the deepest places in the nether world. He showed Zhang, one by one, the mountain of knives and the forest of swords. Finally, they came to a place where they saw a monk hung upside down with his leg holed and strung by a rope. It seemed that the monk must be dying from the way that he was wailing and suffering. Looking more closely at the monk, Zhang discovered that he was his brother. Seeing this, Zhang was both shocked and grief-stricken. He asked, "What sin had this man committed so that he had fallen into such a plight?" The messenger said, "The man was a monk. He went everywhere to beg for alms and squandered all the money on whoring and gambling. So he is thus punished. If he wants to extricate himself from the suffering, he must repent of his sins."

---

1. the life-and-death register: According to Chinese traditional belief, before a person was born, his birth and death dates were written down in the birth-and-death register of the nether world. So, on his day of birth, he would be sent to the world, and on his day of death, he would be brought back to the nether world.

張既蘇，疑兄已死。時其兄居興福寺[3]，因往探之。入門，便聞其號痛聲。入室，見瘡生股間，膿血崩潰，掛足壁上，宛冥司倒懸狀。駭問其故。曰："掛之稍可，不則痛徹心腑。"張因告以所見。僧大駭，乃戒葷酒，虔誦經咒。半月尋愈。遂為戒僧[4]。

---

3. 興福寺：今在山東省淄博市。
4. 戒僧：恪守各種戒律的僧人。

When Zhang came back to life, he thought his brother was dead, so he went to Xingfu Temple, where his brother lived, to visit him. As soon as he opened the door, he heard his brother's cries. When he entered the room, he saw his brother lying on the bed with a huge sore on his leg, and pus and blood flowing out of it. His brother hung his foot on the wall, and the scene was like what he had seen in the nether world. Zhang was shocked, and he asked his brother why he was in this predicament. The brother answered, "I feel much better this way because otherwise, it is too painful for me to bear." Zhang told his brother of the terrible scenes he had witnessed in the nether world, and the monk was extremely frightened. From then on, the monk gave up meat and alcohol, and he read sutras devoutly every day. Two weeks later, the monk recovered. Afterwards, he became a monk who scrupulously abided by Buddhist taboos and commandments.

四 罵鴨

　　邑西白家莊居民某，盜鄰鴨烹之。至夜，覺膚癢。天明視之，茸生鴨毛，觸之則痛。大懼，無術可醫。夜夢一人告之曰："汝病乃天罰。須得失者罵，毛乃可落。"而鄰翁素雅量，生平失物，未嘗徵[1]於聲色。某詭告翁曰："鴨乃某甲所盜。彼甚畏罵焉，罵之亦可警將來。"翁笑曰："誰有閑氣罵惡人。"卒不罵。某益窘，因實告鄰翁。翁乃罵，其病良已。

---

1. 徵：表露。

12

4   The Man Who Stole a Duck

A certain man in Bai Village on the west of the town one day stole a duck of his neighbour's and cooked it. At night, he felt that his body itched. The next morning, he found his body covered with duck down, and it was painful whenever he touched his skin. He was scared to death. Nothing could cure him. That night, he had a dream in which a man told him, "Your disease is the punishment from heaven. You must be cursed by the owner of the duck before the duck down will shed." However, his neighbour, an old man, was a generous man. Whenever he lost any thing, he never expressed any resentment. The man lied to the old man, "A certain man stole your duck, and he was scared of being cursed. If you curse him, it will warn him against stealing in the future." The old man laughed and said, "I don't have time to swear at bad people." So the old man did not give the curse. The man was embarrassed and told the old man the truth. The old man invoked a curse upon him and the man recovered.

五 鷹虎神

　　郡城東嶽廟，在南郭。大門左右，神高丈餘，俗名
"鷹虎神"，猙獰可畏。廟中道士任姓，每雞鳴，輒起焚
誦。有偷兒預匿廊間，伺道士起，潛入寢室，搜括財物。
奈室無長物，惟於薦底[1]得錢三百，納腰中，拔關[2]而出，
將登千佛山。

　　南竄許時[3]，方至山下。見一巨丈夫，自山上來，左臂
蒼鷹，適與相遇。近視之，面銅青色，依稀似廟門中所習
見者。大恐，蹲伏而戰。神詫曰："盜錢安往？"偷兒益
懼，叩不已。神揪令還，入廟，使傾所盜錢，跪守之。道
士課畢，回顧駭愕。盜歷歷自述。道士收其錢而遣之。

---

1. 薦底：草席的下面。
2. 關：門閂。
3. 南竄許時：向南逃了一段時間。

5　The Eagle and the Tiger Gods

Outside the southern gate of the capital city of Shandong Province stood the Dongyue Temple. Two gods, each over ten feet tall with an awesome, hideous visage, were placed on the two sides of the temple gate. People called them "the eagle and the tiger gods." A Taoist priest named Ren lived there, and every morning, he would rise at cockcrow, burn incense and chant scriptures in front of the gods. A thief hid himself in a corridor in advance and waited until the priest got up. He then sneaked into his bedroom and searched for money and valuables. To his disappointment, he found nothing valuable except three hundred coins under the straw mat. Putting the money into his waist bag, he went out of the temple and escaped towards the Thousand Buddha Mountain south of the temple.

After some time, the thief neared the foot of the mountain. He saw a huge man with an eagle perching on his left arm coming down from the mountain. When they met, the thief recognized on closer look that the bronze-faced man looked familiar, like one of the gods in front of the temple. The thief was terrified, and he crouched on the ground, trembling. The god was surprised and said, "Where are you going after stealing the money?" The thief was even more scared and kept kowtowing. The god grabbed him and brought him back to the temple, where he made him pour out the stolen money and kneel in front of the gods. After finishing his chanting, the priest returned to his room and was surprised to find the thief who confessed everything. At last, the priest retrieved his money and released the thief.

六　瞳人語（一）

　　長安士方棟，頗有才名，而佻脫不持儀節。每陌上見游女，輒輕薄尾綴之。清明前一日，偶步郊郭，見一小車，朱茀繡幰；青衣數輩，款段[1]以從。內一婢，乘小駟[2]，容光絕美。稍稍近覘之，見車幔洞開，內坐二八女郎，紅妝艷麗，尤生平所未睹。目炫神奪，瞻戀弗舍，或先或後，從馳數里。忽聞女郎呼婢近車側，曰："為我垂簾下。何處風狂兒郎，頻來窺瞻！"婢乃下簾，怒顧生曰："此芙蓉城[3]七郎子新婦歸寧[4]，非同田舍娘子，放[5]教秀才胡覷！"言已，掬轍土颺生。

---

1. 款段：行動遲緩的馬。這裏指騎馬慢行。
2. 小駟：小馬。
3. 芙蓉城：傳說中神仙居住的地方。
4. 歸寧：結婚後的婦女回娘家。
5. 放：任憑。

6   The Talking Pupils (1)

In Chang'an, there was a man named Fang Dong who was known as a talented scholar, but he was also known for being frivolous and having no manners. Whenever he met a woman on the road, he would follow her and arouse her attention. The day before the Qingming Festival[1], while he was taking a walk outside the city, he saw a small carriage with red curtains and an embroidered canopy. Several maids on horseback followed the carriage leisurely. One of the maids, riding on a pony, was exceedingly beautiful. Fang went closer to have a better view and found that the carriage curtain was open. Inside sat a young woman of about sixteen in a splendid dress, the most beautiful woman he had ever seen. Dazzled by her beauty, Fang could not take his eyes off her. Now in front, now behind, Fang rode with them for several miles. Suddenly, he heard the young woman call out to her maid to come to the side of her carriage and say, "Let down the curtain for me. Who is that rude young man who keeps on peeping at me?" The maid lowered the curtain and looked at Fang angrily, saying, "This is the bride of the Seventh Prince in the City of Hibiscus. She is on her way to visit her parents and she is not the kind of village girl whom you think you can stare at." After that, she threw a handful of dust at Fang.

---

1. Qingming Festival: the fifth of the twenty-four solar terms in the lunar year, a festival for worshipping ancestors at ancestral graves.

生眯目不可開。纔一拭視，而車馬已渺。驚疑而返。覺目終不快。倩人啟瞼撥視，則睛上生小翳[6]；經宿益劇，淚簌簌不得止；翳漸大，數日厚如錢。右睛起旋螺。百藥無效。懊悶欲絕，頗思自懺悔。聞《光明經》能解厄，持一卷，浼人教誦。初猶煩躁，久漸自安。旦晚無事，惟趺坐捻珠。持之一年，萬緣俱淨。

6. 翳：薄膜。

Fang could not open his eyes as the dust had got into them. A moment later, he opened his eyes again and found that the carriage and horses were gone. He went back home wondering, and feeling very uncomfortable in his eyes. He asked someone to turn up his eyelids and have a look and a thin film was found on each of the pupils. The next day, his eye problem became more acute and tears kept on streaming down. The film grew bigger and a few days later, it was as thick as a coin. On the right pupil, the film formed a spiral. No medicine was effective. Fang was dejected and wished for death. Thinking about his follies, he repented. Hearing that the *Guangming Sutra* could relieve distress, Fang found himself a copy and asked somebody to teach him to chant it. At first, he was still disturbed about what had happened to him. As time went by, he became more composed and whenever he was free, he would sit in meditation, counting his beads. A year later, Fang was free from all desires and attained a state of perfect calm.

七 瞳人語（二）

　　忽聞左目中小語如蠅，曰：“黑漆似，叵耐殺人[1]！”右目中應云：“可同小遨游，出此悶氣。”漸覺兩鼻中蠕蠕作癢，似有物出，離孔而去。久之乃返，復自鼻入眶中。又言曰：“許時不窺園亭，珍珠蘭遽枯瘁死！”生素喜香蘭，園中多種植，日常自灌溉。自失明，久置不問。忽聞此言，遽問妻：“蘭花何使憔悴死？”妻詰其所自知，因告之故。妻趨驗之，花果槁矣。大異之。靜匿房中以俟之。見有小人自生鼻內出，大不及豆，營營[2]然竟出門去。漸遠，遂迷所在。俄，連臂歸，飛上面，如蜂蟻之投穴者。如此二三日。

　　又聞左言曰：“隧道迂，還往甚非所便，不如自啟門。”右應云：“我壁子厚，大不易。”左曰：“我試闢，得與而俱。”遂覺左眶內隱似抓裂。有頃，開視，豁見幾

---

1. 叵耐殺人：叵：不可。令人難以忍耐。
2. 營營：來回飛的聲音。

7   The Talking Pupils (2)

One day, Fang suddenly heard a voice, as soft as a fly's, saying from his left eye, "It's so dark here, and I can't stand this anymore!" A voice from his right eye responded, "Let's go out, take a walk and get some fresh air." Fang then felt a wriggling in his nose, which tickled its nostrils, as if something was coming out. After a while, the thing returned to his eye through his nose and said, "I have not visited the garden for a long time and the orchids have all withered and died." Fang was fond of orchids. He had planted plenty of them in his garden and used to water them himself. However, since he lost his sight, he had long neglected them. Hearing those words, he immediately inquired his wife, "Why have you let the orchids die?" His wife asked how he knew about this and Fang told her what had happened. His wife went to the garden and found that the orchids were indeed dead. Greatly surprised, she concealed herself in the room to see what was happening. She saw two tiny men, no bigger than a bean, came out of her husband's nose. They flew out of the door with a buzz and disappeared in the distance. Soon they came back arm in arm and flew up her husband's face like bees and ants seeking their nests. This went on for two or three days.

One day, Fang heard from his left eye: "It's inconvenient to come in and out through the winding tunnel. Why don't we make a door?" The right eye replied, "The wall in front of me is too thick. It is by no means easy to break open." The left eye said, "I will try to make a door so that we both can use it." Fang felt that something inside his left eye was tearing and splitting. In a moment, Fang opened his eyes and found that he

物。喜告妻。妻審之，則脂膜破小竅，黑睛熒熒，如劈椒[3]。越一宿，障盡消。細視，竟重瞳也。但右目旋螺如故，乃知兩瞳人合居一眶矣。生雖一目眇，而較之雙目者，殊更了了。由是益自檢束。鄉中稱盛德焉。

---

3. 劈椒：裂開的花椒。

could see things. He was very happy and told this to his wife who checked his left eye and discovered an opening in the film through which she could see a small part of the shining black pupil. Next day, the film disappeared completely. A close inspection revealed two pupils in his left eye but the spiral-shaped film on his right eye remained. Fang now realized that the two pupils were living together in one eye. Though he was blind in one eye, he could see better than with two eyes. Since then, Fang was even more restrained in his behaviour, and was praised as a virtuous man in his hometown.

八 于江

　　鄉民于江，父宿田間，為狼所食。江時年十六，得父
遺履，悲恨欲死。夜俟母寢，潛持鐵錘去，眠父所，冀報
父仇。少間，一狼來，逡巡嗅之。江不動。無何[1]，搖尾掃
其額，又漸俯首舐其股。江迄不動。既而歡躍直前，將齕
其領。江急以錘擊狼腦，立斃。起置草中。

　　少間，又一狼來，如前狀。又斃之。以至中夜，杳無
至者。忽小睡，夢父曰：「殺二物，足泄我恨。然首殺我
者，其鼻白；此都非是。」江醒，堅臥以伺之。既明，無
所復得。欲曳狼歸，恐驚母，遂投諸眢井[2]而歸。至夜復
往，亦無至者。如此三四夜。忽一狼來，嚙其足，曳之以

---

1. 無何：沒多久。
2. 眢井：枯井。

24

8　Yu Jiang

Yu Jiang was a peasant. One day, his father, while taking a rest in the field, was eaten by a wolf. Jiang was then sixteen. When he saw the shoes left by his father, he was filled with grief and hatred, and he wished for death. That night, Jiang waited until his mother was asleep, and went out quietly, carrying an iron hammer with him. He lay on the field where his father lay before and expected to avenge his father. After a while, a wolf came to the field. Hesitatingly, it got near Jiang and sniffed him. Jiang remained motionless. A moment later, the wolf swept his forehead with its tail and lowered its head to lick his thigh. Jiang still remained motionless. The wolf jumped for joy and sprang on Jiang's neck. At this moment, Jiang suddenly hit it on the head with his hammer and the wolf died immediately. Jiang stood up and dragged the dead wolf among the weeds. Later, another wolf came and Jiang killed it as he did with the first wolf.

It was about midnight and there was no sign of any other wolves. Jiang fell asleep and had a dream in which his father said to him, "You have killed two wolves, which is enough to release my hatred. However, neither of them is the one that ate me. That wolf has a white nose." After waking up, Jiang kept on lying there waiting for the white-nosed wolf. It was light already; however, the white-nosed wolf did not appear. Jiang wanted to drag the two dead wolves home, but he was afraid that his mother would be scared. So he threw them into a dry well. The next evening, Jiang went to the field again waiting for the white-nosed wolf, but it did not come. Three or four nights later, a wolf suddenly came to the field. It snapped at

行。行數步，棘刺肉，石傷膚。江若死者。狼乃置之地上，意將齕腹。江驟起錘之，仆；又連錘之，斃。細視之，真白鼻也。大喜，負之以歸，始告母。母泣從去，探眢井，得二狼焉。

Jiang's foot and dragged him along. After a certain distance, Jiang was scratched by rocks, thistles and thorns. He feigned death. The wolf finally relaxed its bite and laid him on the ground. When the wolf was about to bite into his belly, Jiang suddenly stood up and struck the wolf with his hammer. The wolf fell. Jiang hit it again several times and it died. Looking closely, Jiang found that this wolf had a white nose. He was overjoyed. Carrying the dead wolf on his back, Jiang went back home. It was not until then that he told his mother what he had done and his mother wept with joy. Following her son, the mother came to the dry well and saw the two dead wolves.

九 喬女 (一)

　　平原喬生，有女黑醜：窪[1]一鼻，跛一足。年二十五六，無問名者。邑有穆生，四十餘，妻死，貧不能續，因聘焉。三年，生一子。未幾，穆生卒，家益索[2]；大困，則乞憐其母。母頗不耐之。女亦憤不復返，惟以紡織自給。

　　有孟生喪耦，遺一子烏頭，裁周歲，以乳哺乏人，急於求配；然媒數言，輒不當意。忽見女，大悅之，陰使人風示[3]女。女辭焉，曰："飢凍若此，從官人得溫飽，夫寧不願？然殘醜不如人，所可自信者，德耳；又事二夫，官

---

1. 窪：凹下。
2. 索：衰敗。
3. 風示：透露點意思。

9 Qiao's Daughter (1)

In Pingyuan, there was a man named Qiao. He had an ugly daughter who had dark skin and a flat nose and was lame in one leg. No one proposed marriage to her until she was over twenty-five. In the same county, there was a man named Mu who was then forty. He was poor and had no money to remarry a normal girl after his wife's death, so he took the ugly daughter of Qiao. Three years later, the woman gave birth to a boy. Soon Mu died and the woman and her son were getting poorer and poorer, and finally they were broke. She went to her mother for help, but her mother showed reluctance. She left in anger and never went back to her mother again. She made a living by spinning and weaving.

In the same place, there was a man named Meng whose wife died and left him a son called Dark Head, who was less than a year old. Since his son still needed breast-feeding, Meng was badly in need of a wife. Though matchmakers proposed several girls to him, he liked none of them. One day, seeing the ugly woman, Meng liked her very much and sent someone to sound her out about a marriage proposal. However, the ugly woman refused his proposal and said, "How can a poor woman like me not want to marry you who can give me adequate food and clothing? But I am inferior to others because I am ugly and have a deformed leg. The only thing I am proud of myself is my virtue. If I married again, what virtue would I possess[1] to

---

1. what virtue would I possess: According to Chinese tradition, if a woman married again after her husband died, she was regarded as having lost her moral integrity.

人何取焉！"孟益賢之，向慕尤殷，使媒者函金加幣[4]而說其母。母悅，自詣女所，固要之；女志終不奪。母慚，願以少女字孟；家人皆喜，而孟殊不願。

---

4. 函金加幣：函，成封的。幣，繒帛。成封的金銀繒帛。

make you want to marry me?" Meng had respect for her after hearing her words and liked her even more. He sent a matchmaker to persuade her mother by offering her a lot of money and silk. Her mother was very happy. She went to her daughter's house and asked her to marry Meng. But the ugly woman insisted on her own decision. Her mother felt embarrassed and was willing to let Meng take her younger daughter. Meng's family also agreed but Meng refused.

十　喬女（二）

居無何，孟暴疾卒，女往臨哭盡哀。孟故無戚黨，死後，村中無賴悉憑陵之，家具攜取一空，方謀瓜分其田產。家人亦各草竊[1]以去，惟一嫗抱兒哭幃中。女問得故，大不平。聞林生與孟善，乃踵門而告曰：「夫婦、朋友，人之大倫也。妾以奇醜，為世不齒，獨孟生能知我；前雖固拒之，然固已心許之矣。今身死子幼，自當有以報知己。然存孤易，御侮難；若無兄弟父母，遂坐視其子死家滅而不一救，則五倫中可以無朋友矣。妾無所多須[2]於君，但以片紙告邑宰；撫孤，則妾不敢辭。」林曰：「諾。」女別而歸。

---

1. 草竊：亂偷，乘亂偷竊。
2. 須：期待。

10 Qiao's Daughter (2)

Not long afterwards, Meng died of a sudden illness. The ugly woman wept bitterly to mourn his death. Since Meng did not have any blood relatives, many rascals of the village took advantage of his death to loot his furniture. They also plotted to carve up his field. His servants all left, taking away whatever they could with them. Only the nanny, holding Meng's son, wept in the mourning hall. After learning what had happened, the ugly woman was very indignant. She heard that Meng used to have a good friend named Lin, so she went to see him and said, "Relations between husbands and wives and relations between friends are the basic human relations[1]. People dislike me because I am ugly. Meng was the only person who understood me. Though I refused his proposal, I have given my heart to him. Now he is dead, leaving a baby behind. I should repay him for his recognition and appreciation. It is easy to bring up his baby, but hard to protect him from the rascals' bullying. Since Meng has no parents and brothers, if we, as his friends, just sit back and watch those rascals loot his property and kill his son without going to the rescue, we might as well do away with friendship, one of the five basic human relations. I don't expect you to do more than write an indictment and take it to the official of the county. I will take the responsibility of looking after the baby." Lin agreed and the ugly woman took leave.

---

1. the basic human relations: According to Chinese tradition, the five cardinal human relations include relations between ruler and subject, father and son, husband and wife, between brothers and between friends.

林將如其所教；無賴輩怒，咸欲以白刃相仇。林大懼，閉戶不敢復行。女聽之數日，寂無音；及問之，則孟氏田產已盡矣。女忿甚，挺身自詣官。官詰女屬孟何人，女曰：“公宰一邑，所憑者理耳。如其言妄，即至戚無所逃罪；如非妄，則道路之人可聽也。”

　　官怒其言戇，訶逐而出。女冤憤無以自伸，哭訴於搢(縉)紳之門。某先生聞而義之，代剖[3]於宰。宰按[4]之，果真，窮治諸無賴，盡返所取。

---

3. 剖：辯白。
4. 按：審查。

Lin was going to do what the ugly woman told him, but the rascals were angry and threatened to kill him. Lin was scared, he locked himself in, and dared not report the case. Several days passed, the ugly woman heard nothing from Lin. When she learned what had happened, Meng's field had been carved up. The ugly woman was enraged and went straight to court to see the official herself. The official asked whether she was a relative of Meng's. She said, "Being an official of the county, you should listen to reason. If I talk nonsense, I should be punished even though I am the closest relative of Meng's; if I tell the truth, you should listen to me though I am only a passerby."

The official was angry at her outspoken and rash remarks. He scolded her and drove her out. The ugly woman had nowhere to vent her grievances, so she complained tearfully in front of some country gentlemen's homes. One of the gentlemen was moved by her righteousness, so he explained the case to the official on her behalf. The official investigated the case and found the truth was just as she had described, so he punished the rascals and forced them to return everything that belonged to Meng.

十一 喬女（三）

　　或議留女居孟第，撫其孤；女不肯。扃其戶，使媼抱烏頭，從與俱歸，另舍之。凡烏頭日用所需，輒同媼啟戶出粟，為之營辦；己錙銖無所沾染，抱子食貧，一如曩日。

　　積數年，烏頭漸長，為延師教讀；己子則使學操作。媼勸使並讀，女曰：“烏頭之費，其所自有；我耗人之財以教己子，此心何以自明？”

　　又數年，為烏頭積粟數百石，乃聘於名族，治其第宅，析令歸。烏頭泣要同居，女乃從之；然紡績如故。烏頭夫婦奪其具，女曰：“我母子坐食，心何安矣。”遂早暮為之紀理，使其子巡行阡陌，若為傭然。烏頭夫婦有小過，輒斥譴不少貸；稍不悛[1]，則怫然欲去。夫妻跪道悔

---

1. 不悛：不悔改。

11   Qiao's Daughter (3)

Some suggested that the ugly woman live in Meng's house to take care of the orphan, but the ugly woman refused. She locked Meng's house and asked the nanny to take Meng's son, Dark Head, to her home and put them up in another house. Whenever Dark Head needed anything, she would, accompanied by the nanny, unlock his house, and take out some grain for his use. She and her son never took any money from Meng's property for their own use and still stayed poor as before.

Several years later, Dark Head grew up. The ugly woman found him a teacher, while her own son only learned how to work in the field. The nanny advised her to let her son study with Dark Head. The ugly woman said, "Dark Head is spending his own money. How can I explain my motive if I spend another's money to educate my son?"

Several more years passed, the ugly woman had saved hundreds of hectolitres of grain for Dark Head. She renovated Meng's house for Dark Head, and arranged for him to marry a daughter of an eminent family. Then she told him to move back to his own house. Dark Head wept and asked her to live with him. The ugly woman agreed. After moving into his house, the ugly woman still spun and wove as usual. Dark Head and his wife took the instruments away from her. The ugly woman said, "My son and I can't stand living off others." Since then, she worked as a housekeeper from dawn to dusk and her son worked as a servant in the field. Whenever Dark Head and his wife made a small mistake, she would reproach them sternly. If they showed no sign of repentance, she would angrily prepare to leave them until the couple knelt down promising they would

詞，始止。未幾，烏頭入泮[2]，又辭欲歸。烏頭不可，捐聘幣，為穆子完婚。女乃析子令歸。烏頭留之不得，陰使人於近村為市恆產百畝而後遣之。

後女疾求歸。烏頭不聽。病益篤，囑曰："必以我歸葬！"烏頭諾。既卒，陰以金啗穆子，俾合葬於孟。及期，棺重，三十人不能舉。穆子忽仆，七竅血出，自言曰："不肖兒，何得遂賣汝母！"烏頭懼，拜祝之，始愈。乃復停數日，修治穆墓已，始合厝之。

2. 入泮：考入縣學，即考取秀才。

repent. Soon Dark head became a *xiucai*[1]. The ugly woman wanted to go again but Dark Head kept her. Later Dark Head paid out some betrothal money to enable the ugly woman's son to get married. After that, the ugly woman told her son to move back to her own house. Dark Head had no way to stop them so he privately bought them a hundred *mu*[2] of land in a nearby village before he allowed them to move out.

Later the ugly woman was ill and asked to return to her place, but Dark Head did not agree. Her illness was getting worse and worse. One day, she said to Dark Head, "After I die, bury me with my husband Mu!" Dark Head agreed. But after her death, Dark Head secretly gave some money to her son so that the latter agreed to bury her with his father Meng. On the funeral day, the coffin became so heavy that thirty people could not lift it. The ugly woman's son suddenly fell down and blood came out from his eyes, ears, nose and mouth. People heard him talking to himself, "You, unworthy son, how dare you betray your mother!" Dark Head was scared and kept on kowtowing to the coffin. It was not until then that the ugly woman's son recovered. Dark Head delayed the burial for several days until he had renovated Mu's tomb. Finally he buried the ugly woman with her own husband Mu.

---

1. *xiucai* : a title for one who passed the imperial examination at the county level.
2. *mu* : = 0.165 acre.

十二　孝子

　　青州東香山之前，有周順亭者，事母至孝。母股生巨疽，痛不可忍，晝夜嚬呻。周撫肌進藥，至忘寢食。數月不痊，周憂煎無以為計。

　　夢父告曰：「母疾，賴汝孝。然此瘡非人膏塗之不能愈，徒勞焦惻也。」醒而異之。乃起，以利刀割脅肉；肉脫落，覺不甚苦。急以布纏腰際，血亦不注。於是烹肉持膏，敷母患處，痛截然頓止。母喜問：「何藥而靈效如此？」周詭對之。母瘡尋愈。周每掩護割處，即妻子亦不知也。既痊，有巨痕如掌。妻詰之，始得其情。

12 A Filial Son

In the vicinity of Dong Xiang Mountain, Qingzhou[1], there was a man named Zhou Shunting who was extremely filial toward his mother. Once his mother suffered from a huge ulcer on her thigh, which caused her so much pain that she moaned and groaned day and night. Zhou massaged his mother's leg and applied medicine. Such good care of his mother he took that he often forgot to eat and sleep. Several months passed and his mother remained ill. Zhou was burning with anxiety but could do nothing about it.

One night, he had a dream in which his father told him, "Your mother's recovery depends on your filial piety. However, she will not recover from her ulcer unless you put human fat on it. It is in vain to be anxious." Zhou woke up and felt very strange. Without any hesitation, he rose from the bed, took a knife and cut off a piece of flesh from his side. But he felt little pain. He hurriedly wrapped his waist with a piece of cloth, and it stopped bleeding. He cooked the flesh and smeared the fat on the ulcer. His mother's pain stopped immediately. She was very happy and asked, "What kind of drug is it that is so efficacious?" Zhou did not tell her the truth. Soon the mother recovered. Zhou kept on hiding his wound so that even his wife did not know what had happened. When he recovered, there was a scar the size of a palm left on his waist. His wife asked him how he got it, and he told her everything.

---

1. Qingzhou: now in Yidu County of Shangdong Province.

十三　杜小雷

　　杜小雷，益都之西山人。母雙盲。杜事之孝，家雖
貧，甘旨無缺。一日，將他適，市肉付妻，令作餺飥[1]。妻
最忤逆，切肉時雜蜣蜋[2]其中。母覺臭惡不可食，藏以待
子。杜歸，問："餺飥美乎？"母搖首，出示子。杜裂視，
見蜣蜋，怒甚。入室，欲撻妻，又恐母聞。上榻籌思，妻
問之，不語。妻自餒，徬徨榻下。久之，喘息有聲。杜叱
曰："不睡，待敲撲[3]耶！"亦覺寂然。起而燭之，但見一
豕，細視，則兩足猶人，始知為妻所化。邑令聞之，縶
去，使游四門，以戒眾人。譚微臣曾親見之。

---

1. 餺飥（bó tuō）：一種麪食，這裏指餃子。
2. 蜣蜋：一種黑色的昆蟲，喜歡食糞。
3. 敲撲：杖打。

13   A Man Named Du Xiaolei

Du Xiaolei was a native of Xishan, Yidu[1]. His mother was blind in both eyes. Du was a filial son, and though he was poor, he always prepared delicious food for his mother. One day, he had to go out, so he bought some meat and told his wife to make some dumplings for his mother. However, his wife was mean and unfilial. While chopping the meat, she added some dung beetles in it. Presented with the dumplings, the mother smelled their stink and did not eat them. Instead, she hid the dumplings in order to be able to show them to her son later. When her son returned, he asked his mother, "Were the dumplings delicious?" His mother shook her head and showed the dumplings. Du broke one and found dung beetles inside. He was very angry. Entering his room, he wanted to beat up his wife, but worried that his mother would hear it. He reclined on the bed to think about what to do. His wife asked him what was bothering him, but he said nothing. His wife was discouraged, walking back and forth beside the bed. After quite a long time, Du heard the sound of breathing. He rebuked his wife, "Why don't you go to bed? Are you waiting for me to beat you?" There was no response. Du rose from the bed, lit the lamp and found a pig-like creature on the ground. Looking carefully, he saw that the creature had two human feet. Now he realized that it was the incarnation of his wife. The county official heard about this. He tied it up, paraded it at the four gates of the city to warn people against being disobedient to their parents. A man named Tan Weichen saw it with his own eyes.

---

1. Yidu: in Shandong Province.

十四　祿數

　　某顯者多為不道，夫人每以果報勸諫之，殊不聽信。適有方士，能知人祿數，詣之。方士熟視曰：“君再食米二十石、麵四十石，天祿乃終。”歸語夫人。計一人終年僅食麵二石，尚有二十餘年天祿，豈不善所能絕耶？橫如故。逾年，忽病“除中”[1]，食甚多而旋飢，一晝夜十餘食。未及周歲，死矣。

---

1. 除中：疾病的名稱。其癥狀主要是病人在臨死之前食量反而非常大。

14 The Allotted Life Span

Once upon a time, there was a high official who did a lot of bad things. His wife told him that there would be retribution for evil deeds; however, he would not listen. One day, a fortune-teller, who claimed that he knew the allotted life span of people, came to the place. The official went to see him. The fortune-teller looked at him closely for a while and said, "As soon as you finish eating twenty *dan*[1] of rice and forty *dan* of flour, you will die." The official returned home and told this to his wife. He calculated that a person could eat only two *dan* of flour a year, so he still had more than twenty years of life. How could doing bad deeds shorten his life? So he behaved as usual. The next year he suddenly suffered from bulimia. No matter how much he ate, he was soon hungry. In one day, he would eat about a dozen meals. Finally, he died before the end of the year.

---

1. *dan* : a hectolitre.

十五　醜狐（一）

　　穆生，長沙人。家清貧，冬無絮衣。一夕枯坐[1]，有女子入，衣服炫麗而顏色黑醜，笑曰：“得毋寒乎？”生驚問之，曰：“我狐仙也。憐君枯寂，聊與共溫冷榻耳。”生懼其狐，而厭其醜，大號。女以元寶置几上，曰：“若相諧好，以此相贈。”生悅而從之。牀無裯褥，女代以袍。將曉，起而囑曰：“所贈，可急市軟帛作臥具；餘者絮衣作饌，足矣。倘得永好，勿憂貧也。”遂去。

　　生告妻，妻亦喜，即市帛為之縫紉。女夜至，見臥具一新，喜曰：“君家娘子劬勞哉！”留金以酬之。從此至無虛夕。每去，必有所遺。

---

1. 枯坐：寂寞地坐着。

15　An Ugly Fox Fairy (1)

Mu, a native of Changsha, was so poor that he did not even have padded-cotton clothes for the winter season. One night, while he was sitting in his room alone, a lady, who was dark and ugly but wearing a gorgeous dress, came in. She smiled at Mu and said, "Do you feel cold?" Mu was taken aback and asked who she was. The lady said, "I am a fox fairy. I feel sorry for you being so lonely here. Maybe we can warm your cold bed together." Mu was scared as she was a fox and disliked her ugly looks, so he screamed. The fox fairy took out a silver ingot, put it on the table, and said, "If you agree to be my lover, I will give it to you." Mu was happy and agreed. There was no mattress on the bed, so the fox fairy covered the bed with her gown. At dawn, the fox fairy got up and told Mu, "You can use that money to buy some silk and make a quilt and a cotton-padded mattress. You can also buy some food and clothes with the rest of the money, which should be enough. If you will continue to be my lover, you will never be poor again." After that, the fox fairy left.

Mu told this to his wife and she was happy too. Immediately she went out and bought some silk and made a quilt and a mattress. At night, the fox fairy came again. Seeing the new quilt and mattress, she was pleased and said, "Your wife has been working hard!" She left some money as a reward to Mu's wife. Since then, the fox fairy would come every night and whenever she came, she would leave Mu some money.

年餘，屋廬修潔，內外皆衣文錦繡，居然素封[2]。女賂貽漸少，生由此心厭之，聘術士至，畫符於門。女嚙折而棄之，入指生曰："背德負心，至君已極！然此奈何我！若相厭薄，我自去耳。但情義既絕，受於我者，須要償也！"忿然而去。

生懼，告術士。術士作壇，陳設未已，忽顛地下，血流滿頰；視之，割去一耳。眾大懼，奔散；術士亦掩耳竄去。室中擲石如盆，門窗釜甑，無復全者。生伏牀下，搐縮汗聳[3]。

---

2. 素封：無官職的有錢人。
3. 搐縮汗聳，身體發顫，直冒冷汗。

More than a year passed. With the money given by the fox fairy, Mu renovated his house and the whole family was able to put on beautiful clothes. Mu became rich. However, the money brought by the fox fairy got less and less, and Mu began to feel disgusted with her. So he asked a Taoist priest to write a charm and paste it on the door of his house. When the fox fairy came, she bit the charm off and discarded it. She entered the room, pointed her finger at Mu and said, "You have gone to the extreme of ingratitude! What can this charm do to me? If you dislike me, I will leave by myself. But I will take away everything I gave you since you have cut off the ties of our relationship!" The fox fairy left angrily.

Mu was scared to death, and told this to the Taoist priest. The priest decided to build an altar to exorcise the fox fairy. Before he finished it, the priest suddenly fell down and blood was all over his face. People came close and found that one of his ears was cut off. They all ran away terrified. Covering his ear with his hand, the priest scurried away too. Stones as big as basins were thrown into Mu's house and shattered almost everything such as doors, windows, furniture and pots. Mu, hiding under the bed, huddled up in fright and in a cold sweat.

十六　醜狐（二）

　　俄見女抱一物入，貓首猈尾[1]，置牀前，嗾[2]之曰：
"嘻嘻！可嚼奸人足。"物即齕履，齒利於刃。生大懼，將
屈藏之，四肢不能動。物嚼指，爽脆有聲。生痛極，哀
祝。女曰："所有金珠，盡出勿隱。"生應之。女曰："呵
呵！"物乃止。生不能起，但告以處。

　　女自往搜括，珠鈿衣服之外，止得二百餘金。女少
之，又曰："嘻嘻！"物復嚼。生哀鳴求恕。女限十日，償
金六百。生諾之，女乃抱物去。

　　久之，家人漸聚，從牀下曳生出，足血淋漓，喪其二
指。視室中，財物盡空，惟當年破被存焉。遂以覆生，令
臥。又懼十日復來，乃貨婢鬻衣，以足其數。至期，女果

---

1. 猈（wō）：小狗。
2. 嗾（sǒu）：讓狗咬人時發出的聲音。

16   An Ugly Fox Fairy (2)

Soon the fox fairy came in, holding an animal which had a cat's head and dog's tail. She put the animal beside the bed and said to it, "Go! Bite the scoundrel's feet." The animal went to bite one of Mu's shoes, and its teeth were as sharp as a blade. Mu was terrified and wanted to withdraw his feet, but he was unable to move any of his limbs. The animal began to bite his toes, and Mu could even hear the crunchy sound of biting. It was extremely painful and Mu begged the fox fairy to forgive him. The fox fairy said, "You must give me back everything including gold, silver and jewelry. Don't hide anything!" Mu agreed. The fox fairy said, "Stop! Stop!" and the animal stopped biting. Mu was unable to stand up, so he told the fox fairy the place where he had hidden his property.

The fox fairy went to search for the property by herself and found all the clothes and jewelry. However, there were only two hundred taels of silver. She was not satisfied with such a small amount, so she said to the animal again, "Go! Go!" The animal went to bite Mu again. Mu wept and implored the fox fairy for forgiveness. The fox fairy gave him ten days to pay back six hundred taels of silver and Mu agreed. The fox fairy left, holding the animal in her arms.

After some time, the family came to Mu's room and dragged him out from under the bed. His foot was dripping with blood and two toes were bitten off. Looking around, the family members found that all the property was taken away except the old quilt they had in the past. They helped Mu lie down and covered him with the quilt. Mu was afraid that the fox fairy would come back ten days later, so he sold all the servants and

至；急付之，無言而去。自此遂絕。生足創，醫藥半年始愈，而家清貧如初矣。

　　狐適近村于氏。于業農，家不中資；三年間，援例納粟[3]，夏屋[4]連蔓，所衣華服，半生家物。生見之，亦不敢問。偶適野，遇女於途，長跪道左。女無言，但以素巾裹五六金，遙擲去，反身徑去。後于氏早卒，女猶時至其家，家中金帛輒亡去。于子睹其來，拜參之，遙祝：“父即去世，兒輩皆若子，縱不撫恤，何忍坐令貧也？”女去，遂不復至。

---

3. 援例納粟：照過去的例子，通過捐獻財物給官府，可獲得監生（國子監肄業）的稱號。監生可不經過府州縣學考試而直接參加鄉試。
4. 夏屋：大屋。

clothes, and gathered enough money. Ten days later, as expected, the fox fairy came back. Mu gave her the money, and the fox fairy left without saying a word. Since then, she never came again. After half a year's treatment, Mu's foot was healed. He was as poor as before.

Later the fox fairy married a peasant farmer named Yu who lived in a neighbouring village. Yu was not rich then, but in three years after his marriage, he acquired many big houses, and he even bought the academic title of "*jiansheng*[1]". Most of the beautiful clothes of Yu's family were once Mu's. Mu dared not say a word. One day, Mu went out and met the fox fairy on the road. He knelt down at the side of the road. The fox fairy said nothing but threw him five or six taels of silver wrapped in a piece of white cloth from a distance and turned away. Later Yu died early and the fox fairy still went to Yu's home often. Every time she went there, Yu's family would lose some property. One day the fox fairy went to Yu's home again. Seeing her coming, Yu's son knelt down from a distance and said to her, "Though our father died, we are still your sons. You may not take care of us, but how can you let us get poor?" The fox fairy left and never came back again.

---

1. *jiansheng* : a kind of title for scholars who were selected as students of the Imperial College in the Ming and Qing Dynasties. Only those who passed the imperial examination at the county level '   opportunity. However, sometimes rich people could h   title with money.

十七　青鳳（一）

　　太原耿氏，故大家，第宅弘闊。後凌夷[1]，樓舍連亙，半曠廢之。因生怪異，堂門輒自開掩，家人恆中夜駭譁。耿患之，移居別墅，留老翁門焉。由此荒落益甚。或聞笑語歌吹聲。

　　耿有從子[2]去病，狂放不覊，囑翁有所聞見，奔告之。至夜，見樓上燈光明滅，走報生。生欲入覘其異。止之，不聽。門戶素所習識，竟撥蒿蓬，曲折而入。登樓，殊無少異。穿樓而過，聞人語切切。潛窺之，見巨燭雙燒，其明如晝。一叟儒冠南面坐，一媼相對，俱年四十餘。東向一少年，可二十許；右一女郎，裁及笄[3]耳。酒胾[4]滿案，

---

1. 凌夷：衰敗。
2. 從子：侄兒。
3. 及笄：笄，盤頭髮用的簪子。古代女子十五歲開始把頭髮盤起來，表示已成年，稱為及笄。
4. 胾（zì）：古代人稱大塊肉為胾，小塊肉為臠。

17 Qingfeng (1)

The Geng family of Taiyuan was a big and wealthy family living in a large mansion. Later, this family declined and most of the rooms in its mansion were empty. Thus, some strange things happened. For instance, the door of the central room often opened and closed by itself. During the night, family members often screamed after being frightened by things like this. Plagued by these strange occurrences, the Geng family moved out of the mansion to another villa, leaving behind an old doorkeeper. From that time on, the mansion had grown even more desolate. Sometimes, sounds of laughing and singing could be heard inside the mansion.

The Geng family included a nephew named Qubing who was an unruly person. He told the old doorkeeper to inform him if he noticed anything strange. One night, upon seeing lights flashing on and off upstairs, the doorkeeper notified Qubing. Qubing wanted to go and see the strange phenomenon. The old doorkeeper tried to stop him, but he would not listen. Since Qubing was very familiar with the mansion, he wound his way through the wormwood and entered the mansion. Nothing seemed strange upstairs. But as he was walking through one of the hallways, Qubing suddenly heard the sound of chatter coming from one of the rooms. He peeped into the room and found that there was a pair of big red candles burning, making the room as bright as if it were daylight. An old man dressed like a scholar sat on the south side of a table. Sitting opposite the old man was a lady. Both were over forty. A young man of about twenty sat on the east side. On the right side was a girl who was about fifteen years old. Beverages and food covered

團坐笑語。生突入，笑呼曰："有不速之客一人來！"群驚奔匿。獨叟出，叱問："誰何入人閨闥[5]？"生曰："此我家閨闥，君佔之。旨酒自飲，不一邀主人，毋乃太吝？"

---

5. 閨闥：內寢。

the table, and the four of them were sitting there chatting and laughing. Qubing burst into the room, laughed and said, "Here comes an uninvited guest!" The people at the table were terrified and ran for hiding, but the old man alone stepped forward and said angrily, "Who are you, and how dare you come to our inner room?" Qubing said, "This is my inner room. You occupy my place, and drink merrily without inviting the host. Don't you think you are too stingy?"

十八　青鳳（二）

　　叟審諦，曰：“非主人也。”生曰：“我狂生耿去病，主人之從子耳。”叟致敬曰：“久仰山斗[1]！”乃揖生入，便呼家人易饌。生止之。叟乃酌客。生曰：“吾輩通家[2]，座客無庸見避，還祈招飲。”叟呼：“孝兒！”俄少年自外入。叟曰：“此豚兒也。”揖而坐。

　　略審門閥[3]。叟自言：“義君姓胡。”生素豪，談議風生，孝兒亦倜儻；傾吐間，雅相愛悅。生二十一，長孝兒二歲，因弟之。叟曰：“聞君祖纂《涂山[4]外傳》，知之乎？”答：“知之。”叟曰：“我涂山氏之苗裔[5]也。唐以

---

1. 久仰山斗：久仰大名。
2. 通家：世交。
3. 門閥：家庭出身。
4. 《涂山外傳》：傳說禹曾在涂山娶九尾白狐為妻，稱為涂山氏。
5. 苗裔：後代子孫。

18 Qingfeng (2)

Looking Qubing up and down, the old man said, "You are not the host." Qubing said, "I am the nephew of the Geng family, and my name is Qubing." The old man bowed and said, "I have heard about you for a long time." He invited Qubing to join them, and ordered the servants to bring more dishes. But Qubing stopped him. As the old man poured him a glass of wine, Qubing said, "You are old friends of my family, so those who were sitting here just now do not have to hide. Please let them come out and drink with us." Then the old man called out, "Xiao'er!" Soon the young man came in from outside. The old man said, "This is my son, Xiao'er." The young man bowed to Qubing and sat down.

Qubing asked about the old man's family and the old man replied, "My family name is Hu, and my given name is Yijun." Qubing was by nature bold and uninhibited, and he began to talk cheerfully and freely. Xiao'er was also a free and easy-going person. In the conversation, Qubing and Xiao'er developed a liking for each other. Qubing being twenty-one was two years older than Xiao'er, so he referred to Xiao'er as his younger brother. The old man said, "I have heard that your grandfather wrote a book called *Anecdotes of the Tushan Family*[1]. Do you know the book?" Qubing replied, "Yes, I know it." The old man said, "I am a descendant of Tushan. I can only

---

1. *Anecdotes of the Tushan Family* : In fact, this book is entirely fictitious. According to some Chinese myths, Tushan, a fox fairy, was the wife of Yu, the founder of the Xia Dynasty (c. 21st-16th century B.C.).

後，譜系猶能憶之；五代而上無傳焉。幸公子一垂教也。"
生略述涂山女佐禹之功，粉飾多詞，妙緒泉湧。叟大喜，
謂子曰："今幸得聞所未聞，公子亦非他人，可請阿母及
青鳳來，共聽之，亦令知我祖德也。"孝兒入幃中。少
時，媼偕女郎出。

trace the genealogy of my family up to the Tang Dynasty, and know nothing about it before the Five Dynasties. I hope you can tell me something about it." Qubing described in an exaggerated manner, the Tushan family's contribution in helping Yu to regulate rivers. He talked on and on with great eloquence. The old man was very happy and said to his son, "We are lucky today to hear so many things that we have never known before. Qubing is not a stranger, so go and ask your mother and Qingfeng in and let them also know the merits and virtues of our ancestors." His son went behind a curtain into the boudoir. Soon, the old lady came out with the girl.

十九　青鳳（三）

　　審顧之，弱態生嬌，秋波流慧，人間無其麗也。叟指婦云：“此為老荊。”又指女郎：“此青鳳，鄙人之猶女[1]也。頗惠，所聞見輒記不忘，故喚令聽之。”生談竟而飲，瞻顧女郎，停睇不轉。女覺之，輒俯其首。生陰躡蓮鉤，女急斂足，亦無慍怒。生神志飛揚，不能自主，拍案曰：“得婦如此，南面王[2]不易也！”媼見生漸醉，益狂，與女俱起，遽搴[3]幃去。生失望，乃辭叟出。而心縈縈，不能忘情於青鳳也。

　　至夜，復往，則蘭麝猶芳，而凝待終宵，寂無聲咳。歸

---

1. 猶女：姪女。
2. 南面王：帝王。古代帝王的寶座一般都朝南，因此稱南面王。
3. 搴（qiān）：掀開。

19   Qingfeng (3)

Qubing saw that the girl was bewitchingly tender and charming and had a pair of bright, clear eyes. No woman in the world could match her in beauty. The old man pointed at the old lady and said, "This is my wife." Then he pointed at the girl, saying, "This is my niece, Qingfeng, a very smart girl who has an indelible memory of what she hears or sees. So I want her to listen to what you say about our ancestors." Qubing continued speaking for a while, then he sipped from his drink again, his eyes glued to the girl. Becoming aware of Qubing's stare, the girl lowered her head. Qubing then secretly touched the girl's foot under the table with his own, and the girl withdrew her foot quickly, but without becoming angry. Qubing was getting excited and was unable to control himself. Suddenly, he struck the table and cried out, "If I could marry a beautiful girl like you, I would not even exchange her for the throne!" The old lady realized that he was drunk and beside himself, so she and the girl rose from the table, lifted the curtain and hastily returned to the boudoir. Qubing was very disappointed, so he took leave of the old man. Since then, Qubing became obsessed and just could not forget Qingfeng.

The next evening, Qubing went to the same room again and waited there all night. It was so quiet that not the slightest sound was heard, though he could still smell the lingering fragrance[1]. Qubing went back and discussed with his wife the

---

1. lingering fragrance: In the past, a girl's chamber was often perfumed with musk or a variety of fragrant herbs.

與妻謀，欲攜家而居之，冀得一遇。妻不從，生乃自往，讀[4]於樓下。夜方憑几，一鬼披髮入，面黑如漆，張目視生。生笑，染指研墨自塗，灼灼然相與對視。鬼慚而去。

4. 讀：讀書；這裏指讀書的地方。

intention of moving with the family into the mansion because
he wanted to see Qingfeng again. However, his wife refused to
move with him. Thus, Qubing moved back to the mansion by
himself, and found a room as his study on the ground floor.
One night, while he was leaning against a desk, an unkempt
ghost with a jet-black face came in and stared at him. Qubing
laughed. He dipped his finger in some black ink, smeared it on
his face, and gazed back steadily at the ghost with his sparkling
eyes. His stare made the ghost nervous and it finally left.

二十 青鳳 （四）

次夜，更既深，滅燭欲寢，聞樓後發扃[1]，闢之閛然[2]。急起窺覘，則扉半啟。俄聞履聲細碎，有燭光自房中出。視之，則青鳳也。驟見生，駭而卻退，遽闔雙扉。生長跽[3]而致詞曰：“小生不避險惡，實以卿故。幸無他人，得一握手為笑，死不憾耳。”女遙語曰：“惓惓[4]深情，妾豈不知？但叔閨訓嚴，不敢奉命。”生固哀之，云：“亦不敢望肌膚之親，但一見顏色足矣。”女似肯可，啟關出，捉之臂而曳之。

生狂喜，相將入樓下，擁而加諸膝。女曰：“幸有夙分；過此一夕，即相思無用矣。”問：“何故？”曰：“阿叔畏君狂，故化厲鬼以相嚇，而君不動也。今已卜居[5]他

---

1. 發扃（jiōng）：拔掉門閂。
2. 閛（pēng）然：門被推開的聲音。
3. 長跽：長跪。直挺挺地跪着。
4. 惓惓：拳拳，形容懇切。
5. 卜居：擇居，這裏指遷居。

20 Qingfeng (4)

The next evening after midnight, Qubing blew out the candle and was about to go to bed. Suddenly, he heard from the back of the house the noise of a bolt being unlocked, followed by the sound of a door being pushed open. He quickly rose to see what it was and saw that the door was half opened and that someone carrying a lighted candle was walking out of the room in quick short steps. It was Qingfeng. Startled to see Qubing all of a sudden, Qingfeng hastily stepped back and closed the door. Qubing knelt and said sincerely, "I am risking my life to be here to see you, and I am so lucky that no one else is here. If you can let me hold your hand and see your smiling face, I would die without any regret." Qingfeng replied from inside the room, "How can I not know your deep feelings about me? But my uncle disciplines me strictly, so I cannot fulfill your request." Qubing implored her persistently and said, "I entertain no high hopes of marrying you, but only ask to see your face." It seemed that the girl agreed because she opened the door, came out, and helped Qubing stand up.

Qubing was wild with joy, and holding hands, they both went downstairs. After entering his room, Qubing held her in his arms and made her sit on his lap. Qingfeng said to him, "It is lucky that we have this opportunity to see each other tonight. After tonight, we will never have the chance no matter how hard you want to see me." "Why?" Qubing asked. Qingfeng replied, "My uncle was scared by your wild behaviour, so he transformed himself into a hideous ghost to scare you away. However, he was not able to frighten you. Therefore, today he found us a new house, and they are busy moving things to the

所，一家皆移什物赴新居，而妾留守，明日即發矣。"言已，欲去，云："恐叔歸。"生強止之，欲與為歡。方持論[6]間，叟掩入。女羞懼無以自容，俯首倚牀，拈帶不語。

---

6. 持論：持，拉拉扯扯；論，爭論。

new house. I am staying behind to take care of the rest of the things. I will leave tomorrow." After that, Qingfeng wanted to leave, saying, "I am afraid my uncle will come back." Qubing stopped her and wanted to sleep with her. While Qubing was dragging her, the old man came in. Qingfeng felt too ashamed to raise her head. Leaning on the bed, she held the belt of her dress without saying a word.

二十一　青鳳（五）

　　叟怒曰：“賤輩辱吾門戶！不速去，鞭撻且從其後！”女低頭急去，叟亦出。尾而聽之，訶詬萬端。聞青鳳嚶嚶啜泣，生心意如割，大聲曰：“罪在小生，於青鳳何與？倘宥[1]鳳也，刀鋸鈇鉞，小生願身受之！”良久寂然，生乃歸寢。

　　自此第內絕不復聲息矣。生叔聞而奇之，願售以居。不較直[2]。生喜，攜家口而遷焉。居逾年，甚適，而未嘗須臾忘鳳也。

　　會清明上墓歸，見小狐二，為犬逼逐。其一投荒竄去，一則皇急道上。望見生，依依哀啼，聳耳輯首[3]，似乞其援。生憐之，啟裳衿，提抱以歸。

---

1. 宥：原諒。
2. 不較直：不計較價錢。
3. 聳耳輯首：縮頭順耳，形容動物非常害怕，乞求憐憫的樣子。

70

21 Qingfeng (5)

The old man cried out furiously, "You have brought disgrace to this family! Get out of here, and wait for me to lash you!" Qingfeng ran out of the room with her head lowered, followed by the old man. Qubing could hear from behind the old man scolding Qingfeng abusively in every possible way, causing her to weep. Qubing felt hurt as if a knife were piercing his heart, so he said loudly, "It is my fault, and it has nothing to do with Qingfeng. If you could forgive her, I would accept any kind of punishment; kill me with a knife or an axe, whatever you want!" After quite a while, the room was quiet, and Qubing fell asleep.

From then on, nothing unusual happened again in the mansion. Qubing's uncle felt very strange about the events, so he sold the mansion to Qubing at a low price. Qubing was happy to move his whole family there. More than a year had passed, and Qubing felt very comfortable living there, but he could not forget Qingfeng for a moment.

At the Qingming Festival[1], Qubing went to pay respects at his ancestors' tombs. On his way back, he saw two small foxes being chased by a dog. One of the foxes ran into the wilderness, and the other dashed along the road in panic. Upon seeing Qubing, the fox came up to him, drooping its head and crying piteously as if it were imploring him for help. Qubing felt pity for the fox. He took it in his arms, covered it with his sleeves and went home.

---

1. Qingming Festival: see Passage 6, Note 1.

閉門，置牀上，則青鳳也。大喜，慰問。女曰：“適與婢子戲，遭此大厄[4]。脫非郎君，必葬犬腹。望無以非類見憎[5]。”生曰：“日切懷思，繫於魂夢。見卿如獲異寶，何憎之云！”女曰：“此天數也，不因顛覆[6]，何得相從？然幸矣，婢子必以妾為已死，可與君堅永約[7]耳。”生喜，另舍舍之。

　　……[8]

―――――――

4. 遭此大厄：遭遇災禍。
5. 望無以非類見憎：希望不要因為我為異類而嫌惡。
6. 顛覆：災禍。
7. 堅永約：堅守盟約，白頭偕老。
8. 後來，青鳳的叔叔，一隻黑狐，被去病的朋友獵獲了。孝兒求去病救救自己的父親。去病救了黑狐。兩家盡釋前嫌，黑狐一家又搬了回來。

72

On returning home he closed the door, and put the fox on the bed. Suddenly, the fox turned into Qingfeng. Qubing was overjoyed and comforted her. Qingfeng said, "While I was taking a walk with my maid, I fell upon this misfortune. Had it not been for you, I would have been swallowed by the hounds. I hope you won't dislike me because I am a fox." Qubing said, "I have been thinking about you day and night, even in my dreams. Finding you has made me feel as if I have discovered a priceless treasure. How could you think that I would dislike you?" Qingfeng said, "This is fate. If I had not encountered the disaster, I would never have had the chance to meet you again. I am so lucky because my maid must think that I am dead, and so we can stay together for the rest of our lives." Qubing was very happy and found another house for Qingfeng.

...²

---

2. Later, Qingfeng's uncle, a black fox, was caught by Qubing's friend. Xiao'er asked Qubing to save his father, and he did so. Qubing and Qingfeng's uncle reconciled with each other. Finally, the fox family moved into the mansion again and they lived together peacefully thereafter.

二十二　嬰寧（一）

　　王子服，莒之羅店人。早孤。絕惠，十四入泮[1]。母最愛之，尋常不令游郊野。聘蕭氏，未嫁而夭，故求凰未就也。

　　會上元，有舅氏子吳生，邀同眺矚[2]。方至村外，舅家有僕來，招吳去。生見游女如雲，乘興獨遨。有女郎攜婢，拈梅花一枝，容華絕代，笑容可掬。生注目不移，竟忘顧忌。女過去數武[3]，顧婢曰：“個兒郎目灼灼似賊！”遺花地上，笑語自去。

---

1. 入泮：見第十一篇註2。
2. 眺矚：登高遠望。這裏是遊覽的意思。
3. 數武：幾步。武，半步。

22   A Laughing Girl Named Yingning (1)

In Luodian of Ju county, Shandong Province, there was a man named Wang Zifu. His father died when he was a child. Wang was very clever and at the age of fourteen, he had already become a *xiucai*[1]. His mother doted on him very much and would not even allow him to play on the outskirts of the village. Wang entered into an engagement with a girl from the Xiao family, but the girl died before the wedding, so Wang was unmarried.

Now it was the day of the Lantern Festival[2]. Wang's cousin Wu invited him to go sightseeing. When they walked out of the village, a servant of the Wu family overtook them and called Wu back. Seeing many beautiful girls in the crowd, Wang decided to stay and enjoy the sights alone. Suddenly, he saw a matchless beauty holding a spray of plum blossoms. She was radiant with smiles and was followed by her maid. Free from all inhibitions, Wang kept his eyes fixed on the girl. Passing by him a few steps away, the girl turned to the maid and said, "This young man has greedy eyes like a thief!" She then threw the flowers on the ground and walked away talking and laughing.

---

1. *xiucai* : see Passage 11, Note 1.
2. Lantern Festival: a festival on the the fifteenth of the first lunar month, a day of the full moon, when people celebrate with lanterns and visit lantern fairs. In old China, girls had to stay home on normal days to avoid male strangers and were allowed to go out only on holidays like this.

生拾花悵然，神魂喪失，怏怏遂返。至家，藏花枕底，垂頭而睡，不語亦不食。母憂之。醮禳[4]益劇，肌革銳減。醫師診視，投劑發表，忽忽若迷。母撫問所由，默然不答。

適吳生來，囑密詰之。吳至榻前，生見之淚下。吳就榻慰解，漸致研詰。生具吐其實，且求謀畫。吳笑曰："君意亦復癡！此願有何難遂？當代訪之。徒步於野，必非世家。如其未字，事固諧矣；不然，拼以重賂，計必允遂。但得痊瘳，成事在我。"生聞之，不覺解頤[5]。

---

4. 醮禳：請和尚、道士等作法驅鬼，避邪。
5. 解頤：臉上露出笑容。

Wang picked up the flowers and stared blankly as if he had lost his soul. Returning home in low spirits, he put the flowers under his pillow and lay on the bed. He would neither talk nor eat. His mother was extremely worried about him. She invited some Taoist priests and monks to come to exorcize evil spirits[3], but it seemed that her son's condition continued to worsen. Wang was getting thinner rapidly. His mother asked a doctor to give him medical treatment. After taking some medicine, Wang was still in a trance and seemed to have lost his consciousness. His mother asked him the cause of his sickness, but he did not say anything.

One day, Wu came to see Wang and Wang's mother asked him to inquire the cause of her son's illness. Wu came to Wang's room. On seeing Wu, Wang wept. Wu said a few words to comfort him and gradually led up to the point in question. Wang told him the truth and asked for help. Wu laughed and said, "How foolish you are to pine for her! I see no difficulty in fulfilling your wish. I will find the girl for you. Travelling alone on foot, she could not be a daughter of an aristocratic family. It she is not yet betrothed, it will be easy. Otherwise, we can offer her family a huge sum of betrothal money. I am sure they will approve of the marriage. All you have to do is to get well. I will take care of the rest." After hearing this, Wang smiled.

---

3. exorcize evil spirits: In the past, people believed that sickness was the result of evil influences.

吳出告母，物色女子居里，而探訪既窮，並無蹤緒。母大憂，無所為計。然自吳去後，顏頓開，食亦略進。數日，吳復來。生問所謀。吳紿之曰：「已得之矣。我以為誰何人，乃我姑氏女，即君姨妹行，今尚待聘。雖內戚有婚姻之嫌，實告之，無不諧者」。生喜溢眉宇，問：「居何里？」吳詭曰：「西南山中，去此可三十餘里。」生又付囑再四，吳銳身自任而去。

Wu came out and told everything to Wang's mother. The mother spared no effort to look for the girl but found no trace of her. She was extremely worried; however, there was nothing she could do. After Wu's visit, Wang became happy and started to eat a little. Several days later, Wu came again. Wang asked him how the thing was going. Wu lied to him, "I have found her. Guess who she is? She is my aunt's daughter, and also your cousin. She is now waiting to be betrothed. Though marriages between cousins are not generally acceptable, if we tell them the truth, I am sure the difficulty will be overcome." Wang was radiant with joy. He asked Wu, "Where does she live?" Wu lied to him again, "She lives in the southwest mountains. It is about ten miles from here." Wang urged Wu again and again to do his best for him. Wu said that he would definitely be responsible for everything and left.

二十三 嬰寧（二）

　　生由是飲食漸加，日就平復。探視枕底，花雖枯，未便凋落。凝思把玩，如見其人。怪吳不至，折柬招之。吳支託不肯赴招。生恚怒，悒悒不歡。母慮其復病，急為議姻；略與商榷，輒搖首不願，惟日盼吳。吳迄無耗，益怨恨之。轉思三十里非遙，何必仰息他人？懷梅袖中，負氣自往，而家人不知也。

　　伶仃獨步，無可問程，但望南山行去。約三十餘里，亂山合沓[1]，空翠爽肌，寂無人行，止有鳥道[2]。遙望谷底，叢花亂樹中，隱隱有小里落。下山入村，見舍宇無多，皆茅屋，而意甚修雅。北向一家，門前皆絲柳，牆內

---

1. 合沓：重迭。
2. 止有鳥道：只有險峻狹窄的山間小路。

23 A Laughing Girl Named Yingning (2)

From that moment on, Wang's appetite and health gradually improved. Though the plum blossoms under his pillow withered, the petals had not fallen off. Looking at the flowers, he was lost in thought and it seemed that he saw the girl again. Soon he started to blame Wu for not coming to see him. He wrote a letter and asked him to come, but Wu refused by saying that he had something to do. Wang got angry and depressed. His mother worried that he would relapse into his old illness, so she asked someone to propose a marriage for him. However, each time this was mentioned, Wang would shake his head, and sat day after day waiting for Wu. Hearing nothing from Wu, Wang hated him all the more. Then he thought that ten miles was no great distance. Why should he rely on someone else? So concealing the plum blossoms in his sleeve, he went out looking for the girl in a fit of pique. His family knew nothing about his departure.

Walking all alone, Wang found no one to show him the way to the girl's home. So he went towards the south mountains. After walking about ten miles, he came to a place where he saw mountains upon mountains. Here the verdant trees were refreshing. It was so quiet; not a single person passed by. The mountain path was so narrow and precipitous. Down in the valley below, he vaguely saw among the flowering shrubs and thickets, a small village. So he descended from the hill to the village. There were not too many houses there, and most of them were thatched cottages elegantly laid out. Among them, there was a north-facing cottage with weeping willow trees in

桃杏尤繁，間以修竹；野鳥格磔[3]其中。意其園亭，不敢遽入。回顧對戶，有巨石滑潔，因據坐少憩。

俄聞牆內有女子，長呼"小榮"，其聲嬌細。方佇聽間，一女郎由東而西，執杏花一朵，俯首自簪。舉頭見生，遂不復簪，含笑拈花而入。審視之，即上元途中所遇也。心驟喜。但念無以階進[4]；欲呼姨氏，顧從無還往，懼有訛誤。門內無人可問。坐臥徘徊，自朝至於日昃，盈盈望斷，並忘飢渴。時見女子露半面來窺，似訝其不去者。

忽一老嫗扶杖出，顧生曰："何處郎君，聞自辰刻便來，以至於今。意將何為？得勿飢耶？"生急起揖之，答云："將以盼親[5]。"嫗聾聵不聞。又大言之。乃問："貴戚何姓？"生不能答。

---

3. 格磔（zhé）：形容鳥的叫聲。
4. 階進：進見的原因。
5. 盼親：探訪親戚。

front of the gate. Inside the wall were peach and apricot trees in full bloom interspersed with tall bamboos. Birds were chirping among the trees. Wang thought that this must be a private garden, so he did not venture to go in. He turned to the opposite house and saw a huge smooth stone, so he sat on it to have a rest.

Soon he heard a girl inside the wall calling "Xiaorong" in a soft, sweet voice. While he was listening, he saw a girl walking across the garden, holding an apricot flower in her hand. She was about to put the flower in her hair. When she raised her head and saw Wang, she stopped and entered the house with a smile on her face and the flower in her hand. Looking carefully, Wang recognized that this was exactly the girl whom he had met at the Lantern Festival. Filled with joy, he wanted to follow the girl, but there was no excuse for him to do so. He wanted to say that he was here to visit his aunt; however, since they never had any contact before, Wang was afraid that he might make a mistake. There was no one around whom he could ask about the girl's family. He felt very uneasy whether sitting or standing. From morning till night, he paced up and down, waiting to see someone, while even forgetting his hunger and thirst. Occasionally, the girl, half showing her face, peeped at him, and it seemed that she was surprised to see him still there.

Suddenly, an old lady leaning on a stick came out. She asked Wang, "Where do you come from? I heard that you came this morning and stayed here until now. What do you want? Don't you feel hungry?" Wang got up hurriedly and bowed to her, saying, "I am here looking for my relatives." The old lady was partially deaf and did not catch his words. So Wang spoke again loudly. The old lady asked, "Can you tell me their names?" Wang was unable to answer.

二十四　嬰寧（三）

　　媼笑曰："奇哉！姓名尚自不知，何親可探？我視郎君，亦書癡耳。不如從我來，啖以粗糲，家有短榻可臥。待明朝歸，詢知姓氏，再來探訪，不晚也。"生方腹餒思啖，又從此漸近麗人，大喜。從媼入，見門內白石砌路，夾道紅花，片片墮階上；曲折而西，又啟一關，豆棚花架滿庭中。

　　肅客入舍[1]，粉壁光明如鏡；窗外海棠枝朵，探入室中；裀藉[2]几榻，罔不潔澤。甫坐，即有人自窗外隱約相窺。媼喚："小榮！可速作黍。"外有婢子嗷聲[3]而應。坐次，具展宗閥。媼曰："郎君外祖，莫姓吳否？"曰："然。"媼驚曰："是吾甥也！尊堂，我妹子。年來以家竇貧[4]，又無三尺男，遂至音問梗塞。甥長成如許，尚不相識。"生曰："此來即為姨也，匆遽遂忘姓氏。"媼曰："老

---

1. 肅客入舍：請客人先進屋。
2. 裀藉：坐墊。
3. 嗷（jiào）：高聲。
4. 竇貧：貧窮。

24   A Laughing Girl Named Yingning (3)

The old lady laughed and said, "It is strange. How can you find your relative when you do not even know his name? I guess you are just a bookworm. You'd better come with me, we have some simple food and a bed for you. Tomorrow you can return and find out the names of your relatives before you come back here. It is never too late." It was not until now that Wang began to feel hungry, and besides, this invitation would bring him nearer to the beautiful girl, so he happily accepted it. Following the old lady, Wang walked in. Inside the door was a path paved with white stones and flanked with many red flowers. Petals scattered on the path. Following the winding path, they came to another door, through which they entered a courtyard full of trellised climbing plants of peas and flowers.

The old lady politely asked Wang to enter the room. The whitewashed walls of the room were bright and clean. A branch of begonia blossoms stretched into the room through a window. Everything inside the room such as cushions, tables and couches was nice and clean. Hardly had Wang sat down when he felt that someone was peeking at him through a window. The old lady cried out, "Xiaorong, go and cook the millet meal quick." Immediately, a maid answered loudly from outside. The old lady took a seat opposite Wang. They told each other their family names. The old lady said, "Is your maternal grandfather named Wu?" Wang answered, "Yes." The old lady cried out in surprise, "You are my nephew! Your mother is my sister. Since we have been poor for years and have no son, your mother and I lost contact. You have grown up and I don't even know you." Wang said, "I am here looking for you. In a hurry, I forgot your name."

身秦姓，並無誕育；弱息僅存，亦為庶產。渠母改醮，遺我鞠養。頗亦不鈍，但少教訓，嬉不知愁。少頃，使來拜識。”

　　未幾，婢子具飯，雛尾盈握[5]。媼勸餐已，婢來斂具。媼曰：“喚寧姑來。”婢應去。良久，聞戶外隱有笑聲。媼又喚曰：“嬰寧，汝姨兄在此。”戶外嗤嗤笑不已。婢推之以入，猶掩其口，笑不可遏。媼嗔目曰：“有客在，咤咤叱叱，是何景象？”女忍笑而立，生揖之。媼曰：“此王郎，汝姨子。一家尚不相識，可笑人也。”生問：“妹子年幾何矣？”媼未能解。生又言之。女復笑，不可仰視。媼謂生曰：“我言少教誨，此可見矣。年已十六，呆癡裁如嬰兒。”生曰：“小於甥一歲。”曰：“阿甥已十七矣，得非庚午屬馬者耶？”生首應之。

────────────

5. 雛尾盈握：肥嫩的小雞。

The old lady said, "My family name is Qin, and I have no son, only a daughter. She is the child of a concubine who remarried after our husband's death. She left the girl with me. The girl is quite clever, but not disciplined. She never worries about anything but laughs all the time. Soon I will introduce her to you."

After a while, the maid brought in a meal of scrumptious chicken. The old lady pressed him to eat. When they had finished, the maid came in to clear the table. The old lady said to her, "Call Miss Yingning." The maid said "yes" and left. After a while, someone was heard giggling at the door. The old lady called again, "Yingning, your cousin is here." The girl kept on laughing. When the maid pushed her into the room, she, covering her mouth with her hands, still could not stop laughing. The old lady gave her an angry look and said, "We have a guest here. What kind of manners is this, laughing and giggling?" The girl held her laughter and stood there. Wang made a bow to her. The old lady said, "This is your aunt's son Wang. It is so funny that we, as a family, don't know each other." Wang asked, "How old is she?" The old lady did not hear him, so Wang asked again. The girl laughed, and could not even raise her head. The old lady said to Wang, "I told you that she lacks discipline. Though she is sixteen, she behaves as foolishly as a child." Wang said, "She is one year younger than I." The old lady asked, "You are seventeen, then? Weren't you born in the Year of the Horse?" Wang nodded.

二十五　嬰寧（四）

又問：“甥婦阿誰？”答云：“無之。”曰：“如甥才貌，何十七歲猶未聘？嬰寧亦無姑家，極相匹敵；惜有內親之嫌。”生無語，目注嬰寧，不遑他瞬。婢向女小語云：“目灼灼，賊腔未改！”女又大笑，顧婢曰：“視碧桃開未？”遽起，以袖掩口，細碎連步而出。至門外，笑聲始縱。媼亦起，喚婢襆被，為生安置。曰：“阿甥來不易，宜留三五日，遲遲送汝歸。如嫌幽悶，舍後有小園，可供消遣；有書可讀。”

次日，至舍後，果有園半畝，細草鋪氈，楊花糝[1]徑；有草舍三楹，花木四合其所。穿花小步，聞樹頭蘇蘇有

---

1. 糝（sǎn）：點點撒落。

25 A Laughing Girl Named Yingning (4)

The old lady asked again, "Who is your wife?" Wang answered, "I am not married." The old lady said, "How can a handsome and clever young man like you not be married at the age of seventeen[1]? Yingning is not engaged either. You two would make a very good couple, were you not relatives." Wang said nothing, and he stared at Yingning without taking his eyes off her for a second. The maid said to Yingning in a low voice, "You see, he still gets those wicked eyes without changing a bit." Yingning laughed and said to the maid, "Let's go and see if the peach trees are in blossom." After that, covering her mouth with her sleeve, she went out in quick short steps. As soon as she went out of the room, she burst into a hearty fit of laughter. The old lady stood up and told the maid to make the bed for Wang and said to him, "You don't come here often, and you really should stay here for several days. We will send you home later. If you feel bored, you can go to the small garden behind the house. There you can take a walk and read some books."

The next day, Wang went to the back of the house, and as expected, there was a small garden about the size of half a *mu*[2]. The lush green grass soft like a carpet was strewn with the catkins of the poplars. There were three thatched cottages surrounded by trees and flowers. While walking through the

---

1. the age of seventeen: In old China, people usually married at the age of fifteen or sixteen. In order to have grandsons to perpetuate the family, parents liked to have their sons married as early as possible.
2. *mu* : see Passage 11, Note 2.

聲，仰視，則嬰寧在上。見生來，狂笑欲墮。生曰：「勿
爾，墮矣！」女且下且笑，不能自止。方將及地，失手而
墮，笑乃止。生扶之，陰捘[2]其腕。女笑又作，倚樹不能
行，良久乃罷。

　　生俟其笑歇，乃出袖中花示之。女接之，曰：「枯矣。
何留之？」曰：「此上元妹子所遺，故存之。」問：「存之
何意？」曰：「以示相愛不忘也。自上元相遇，凝思成病，
自分化為異物[3]；不圖得見顏色，幸垂憐憫。」女曰：「此
大細事。至戚何所靳惜[4]？待郎行時，園中花，當喚老奴
來，折一巨捆負送之。」生曰：「妹子癡耶？」女曰：「何
便是癡？」生曰：「我非愛花，愛拈花之人耳。」女曰：「葭
莩[5]之情，愛何待言。」生曰：「我所謂愛，非瓜葛[6]之愛，
乃夫妻之愛。」女曰：「有以異乎？」曰：「夜共枕席耳。」
女俯思良久，曰：「我不慣與生人睡。」語未已，婢潛至，
生惶恐遁去。

2. 捘（zùn）：捏。
3. 自分化為異物：自以為不久於人世。
4. 靳惜：吝惜。
5. 葭莩（jiāfú）：親戚。
6. 瓜葛：親戚。

flowering shrubs, Wang heard a noise from a tree. Raising his head, he found Yingning on the tree. Upon seeing Wang coming, Yingning burst out laughing and nearly fell down the tree. Wang said to her, "Don't! You will fall." Yingning came down, laughing all the way, unable to control herself, until when she was near the ground, she lost hold and fell off the tree and stopped laughing. Wang helped her to her feet and took this opportunity to squeeze her wrist. Leaning against a tree, Yingning laughed again, so much that she could hardly move for a long while.

Wang waited until she stopped laughing, and took the branch of withered flowers out from his sleeve and handed it to Yingning. Taking the flowers, Yingning said, "They are withered. Why are you still keeping them?" Wang said, "I am keeping them because you dropped them during the Lantern Festival." Yingning asked again, "What's your purpose of keeping them?" Wang said, "To show my love. From the day we met, I was lovesick and almost died. I never thought that I could see you again. I hope you have pity on me." Yingning said, "It's nothing. Since we are cousins, I won't grudge giving you anything. Before you leave, I will tell the old servant to pick a huge bunch of flowers from the garden for you." Wang said, "How foolish you are!" Yingning asked, "What makes you say that?" Wang replied, "I don't care about the flowers. I love the person who holds the flowers." Yingning said, "Of course you love me. We are relatives." Wang said, "I am not talking about the love between cousins. It is the love between husband and wife." Yingning asked, "So what's the difference?" Wang replied, "Husband and wife sleep together at night." Yingning lowered her head and thought about it for a while, and said, "I am not used to sleeping with strangers." At that moment, the maid came in quietly. Wang was scared, so he left.

二十六　嬰寧（五）

　　少時，會母所。母問："何往？"女答以園中共話。媼
曰："飯熟已久，有何長言，周遮[1]乃爾。"女曰："大哥
欲我共寢。"言未已，生大窘，急目瞪之。女微笑而止。
幸媼不聞，猶絮絮究詰。生急以他詞掩之，因小語責女。
女曰："適此語不應說耶？"生曰："此背人語。"女曰：
"背他人，豈得背老母。且寢處亦常事，何諱之？"生恨其
癡，無術可以悟之。食方竟，家中人捉雙衛[2]來尋生。

　　先是，母待生久不歸，始疑；村中搜覓幾遍，竟無蹤
兆。因往詢吳。吳憶曩言，因教於西南山村行覓。凡歷數
村，始至於此。生出門，適相值，便入告媼，且請偕女同

---

1. 周遮：囉囉嗦嗦，話多的意思。
2. 捉雙衛：牽着兩頭驢。

26 A Laughing Girl Named Yingning (5)

After a while, they both came to the old lady's room. The lady asked Yingning, "Where have you been?" Yingning replied, "I was chatting with my cousin in the garden." The lady said, "Dinner has been ready for a long time. What made you talk for so long?" Yingning said, "He wanted to sleep with me." Yingning had hardly finished her words when Wang felt very embarrassed. He gave Yingning a stare, and Yingning smiled at him and stopped talking. Fortunately, the old lady did not catch her words and kept on asking the same question. Immediately, Wang put her off by saying something else. Wang whispered to Yingning, blaming her for telling that to the old lady. Yingning said, "Shouldn't I tell my mother that?" "No, you can only talk about it behind people's backs," Wang said. Yingning replied, "Behind others' backs, yes; but not behind my mother's back. Besides, sleeping is an ordinary thing, why shouldn't people talk about it?" Wang was exasperated by her dullness but did not know how to explain to her. When he finished his dinner, Wang found that his family had sent several servants with two donkeys coming to the place to look for him.

It appeared that when Wang's mother noticed that Wang had gone for a long time, she got worried and had people search for him several times in the village. However they found no trace of him, so she went to ask Wu. Wu recollected that he once told Wang that the girl lived in the southwest mountains, so they sent some servants there to look for him. They went to several villages, and finally came to this one and saw him walk out of the old lady's house incidentally. Wang went inside and

歸。嫗喜曰：“我有志，匪伊朝夕。但殘軀不能遠涉，得甥攜妹子去，識認阿姨，大好！”呼嬰寧。寧笑至。嫗曰：“有何喜，笑輒不輟？若不笑，當為全人。”因怒之以目。乃曰：“大哥欲同汝去。可便裝束。”又餉家人酒食，始送之出，曰：“姨家田產豐裕，能養冗人。到彼且勿歸，小學詩禮，亦好事翁姑。即煩阿姨，為汝擇一良匹。”二人遂發。至山坳，回顧，猶依稀見嫗倚門北望也。

......3

---

3. 王子服把嬰寧帶回家以後，他的母親很奇怪，因為她只有一個姐姐，曾嫁給秦家，但是已經死去多年了。後來，他們才明白，嬰寧是秦家狐妾的女兒，由鬼母撫養長大。王的母親開始還有些疑懼，久而久之，見嬰寧與常人無異，便讓二人結為夫妻。

told the old lady that he was going to take Yingning home with him. The old lady was very happy and said, "I have had this idea in my head for a long time. However, I am too old to withstand long journeys. If you can take her to see her aunt, that will be wonderful." After that, she called Yingning, who was laughing while she came out. The old lady stared at her angrily, saying, "What's so funny that makes you laugh all the time? You would be perfect if you did not behave like this." Then she said again, "Your cousin wants to take you home with him, you had better get yourself dressed."

The old lady provided the servants with some food and drink. Finally, she walked them to the door, and said to Yingning, "Your aunt is rich enough to support your living, so you don't have to come back. You should read some books and learn how to behave properly in order to take good care of your future parents-in-law. Later, you should ask your aunt to find you a good husband." The two left, and when they reached the foot of the mountain, looking back, they could faintly see the old lady leaning against the door still looking in their direction.

...[1]

---

1. After Wang brought Yingning home, his mother was surprised, for her sister, who married a man named Qin, died many years ago. Later, they figured out that Yingning was Qin's child and a fox fairy. She was brought up by Wang's mother's ghostly sister. Later Yingning became normal and was married to Wang and they had a son.

二十七　聶小倩（一）

　　寧采臣，浙人。性慷爽，廉隅自重[1]。每對人言：“生平無二色。”適赴金華，至北郭，解裝蘭若[2]。寺中殿塔壯麗；然蓬蒿沒人，似絕行蹤。東西僧舍，雙扉虛掩；惟南一小舍，扃鍵如新。又顧殿東隅，修竹拱把[3]；階下有巨池，野藕已花。意甚樂其幽杳。

　　會學使案臨[4]，城舍價昂，思便留止，遂散步以待僧歸。日暮，有士人來，啟南扉。寧趨為禮，且告以意。士人曰：“此間無房主，僕亦僑居。能甘荒落，旦晚惠教，幸甚。”

　　寧喜，藉藁[5]代牀，支板作几，為久客計。是夜，月明

---

1. 廉隅自重：廉隅，稜角。品行端正。
2. 蘭若：寺廟。
3. 拱把：一手滿握，喻粗壯。
4. 學使案臨：學使，提督學使，科舉時代各省主持教育和考試的官員。學使在三年任職期間到所轄各地主持考試稱案臨。
5. 藉藁：藉，鋪。藁，稻草。

27   Nie Xiaoqian (1)

Ning Caichen was a native of Zhejiang. Being a frank and generous person, he was reputed for his personal integrity. He often told others that he would never take concubines or have any lover except his wife. One year, he happened to go to Jinhua city to do some business and took shelter in a temple to the north of the city. The halls and pagodas of the temple were magnificent, but the courtyard was bleak and desolate with seemingly no trace of human beings. On either side were the Buddhist monks' abodes, the doors of which were ajar. Only the door of a small house on the south side was bolted with a new lock. In the east corner of the hall were groves of tall bamboos growing thick and strong. A few steps down the hall, there was a small pond in which lotuses were in bloom. The whole place was secluded and peaceful.

It was about the time when the scholars of Zhejiang Province would flock to the city to take the imperial examination held there. Ning thought that the cost of accommodation in the city would be very high, so he decided to stay here. While waiting for the monks to come back, he took a walk in the temple. At dusk, a man returned and opened the locked door. Ning approached him and with a bow, he told him his intention. The man said, "This is an abandoned temple. I am also lodging here for the time being. If you can put up with the loneliness and desolation here, it will be my pleasure to have your company and I may learn from you."

Ning was very happy. He laid some straw on the ground as his bed and put up a table with boards because he planned to

高潔，清光似水，二人促膝殿廊，各展姓字。士人自言：
"燕姓，字赤霞。"寧疑為赴試諸生，而聽其音聲，殊不類
浙。詰之，自言："秦人。"語甚樸誠。既而相對詞竭，
遂拱別歸寢。

　　寧以新居，久不成寐。聞舍北喁喁，如有家口。起伏
北壁石窗下，微窺之。見短牆外一小院落，有婦可四十
餘；又一媼衣㡠緋[6]，插蓬沓[7]，鮐背龍鍾，偶語月下。
婦曰："小倩何久不來？"媼曰："殆好至矣。"婦曰：
"將無向姥姥有怨言否？"曰："不聞，但意似蹙蹙[8]。"
婦曰："婢子不宜好相識[9]。"言未已，有一十七八女
子來，仿佛艷絕。

---

6. 㡠緋（yè fēi）：退了色的紅衣服。
7. 蓬沓：一種頭飾。
8. 蹙蹙：不太高興。
9. 相識：對待。

live here for some time. That night, the moon was clear and bright and the moonlight streamed down. The two men sat side by side in the corridor and told each other their names. The man said, "My family name is Yan, and my given name is Chixia." Ning thought that he must be a scholar who came to take the imperial examination. But from his accent, Ning knew that he was not from Zhejiang Province[1], so he asked Yan who told him that he was from Shanxi. Through the conversation, Ning felt that he was an honest and sincere person. After a while, they had nothing more to talk about, so they took leave and went to bed.

Being in a strange place, Ning was unable to fall asleep. Suddenly, he heard low sounds of talking outside, north of his room, and it seemed that a family was living there. He got out of bed and peeped through the north stone window. He saw on the other side of a low wall a small courtyard. A woman of about forty and a hunchbacked doddering woman, wearing a faded red gown and a big silver hair clasp, were chatting in the moonlight. One woman said, "Why has Xiaoqian not come yet?" The old woman said, "She will be here soon." "Did she complain to you?" The woman asked. "No, I haven't heard of any complaints, but she looked unhappy." The old woman answered. "We should not treat her too well." Hardly had the woman finished her words when a girl who was about seventeen or eighteen years old came over, and she looked exceedingly beautiful.

---

1. not from Zhejiang Province: Scholars usually took the imperial examinations in their home provinces.

二十八 聶小倩（二）

嫗笑曰：“背地不言人，我兩個正談道，小妖婢悄來無跡響。幸不訾[1]著短處。”又曰：“小娘子端好是畫中人，遮莫[2]老身是男子，也被攝魂去。”女曰：“姥姥不相譽，更阿誰道好？”婦人女子又不知何言。寧意其鄰人眷口，寢不復聽。

又許時，始寂無聲。方將睡去，覺有人至寢所。急起審顧，則北院女子也。驚問之。女笑曰：“月夜不寐，願修燕好。”寧正容曰：“卿防物議，我畏人言；略一失足，廉恥道喪。”女云：“夜無知者。”寧又咄之。女逡巡若復有詞。寧叱：“速去！不然，當呼南舍生知。”女懼，乃退。至戶外復返，以黃金一錠置褥上。寧掇擲庭墀，曰：“非義之物，污吾囊橐！”女慚，出，拾金自言曰：“此漢

---

1. 訾（zǐ）：談論。
2. 遮莫：假如。

28   Nie Xiaoqian (2)

The old woman laughed and said, "It is wise never to talk behind somebody's back, and it is true. We were talking about you when you, little bogey, stealthily arrived. Fortunately we were saying nothing bad about you." Then she continued, "You are so beautiful, just like a painted beauty. Were I a man, my spirit would have been summoned by you." The girl said, "If you don't praise me, who else will?" Later, they said something again, but Ning did not hear clearly. Thinking that they must be the neighbour's family members, Ning stopped listening and went back to sleep.

After a while, it became quiet outside. When Ning was about to fall asleep, he felt that someone came into his room. He immediately rose from the bed and looked around and saw the girl he had just seen from the north courtyard. He was surprised and asked what she was doing in his room. The girl laughed and said, "I could not fall asleep alone in such a beautiful moonlit night, so I am here to be with you." Ning looked serious and said, "You should behave yourself and beware of others' gossip. I fear gossip. A single slip may cause a lasting sense of shame." The girl said, "It's in the middle of the night, so nobody will know." Ning scolded her again. The girl hesitated and it seemed that she had something to say. Ning shouted at her, "Get out of here! Or, I will call the other man who lives in the south room here." The girl looked scared and left. As soon as she walked out, she turned back and put a small ingot of gold on his bed. Ning picked up the gold and threw it out, saying, "This ill-gotten wealth will dirty my bag!" The girl was ashamed.

當是鐵石。"

　　詰旦，有蘭溪生攜一僕來候試，寓於東廂，至夜暴亡。足心有小孔，如錐刺者，細細有血出。俱莫知故。經宿，僕一死，癥亦如之。向晚，燕生歸，寧質之，燕以為魅。寧素抗直[3]，頗不在意。

　　宵分，女子復至，謂寧曰："妾閱人多矣，未有剛腸如君者。君誠聖賢，妾不敢欺。小倩，姓聶氏，十八夭殂，葬寺側，輒被妖物威脅，歷役賤務；靦顏向人，實非所樂。今寺中無可殺者，恐當以夜叉來。"

---

3. 抗直：剛直。

She went out, picked up the gold and said, "This man must have a heart of stone."

The following morning, a scholar, coming with a servant from Lanxi County to take the examination, lodged in the east wing-room of the temple. That very night, he met his sudden death. In the sole of his foot, there was a small hole, as if bored by an awl, and from which a little blood came out. Nobody knew how he died. The next night, the servant of the dead scholar died like his master. At dusk, Yan came back. Ning asked him who killed those people. Yan told him that they were killed by ghosts. Since Ning was an upright man, he did not pay much attention to Yan's words.

At midnight, the girl came to Ning's room again and said to him, "I have seen many men, but none of them was as upright as you. You are indeed an honest person, and I don't want to deceive you. My name is Xiaoqian, and my family name is Nie. I died when I was eighteen years old and was buried beside this temple. I am often forced by demons to do mean things, seducing people against my wish, which I am ashamed of. Tonight, since there is no one else here to be killed, I am afraid they will send a ghost to kill you off."

二十九　聶小倩（三）

　　寧駭求計。女曰：“與燕生同室可免。”問：“何不惑燕生？”曰：“彼奇人也，不敢近。”問：“迷人若何？”曰：“狎昵我者，隱以錐刺其足，彼即茫若迷，因攝血以供妖飲；又或以金，非金也，乃羅剎鬼骨，留之能截取人心肝：二者，凡以投時好耳。”寧感謝。問戒備之期，答以明宵。

　　臨別泣曰：“妾墮玄海[1]，求岸不得。郎君義氣干雲[2]，必能拔生救苦。倘肯囊妾朽骨，歸葬安宅，不啻再造。”寧毅然諾之。因問葬處，曰：“但記取白楊之上，有烏巢者是也。”言已出門，紛然而滅。

---

1. 玄海：佛教語，指苦海。
2. 干雲：沖天。

29 Nie Xiaoqian (3)

Ning was terrified and asked Xiaoqian what he should do.
Xiaoqian said, "Stay in Yan's room, and you can avoid the
disaster." Ning asked, "Why don't you ensnare him?" The girl
replied, "He is an unusual person. I dare not get near him."
Ning asked, "How did you bewitch people?" The girl answered,
"Whenever a man was improperly familiar with me, I would
drill his foot with an awl. The man would lose consciousness.
After that, I would draw his blood for the demons to drink.
Sometimes I would give the victim gold. In fact, it was not
gold but the bone of the Luosha ghost[1]. Whoever took the gold
would lose his heart and liver. I used both ways, depending on
the taste of the victims." Ning thanked the girl for telling him
everything. He asked the girl when he should watch out. The
girl said that it would be the next evening.

Before she left, the girl wept and said, "I have fallen into
the sea of suffering and there is no way out for me. You are
above the rest in righteousness, so you can help me get out of
the abyss of misery. If you are willing to help me, pick up my
bones and bury them in a peaceful place. This will give me a
new life." Ning readily promised, and asked where her tomb
was. The girl said, "At the foot of a white poplar tree with a
crow's nest." After the words, she went out and disappeared.

---

1. the Luosha ghost: a man-eating ghost.

明日，恐燕他出，早詣邀致。辰後具酒饌，留意察燕。既約同宿。辭以性癖耽寂[3]。寧不聽，強攜臥具來。燕不得已，移榻從之，囑曰："僕知足下丈夫，傾風[4]良切。要有微衷[5]，難以遽白。幸勿翻窺篋襆，違之兩俱不利。"寧謹受教。既而各寢，燕以箱篋置窗上，就枕移時，齁如雷吼。

寧不能寐。近一更許，窗外隱隱有人影。俄而近窗來窺，目光睒閃。寧懼，方欲呼燕，忽有物裂篋而出，耀若匹練，觸折窗上石櫺，颼然一射，即遽斂入，宛如電滅。燕覺而起，寧偽睡以覘之。燕捧篋檢徵，取一物，對月嗅視，白光晶瑩，長可二寸，徑韭葉許。已而數重包固，仍置破篋中。

---

3. 耽寂：喜歡寂靜。
4. 傾風：傾慕你的風度。
5. 要有微衷：總是有些心裏話。要，總歸。

The next day, Ning was afraid that Yan would go out, so he went over early in the morning to invite Yan to a drink. Ning prepared some food and wine. While drinking together, Ning was careful to watch Yan's every mood. Later, Ning asked to stay in his room. Yan refused him, saying that being not a sociable person he would like to stay alone. Ning did not listen and brought his things to Yan's room. Yan had no choice but to make way for him. He said to Ning, "I know you are a decent man, and I really admire your conduct. However, there is something on my mind which I can't make clear now. Please don't open and peep into my chest and baggage because that will do harm to both of us." Ning respectfully consented to his request. They went to bed. Yan put his chest on the window-sill. As soon as he touched the pillow, he fell asleep, snoring thunderously.

Ning could not go to sleep. About midnight, he saw a figure moving outside the window. It approached the window and peeped through it. Its eyes flashed like lightning. Ning was terrified, and before he could call out to Yan, suddenly, something radiant, like a strip of white silk, broke through the chest and flew out, snapping the stone lattice of the window. It shot out and returned at once to the chest and disappeared like a flash of lightning. Yan woke up and rose from his bed. Ning pretended that he was sleeping and watched Yan stealthily. Yan went to check his chest and took out something. He looked at it carefully under the moonlight and sniffed it. It glittered like crystal and was about two inches long with the width of a willow leaf. After that, Yan wrapped it up in several layers and put it back in the broken chest.

三十 聶小倩（四）

　　自語曰：“何物老魅，直爾[1]大膽，致壞篋子。”遂復臥。寧大奇之，因起問之，且以所見告。燕曰：“既相知愛，何敢深隱。我，劍客也。若非石櫺，妖當立斃；雖然，亦傷。”問：“所緘何物？”曰：“劍也。適嗅之，有妖氣。”寧欲觀之。慨出相示，熒熒然一小劍也。於是益厚重燕。

　　明日，視窗外，有血跡。遂出寺北，見荒墳纍纍，果有白楊，烏巢其顛。

　　迨營謀既就[2]，趣裝欲歸。燕生設祖帳[3]，情義殷渥[4]。以破革囊贈寧，曰：“此劍袋也。寶藏可遠魑魅。”寧欲從授其術。曰：“如君信義剛直，可以為此。然君猶富貴中人，非此道中人也。”寧乃託有妹葬此，發掘女骨，斂以衣衾，賃舟而歸。

---

1. 直爾：竟然這樣。
2. 迨營謀既就：迨，等到。營謀，要做的事情。等到要做的事情都做完了以後。
3. 祖帳：祖，祖神，即傳說中的路神。臨行時設帳，祭祀路神，以保平安。這裏是擺酒餞行的意思。
4. 殷渥：友情深厚。

30   Nie Xiaoqian (4)

Yan talked to himself, "What an old ghost! How dare it break my chest." After these words, he went back to sleep. Ning was amazed. He got up and told Yan that he had seen everything. Yan said, "Since we are friends, how can I hide the truth from you? I am a swordsman. A moment ago, had it not been for the stone lattice of the window, I would have killed the ghost. Despite that, it was injured." "What's in your chest?" Ning asked. "It is a sword. When I sniffed it, it smelled of the ghost." Ning asked to have a look at the sword. Yan showed him readily. It was a small glittering sword. From then on, Ning respected Yan even more.

The next day, Ning found traces of blood outside the window. He came to the north of the temple and saw many tombs. As expected, there was a white poplar tree, and at the top of the tree was a crow's nest.

After finishing his business, Ning packed his things and was ready to go home. Yan gave a farewell dinner for him and was very cordial. Before leaving, Yan gave Ning an old leather bag and said, "This is a sack for swords, and if you carry it with you, no ghosts will dare to approach you." Ning told him that he wanted to learn swordsmanship. Yan said, "An honest and upright person like you should learn some such skill. However, you belong to the rich and the powerful, not to us." Ning pretended that he had a sister buried here, so he dug out the bones of the girl, wrapped them up in funerary cloth, hired a boat, and brought them home.

寧齋臨野，因營墳葬諸齋外。祭而祝曰：“憐卿孤魂，葬近蝸居，歌哭相聞，庶不見陵於雄鬼。一甌漿水飲，殊不清旨，幸不為嫌！”祝畢而返。

　　後有人呼曰：“緩待同行！”回顧，則小倩也。歡喜謝曰：“君信義，十死不足以報。請從歸，拜識姑嫜，媵御無悔[5]。”審諦之，肌映流霞，足翹細筍，白晝端相，嬌艷尤絕。

　　遂與俱至齋中。囑坐少待，先入白母。母愕然。時寧妻久病，母戒勿言，恐所駭驚。言次，女已翩然入，拜伏地下。寧曰：“此小倩也。”母驚顧不遑。女謂母曰：“兒飄然一身，遠父母兄弟。蒙公子露覆[6]，澤被髮膚，願執箕

---

5. 媵御無悔：無論是做妾，還是做婢，都無怨無悔。
6. 露覆：露，膏澤。覆，庇蔭。露覆，受膏澤庇蔭，受關懷照顧的意思。

110

Ning's study was facing a tract of wilderness. Ning built a tomb and buried the bones of the girl there. During the memorial ceremony for the girl, he prayed, "I sympathize with you, a lonely ghost and bury you here near my study, so that we can hear from each other, whether we sing or cry. I hope you will never be bullied by male ghosts. Here is a cup of wine for you. Though it is nothing sweet and refreshing, I hope you don't mind this libation." After those words, he proceeded home.

Suddenly, someone called him from behind, "Wait a minute! I will go with you." Ning turned his head and saw Xiaoqian who looked very happy. She thanked him, saying, "You are trustworthy. Dying ten times for you will not be enough to repay your kindness. Please allow me to go with you and meet your parents. I won't regret even to be your maid." Looking her up and down, Ning found that she had very delicate skin and rosy cheeks beautiful as a rainbow, and pointed feet like the tips of bamboo shoots[1]. She looked even more charming by daytime.

They went back to Ning's study together. Ning let her wait there, and he went to tell his mother. After hearing this, his mother was shocked. She advised Ning not to say a word about this to his wife, because she had been ill for a long time. The mother was afraid that this would scare her. While they were talking, Xiaoqian came in lithely and threw herself down on her knees. Ning said, "This is Xiaoqian." The mother was both surprised and alarmed. Xiaoqian said, "I am alone, away from my parents and siblings. Fortunately, I met Ning and he really

---

1. feet like the tips of bamboo shoots: Chinese women used to bind their feet, and the smaller their feet the better-looking they were.

帚，以報高義。"母見其綽約可愛，始敢與言，曰："小娘子惠顧吾兒，老身喜不可已。但平生止此兒，用承桃緒[7]，不敢令有鬼偶。"

---

7. 桃緒：傳宗接代。

cares about me. I am willing to wait upon him to repay his kindness." Seeing that she was such a lovely and beautiful girl, the mother lost her fear of her and said, "I am very glad that you like my son. But I have only one son, and I hope he can keep the family line. So I don't want him to marry a ghost."

三十一　聶小倩（五）

女曰：“兒實無二心，泉下人，既不見信於老母，請以兄事，依高堂，奉晨昏，如何？”母憐其誠，允之。即欲拜嫂。母辭以疾，乃止。女即入廚下，代母尸饔[1]。入房穿榻，似熟居者。

……[2]

一日，俯頸窗前，怊悵若失。忽問：“革囊何在？”曰：“以卿畏之，故緘置他所。”曰：“妾受生氣已久，當不復畏，宜取掛牀頭。”寧詰其意，曰：“三日來，心怔忡[3]無停息，意金華妖物，恨妾遠遁，恐旦晚尋及也。”寧

---

1. 尸饔：料理飲食。
2. 起初，寧的母親非常懼怕小倩，不讓小倩住在家裏。但是小倩的聰慧、體貼、勤快使得寧的母親越來越喜歡小倩，並留小倩與她同住。寧的妻子死後，母親讓二人正式結為夫妻。
3. 怔忡：恐懼不安。

31　Nie Xiaoqian (5)

Xiaoqian said, "I have no other request. If you don't trust me, a person of the Yellow Springs[1], please allow me to serve him as his sister and wait upon you as my mother morning till night. Will that be all right?" Moved by her sincerity, the mother let her stay. Xiaoqian asked to see Ning's wife, but the mother refused her, saying that she was ill. Xiaoqian gave up the thought. Immediately, she went to the kitchen and cooked for the mother. She walked in and out as if she had lived there for a long time. ...[2]

One day, leaning at the window, Xiaoqian was in low spirits. Suddenly she asked Ning, "Where is the leather bag for swords?" "Since you are afraid of it, I hid it." Ning answered. Xiaoqian said, "I have been living in the human world for a long time and I wouldn't be frightened by it anymore. Bring it here and hang it on the bed." Ning asked why, and Xiaoqian answered, "For the last three days, I have been very nervous and flustered. I guess that the demon at the temple in Jinhua was angry at my escape. I am afraid it will come to get me sooner or later."

---

1. Yellow Springs: the nether world.
2. At first, Ning's mother was much afraid of Xiaoqian and would not let her sleep in the house. Later, seeing that Xiaoqian was very smart, industrious and considerate, she gradually forgot that she was a ghost and regarded her as her own daughter. She even allowed Xiaoqian to sleep in her bedroom. After the death of Ning's wife, the mother let Xiaoqian marry Ning.

果攜革囊來。女反復審視，曰："此劍仙將盛人頭者也。敝敗至此，不知殺人幾何許！妾今日視之，肌猶粟慄。"乃懸之。

次日，又命移懸戶上。夜對燭坐，約寧勿寢。欻有一物，如飛鳥墮。女驚匿夾幕[4]間。寧視之，物如夜叉狀，電目血舌，睒閃攫拏而前。至門卻步；逡巡久之，漸近革囊，以爪摘取，似將抓裂。囊忽格然一響，大可合簣[5]；恍惚有鬼物，突出半身，揪夜叉入，聲遂寂然，囊亦頓縮如故。寧駭詫。女亦出，大喜曰："無恙矣！"共視囊中，清水數斗而已。

後數年，寧果登進士。女舉一男。納妾後，又各生一男，皆仕進有聲。

---

4. 夾幕：帷幕。
5. 大可合簣：大小有兩個竹筐合起來那麼大。

Ning brought the bag to her. Looking at it closely, Xiaoqian said, "This is a bag for holding people's heads cut off by the immortal swordsman. Now it looks so worn-out, I don't know how many people have been killed and put in it! Even now as I look at it, my flesh creeps." They hung it on the wall.

The next day, Xiaoqian told Ning to move the bag over the door. At night, Xiaoqian sat beside the candle, and she also asked Ning not to fall asleep. Suddenly, something swooped down like a bird. Xiaoqian was terribly frightened and hid herself behind the curtain. Ning saw the thing which looked like a *yaksha* ghost[3] with a pair of flashing eyes and a bloody tongue. It approached, with eyes glaring and claws stretching. Coming to the door, it stopped. Hesitantly it drew closer to the bag and picked it up with its claws. It seemed that it was going to tear the bag in pieces. Suddenly, the bag made a sound and became as big as two baskets put together. A monster half came out and dragged the ghost into the bag. All of a sudden, all was quiet and the bag resumed its original size. Ning was amazed and scared. Xiaoqian came out happily and said, "We won't have any trouble anymore!" Inside the bag, they found only some clear water.

After several years, Ning passed the imperial examination and Xiaoqian gave birth to a son. Later, Ning took in a concubine, and the concubine and Xiaoqian each gave birth to a son. When they grew up, the three sons became officials and they all had good reputations.

---

3. *yaksha* ghost: an evil spirit in Buddhism.

三十二　竇氏（一）

南三復，晉陽世家也。有別墅，去所居十里餘，每馳騎日一詣之。適遇雨，途中有小村，見一農人家，門內寬敞，因投止焉。近村人固皆威重南。少頃，主人出邀，踽踽[1]甚恭。入其舍，斗如。客既坐，主人始操彗[2]，殷勤汎掃[3]。既而潑蜜為茶。命之坐，始敢坐。問其姓名，自言：「廷章，姓竇。」未幾，進酒烹雛，給奉周至。

有笄女行炙[4]，時止戶外，稍稍露其半體，年十五六，端妙無比。南心動。雨歇既歸，縈念縈切。越日，具粟帛往酬，借此階進。是後常一過竇，時攜肴酒，相與留連。女漸稔，不甚避忌，輒奔走其前。睨之，則低鬟微笑。南益惑焉，無三日不往者。

---

1. 踽（jú）踽（jí）：小心，謹慎。
2. 彗（huì）：掃帚。
3. 汎（fàn）掃：打掃。
4. 行炙：傳遞酒菜。

32   A Girl Named Dou (1)

Nan Sanfu was a son of a big family of Jinyang. Three miles from his home he had a villa, and he rode there every day. One day, he was detained by a rainstorm while he was passing by a small village. Seeing a farmhouse with a spacious courtyard, he went in to seek shelter from the rain. Since people from the neighbouring villages were all afraid of Nan, the host of the house came out, and respectfully and cautiously invited Nan to come into his house. The room was quite small. When Nan took a seat, the host began to dust the room with a broom, and then made Nan some honey tea. He remained standing until Nan told him to sit down. Nan asked his name, and the host replied, "My given name is Tingzhang, and my family name is Dou." Soon Nan was served with wine and chicken with great hospitality.

The daughter of the host who was responsible for bringing dishes to the room occasionally stopped at the door. Nan could see her when she partially showed herself. She was about fifteen or sixteen and was extremely beautiful. Nan was deeply impressed by her beauty. When the rain stopped, Nan went home, still thinking about the girl. The next day, on the pretext of thanking the Dou family for their treat, Nan came again, bringing some silk and millet as gifts. Since then, Nan came very often and sometimes he would bring drinks with him and lingered there. The girl was getting familiar with him and did not dodge him anymore. She often walked back and forth in front of him. Noticing that Nan was looking at her sideways, the girl lowered her head and smiled. Nan was even more infatuated and went there more often.

一日，值寶不在，坐良久，女出應客。南捉臂狎之。女慚急，峻拒曰：“奴雖貧，要嫁，何貴倨凌人也！”時南失偶，便揖之曰：“倘獲憐眷，定不他娶。”女要誓；南指矢天日，以堅永約，女乃允之。

自此為始，瞰寶他出，即過繾綣。女促之曰：“桑中之約[5]，不可長也。日在帡幪[6]之下，倘肯賜以姻好，父母必以為榮，當無不諧。宜速為計！”南諾之。轉念農家豈堪匹偶，故假其詞以因循[7]之。

---

5. 桑中之約：指男女私會。
6. 帡幪（píng méng）：帷帳。
7. 因循：拖延。

One day, Nan went there again but the father was not home, so he stayed there for a long time until the girl came out to receive him. Nan grabbed her arms and wanted to caress her. However the girl felt ashamed and annoyed, and she refused Nan sternly, saying, "Though I am poor, I expect a formal marriage. How can you bully me only because you are rich?" At that time, Nan's wife just died, so he made a bow to her and said, "If you allow me to love you, I will never marry anyone else." The girl asked him to take an oath, and Nan swore, by pointing his finger toward the heavens, that he would keep faith with her forever. The girl agreed to his proposal.

From then on, whenever the father went out, Nan would come to stay with the girl. The girl pressed him, saying, "It is not a permanent solution for us to meet each other secretly. Everything is under your control. If I can marry you, my parents will take it as an honour and never show a sign of disagreement. Please arrange it as soon as possible!" Nan agreed. But when he thought better of it, he realized that a country girl would hardly match him as his wife. So he always stalled the girl with excuses.

三十三　竇氏（二）

　　會媒來為議姻於大家，初尚躊躇；既聞貌美財豐，志遂決。女以體孕，催並益急，南遂絕跡不往。無何，女臨蓐，產一男。父怒搒[1]女。女以情告，且言：「南要我矣。」竇乃釋女，使人問南；南立卻不承。竇乃棄兒，益撲女。女暗哀鄰婦，告南以苦。南亦置之。

　　女夜亡，視棄兒猶活，遂抱以奔南。款關而告閽者[2]曰：「但得主人一言，我可不死。彼即不念我，寧不念兒耶？」閽人具以達南，南戒勿內。女倚戶悲啼，五更始不復聞。質明視之，女抱兒坐僵矣。竇忿，訟之上官，悉以南不義，欲罪南。南懼，以千金行賂得免。

　　大家夢女披髮抱子而告曰：「必勿許負心郎；若許，

---

1. 搒（bǎng）：笞打。
2. 閽（hūn）者：看門人。

33 A Girl Named Dou (2)

At this time, a matchmaker came to propose to Nan a marriage with the daughter of a big family. At first, Nan hesitated, but when he learned that the girl was rich and beautiful, he agreed. Later the girl of Dou was pregnant and pressed for marriage. Nan stopped visiting her altogether. Soon the girl gave birth to a boy. Her father was very angry and beat her up. The girl told him everything and said, "Nan has promised to marry me." The father pardoned her and sent someone to ask Nan about it. Nan denied it. The father abandoned the baby and beat his daughter again. Secretly, the girl implored a woman neighbour to tell Nan of her suffering. However, Nan still disregarded it.

At night, the girl of Dou escaped. Seeing the abandoned baby was still alive, she held the baby in her arms and went to see Nan. She knocked on the door and told the gatekeeper, "One word from your master could save my life. He might not care for me, but wouldn't he care for his own son?" The gatekeeper reported this to Nan, but Nan did not allow the girl in. The girl of Dou sat against the door and wept in grief all night. At dawn, the sound of weeping stopped. In the morning, someone opened the door and found the girl holding her baby, both dead and stiff. Enraged, the girl's father brought a lawsuit against Nan. Learning about Nan's heartless behaviour, the magistrate wanted to punish him. Nan was scared and offered one thousand taels of silver to bribe the magistrate. He was remitted.

One day, the parents of the girl who was engaged to Nan had a dream in which the girl of Dou, with dishevelled hair and holding her baby, told them, "Don't let your daughter marry

我必殺之！"大家貪南富，卒許之。既親迎，而奩妝豐盛，新人亦娟好。然善悲，終日未嘗睹歡容；枕席之間，時復有涕洟。問之，亦不言。過數日，婦翁來，入門便淚，南未遑問故，相將入室。見女而駭曰："適於後園，見吾女縊死桃樹上；今房中誰也？"女聞言，色暴變，仆然而死。視之，則竇女。

the heartless man. Otherwise, I will kill her!" However the parents, covetous of Nan's wealth, decided to marry their daughter to him. On their wedding day, the bride was brought to Nan's home with her generous trousseaux. The bride was beautiful but looked sad. She did not smile at all for the whole day. Even when they were in the wedding bed, there were tears in her eyes. Nan asked her for the reason but the bride said not a word. Several days later the father of the bride came to Nan's house. As soon as he walked into the door he wept. Before Nan had time to ask him what had happened, he helped the father into the room. Seeing the bride, the father was shocked and said, "I saw my daughter hang herself on a peach tree in the back garden. Who is this girl in the room?" On hearing this, the bride suddenly turned pale. She dropped dead on the floor. Nan recognized that it was the girl of Dou.

三十四 竇氏 (三)

急至後園，新婦果自經死。駭極，往報竇。竇發女家，棺啟屍亡。前忿未蠲[1]，倍益慘怒，復訟於官。官以其情幻，擬罪未決。南又厚餌竇，哀令休結；官亦受其賕囑[2]，乃罷。而南家自此稍替[3]。又以異跡傳播，數年無敢字者。

南不得已，遠於百里外聘曹進士女。未及成禮，會民間訛傳，朝廷將選良家女充掖庭，以故有女者，悉送歸夫家。一日，有嫗導一輿至，自稱曹家送女者。扶女入室，謂南曰：“選嬪之事已急，倉卒不能如禮，且送小娘子

---

1. 蠲：消除。
2. 賕囑：賕，賄賂。囑，囑託。
3. 稍替：稍稍有些衰落。

34   A Girl Named Dou (3)

Nan hastily went to the backyard and found that, the bride had hanged herself there just as her father had seen. Nan was terrified and went to tell Dou about this. Dou dug up his daughter's tomb only to find the coffin opened and the dead body gone. While his old hatred for Nan still lingered, Dou was even more enraged and he sued Nan again. The magistrate could not give judgement for the case was too strange. By offering him a lot of money, Nan implored Dou to give up. The magistrate also took Nan's bribe, and so the charge was dropped. Since then, the Nan family declined. Hearing about the weird things that happened to Nan, for several years nobody dared to marry their daughters to Nan.

Nan had no choice but took the daughter of a scholar named Cao who lived some thirty miles away. Before the wedding, it was rumoured that the emperor was selecting girls from respectable families to be his concubines. All of the betrothed girls were sent to their husbands' homes hastily[1]. One day, an old lady, leading a sedan, came to Nan and told him that she was sent by Cao to bring Cao's daughter to him. She helped the girl enter the room and said to Nan, "Since the recruitment of royal concubines is imminent, we are too hurried to arrange a formal wedding. I have to bring the bride here." Nan asked,

---

1. All of the betrothed girls...hastily: Generally, common people were afraid of their daughters being taken into the imperial palace. Therefore, whenever such recruitment took place, the eligible girls would either be sent to their betrothed husbands' homes or hastily married to a man their parents could find.

來。"問："何無客？"曰："薄有奩妝，相從在後耳。"
嫗草草徑去。

南視女，亦風致，遂與諧笑。女俯頸引帶，神情酷類
寶女。心中作惡，第未敢言。女登榻，引被幪首而眠。亦
謂是新人常態，弗為意。日斂昏[4]，曹人不至，始疑。挼被
問女，而女亦奄然冰絕。驚怪莫知其故，馳伻[5]告曹，曹竟
無送女之事。相傳為異。

時有姚孝廉女新葬，隔宿，為盜所發，破材失屍。聞
其異，詣南所徵之，果其女。啟衾一視，四體裸然。姚
怒，質狀於官。官以南屢無行，惡之，坐發冢見屍，論
死。

---

4. 日斂昏：天已經黑了。
5. 伻（bēng）：使者。

"Why are there no other guests?" The old lady replied, "They are behind us, taking care of the trousseaux." After that, the old lady left hurriedly.

The bride was pretty. When Nan teased her, she lowered her head and played with the belt of her dress and looked just like the girl of Dou. Nan felt very uneasy but dared not say a word. The girl went to bed and covered her head with the wedding sheet. Nan thought that was normal for a bride, so he did not take that to heart. It was getting dark, but no one from the Cao family came, and this aroused Nan's suspicion. He lifted the wedding sheet and was going to ask the girl what the matter was. The girl was dead and her body was cold. Nan was shocked and did not know what was going on. He sent a man on horseback to go and ask Cao. Cao said that he had not sent his daughter to Nan. People in the vicinity gossiped about this strange story.

At that time, there was a scholar named Yao who had just buried his daughter. The next day, he found that his daughter's tomb was dug open and the body was gone. When he heard about the strange story, he went to Nan's home to take a look. Lifting the cover sheet, he found that it was his daughter lying there naked. Yao was outraged and sued Nan. The magistrate was disgusted with Nan's repeated crime and sentenced Nan to death on the charge of taking bodies out of tombs.

三十五　晚霞（一）

　　五月五日，吳越間有鬥龍舟之戲。刳[1]木為龍，繪鱗甲，飾以金碧；上為雕甍朱檻[2]；帆旌皆以錦繡；舟末為龍尾，高丈餘。以布索引木板下垂，有童坐板上，顛倒滾跌，作諸巧劇；下臨江水，險危欲墮。故其購是童也，先以金啖其父母，預調馴之，墮水而死，勿悔也。吳門則載美姬，較不同耳。

　　鎮江有蔣氏童阿端，方七歲，便捷奇巧，莫能過，聲價益起，十六歲猶用之。至金山下，墮水死。蔣媼止此子，哀鳴而已。阿端不自知死，有兩人導去，見水中別有

---

1. 刳（kū）：將整木從中間剖開，再挖空。
2. 雕甍（méng）朱檻：甍，屋脊。雕飾的屋脊，朱紅色的欄杆。

35　A Girl Named Wanxia (1)

The fifth day of the fifth lunar month was Duanwu (the Dragon Boat Festival). In the Jiangsu-Zhejiang areas, people held dragon boat races on this day. They often hollowed out a tree trunk to make a dragon-shaped boat. The body of the boat was painted with scales and shells, and was splendidly gilded and decorated. On the boat, there were engraved ridgepoles and vermilion banisters. The sails and banners were colourful embroidery. The stern was shaped like the tail of a dragon, pointing upwards more than ten feet high. From the tip of the tail, a board was hung down by ropes, and a boy sitting on it could roll, tumble and perform difficult acrobatic feats. Below was the river and there was the danger of falling into it. So a boy would be bought for training. His parents would be offered a high price and told that they could not go back on their words if the boy drowned. In Suzhou, the practice was a little different from other places, people would hire a beautiful prostitute instead of a boy.

The Jiang family of Zhenjiang had a boy named A'duan. At the age of seven, he was already famous for being skilful and nimble beyond compare. His reputation and remuneration kept on growing, and he was still hired to perform at the age of sixteen. One year, while passing by the Golden Mountain, A'duan fell into the river and drowned. He was the only son of the Jiang family, so his mother could do nothing but have a good cry. However, A'duan did not know that he was dead. He saw two men guide him forward. The world under the water

天地；回視，則流波四繞，屹如壁立。俄入宮殿，見一人兜牟[3]坐。兩人曰：「此龍窩君也。」便使拜伏。龍窩君顏色和霽，曰：「阿端伎巧可入柳條部。」

　　遂引至一所，廣殿四合。趨上東廊，有諸少年出與為禮，率十三四歲。即有老嫗來，眾呼解姥。坐令獻技。已，乃教以錢塘飛霆之舞，洞庭和風之樂[4]。但聞鼓鉦喤聒，諸院皆響；既而諸院皆息。姥恐阿端不能即嫻，獨絮絮調撥之；而阿端一過，殊已了了。姥喜曰：「得此兒，不讓晚霞矣！」

---

3. 兜牟：頭盔。
4. 洞庭和風之樂：這裏所説的舞蹈和音樂表現的是唐人李朝威的《柳毅傳》中描述的錢塘龍王解救龍女的故事。

was a place of unique beauty. Looking back, he saw the water surround them like a sheer wall. After a while, they entered a palace. A man, wearing a helmet, sat there. The two guides said to A'duan, "This is the Dragon Monarch." They told A'duan to kowtow to the monarch. The monarch looked kind and pleasant. He said to A'duan, "According to your skill, you should be put in the Wicker Department."

After that, the two men took him to another place surrounded by big palace buildings. A'duan walked to the eastern corridor, where many boys came out to greet him. Those boys were about thirteen or fourteen. Soon an old woman came out. People all called her Grandma Xie. Grandma Xie sat down and asked A'duan to perform. The performance finished, she taught those boys "The Thunderbolt of Qiantang River[1] Dance", and the music of "The Gentle Breeze of Dongting Lake". The sound of gongs and drums was heard reverberating throughout the palace. When the lessons were over, the palace returned to quietude. Grandma Xie worried that A'duan could not master the dance skilfully, so she let A'duan stay behind alone and continued to instruct him. She soon realized that A'duan had mastered the dance as soon as he had seen it. Grandma Xie was very happy and said, "We don't have to worry about Wanxia after having you."

---

1. Qiantang River: located in Zhejiang Province, the river is famed for its annual Qiantang bore, a magnificent tidal flood.

三十六　晚霞（二）

　　明日，龍窩君按[1]部，諸部畢集。首按夜叉部：鬼面魚服；鳴大鉦，圍四尺許；鼓可四人合抱之，聲如巨霆，叫噪不復可聞。舞起，則巨濤洶湧，橫流空際，時墮一點星光，及著地消滅。龍窩君急止之，命進乳鶯部：皆二八姝麗，笙樂細作，一時清風習習，波聲俱靜，水漸凝，如水晶世界，上下通明。按畢，俱退立西墀下。

---

1. 按：檢查。

36　A Girl Named Wanxia (2)

The next day, the monarch wanted to check the performance of each department, so all the people were gathered in the palace. First, the monarch ordered the Yaksha Department to perform. The performers all had ghost masks and wore fish costumes. They beat gongs as big as four feet in diameter and drums so big that four men could barely put their arms around them. The deafening sound of gongs and drums was so loud that they could hardly hear anything else. When the Yakshas began to dance, huge waves surged turbulently and splashed up to the skies. Every now and then starlight fell from the skies and vanished as soon as it touched the ground. Hurriedly, the monarch told them to stop. Then he ordered the Young Oriole Department to perform. Dancers of the Young Oriole Department were all beautiful girls, aged fifteen to sixteen. They played the *sheng*[1] and the *xiao*[2]. The music was melodious and clear. There rose a gentle cool breeze, and the waves calmed down. The blue water began to condense, and looked like a world of crystal, translucent and glittering. When they finished their performance, they all stepped down and stood on the west platform.

---

1. *sheng* : a reed instrument with small pipes, a traditional Chinese musical instrument.
2. *xiao* : a vertical bamboo flute, a traditional Chinese musical instrument.

次按燕子部，皆垂髫[2]人，內一女郎，年十四五已來，振袖傾鬟，作散花舞；翩翩翔起，衿袖襪履間，皆出五色花朵，隨風颭下，飄泊滿庭。舞畢，隨其部亦下西墀。

阿端旁睨，雅愛好之。問之同部，即晚霞也。無何，喚柳條部。龍窩君特試阿端。端作前舞，喜怒隨腔，俯仰中節[3]。龍窩君嘉其惠悟，賜五文袴褶[4]，魚鬚金束髮，上嵌夜光珠。阿端拜賜下，亦趨西墀，各守其伍。端於眾中遙注晚霞，晚霞亦遙注之。少間，端逡巡出部而北，晚霞亦漸出部而南[5]；相去數武[6]，而法嚴不敢亂部，相視神馳而已。既按蛺蝶部：童男女皆雙舞，身長短、年大小，服色黃白，皆取諸同。諸部按已，魚貫而出。

---

2. 垂髫：女子未及笄之前，年齡約十四、五歲的小姑娘。不束髮。
3. 喜怒隨腔，俯仰中節：表演時的表情和舞姿與音樂的內容、節拍渾然一體。
4. 五文袴褶（xí）：五文，五彩。袴，褲子與上衣連在一起的一種服裝。
5. 端逡巡出部而北，晚霞亦漸出部而南：阿端慢慢地離開自己的位置而向本部的北邊挪去；晚霞也漸漸地離開自己的位置而向本部的南邊挪去。
6. 數武：幾步。武，半步。

Then it was the turn of the Swallow Department. Dancers of this department were all young girls. Among them was a beautiful girl of about fourteen or fifteen. She raised her long sleeves; and flung her hair in a dance of scattering flowers. While she was dancing lightly, colourful flowers came out from her lapel, her sleeves, her shoes and stockings. Those beautiful flowers drifted in the wind and floated all over the courtyard. When she finished dancing, she stepped down with other girls and stood on the west platform.

A'duan stared at the girl and liked her very much. Asking his companion, he learned that the girl was Wanxia. After a while, the Wicker Department was ordered to perform. The monarch especially wanted to see A'duan's skill. A'duan began to dance what he had learned the day before. His performance expressed the happiness and grief of the music precisely and vividly. His movements were in perfect harmony with the rhythm of the music. The monarch praised A'duan for his intelligence and rewarded him a set of colourful embroidered dress and a gold hair ornament inlaid with a night-luminescent pearl. A'duan kowtowed in thanks and then retired to the west platform where his companions stood. He stared at Wanxia from a distance, and Wanxia also stared at him. Gradually, A'duan moved toward the north while Wanxia moved towards the south. The two were only a few steps away, but they dared not overstep the boundary between the two departments for the rules were strict. What they could do was to stare at each other and have a deep longing for each other. Then it was the turn of the Butterfly Department to perform. Dancers of the department were boys and girls in pairs. They were about the same age and stature and they wore the same white or yellow clothes. When all the performances were over, the departments walked out one after the other.

三十七　晚霞（三）

　　柳條在燕子部後，端疾出部前，而晚霞已緩滯在後。回首見端，故遺珊瑚釵，端急內袖中。

　　既歸，凝思成疾，眠餐頓廢。解姥輒進甘旨，日三四省，撫摩殷切，病不少瘥[1]。姥憂之，罔所為計，曰：“吳江王壽期已促，且為奈何！”薄暮，一童子來，坐榻上與語，自言隸蛺蝶部。從容問曰：“君病為晚霞否？”端驚問：“何知？”笑曰：“晚霞亦如君耳。”端淒然起坐，便求方計。童問：“尚能步否？”答云：“勉強尚能自力。”

　　童挽出，南啟一戶；折而西，又闢雙扉。見蓮花數十畝，皆生平地上；葉大如席，花大如蓋[2]，落瓣堆梗下盈尺。

---

1. 瘥（chài）：痊愈。
2. 蓋：傘。

37 A Girl Named Wanxia (3)

The Wicker Department was behind the Swallow Department. A'duan quickened his steps and came to the front of his department. In the meantime, Wanxia slowed down and fell behind hers. When she turned her head and saw A'duan behind her, she threw a coral hairpin on the ground on purpose. A'duan picked it up and quickly hid it in his sleeve.

Coming back home, A'duan thought of Wanxia persistently. He was lovesick, and did not feel like eating and sleeping. Grandma Xie came to see him three or four times a day. She often brought him something good to eat and comforted him sincerely. However, there was no sign that A'duan was getting better. Grandma Xie was anxious but could do nothing. She said to A'duan, "The day of celebrating the King of Wujiang's birthday is approaching. What shall we do?" At dusk, a boy came to see A'duan. He sat on the bed and told A'duan that he was in the Butterfly Department. He then leisurely asked A'duan, "Are you lovesick for Wanxia?" A'duan was amazed and asked, "How do you know?" The boy laughed and said, "Because Wanxia is sick like you." A'duan rose from the bed sadly and asked the boy to find a way out for him. The boy asked, "Can you still walk?" A'duan answered, "I can manage with an effort."

The boy helped A'duan walk out and pushed the south door open for him. After walking a certain distance, they turned west and opened another door. Outside the door was a tract of lotus a dozen acres in size. The lotus plants were all growing on the ground. Their leaves were large as mats and the flowers were big as umbrellas. The fallen petals were heaped around the stalks a foot thick. The boy brought A'duan among the

童引入其中，曰："姑坐此。"遂去。少時，一美人撥蓮花而入，則晚霞也。相見驚喜，各道相思，略述生平。遂以石壓荷蓋令側，雅可幛蔽；又勻鋪蓮瓣而藉之，忻與狎寢。既，訂後約，日以夕陽為候，乃別。端歸，病亦尋愈。由此兩人日一會於蓮畝。

過數日，隨龍窩君往壽吳江王。稱壽已，諸部悉還，獨留晚霞及乳鶯部一人在宮中教舞。數月，更無音耗，端悵望若失。惟解姥日往來吳江府；端託晚霞為外妹，求攜去，冀一見之。留吳江門下數日，宮禁森嚴，晚霞苦不得出。快快而返。

flowers and said to him, "Stay here." Then he left. After a while, a beautiful girl entered through the lotus blossoms. It was Wanxia. When the two saw each other, they were both surprised and delighted. They told each other of their longings for the other and of their life experiences. After that, they leaned a lotus leaf against a rock, so that it served as a screen. They spread the petals evenly and lay on them in intimacy. Afterwards, they arranged to meet each other at sunset before they parted. A'duan returned to his place and recovered from his illness. Since then, he and Wanxia met every day in the lotus field.

A few days later, the various dancers went to celebrate the birthday of King of Wujiang together with the monarch. When the celebration was over, everyone came back except Wanxia and a girl of the Young Oriole Department, who stayed behind to teach dancing in the palace. Several months passed, there was no news about Wanxia. A'duan was driven to distraction. Only Grandma Xie went to the King's palace often. A'duan pretended that he was Wanxia's cousin and asked Grandma Xie to take him there to see Wanxia. However, the entrance to the palace was carefully guarded so that A'duan waited for several days to no avail. Wanxia tried every means to come out to meet A'duan but failed. A'duan returned in low spirits.

三十八　晚霞（四）

　　積月餘，癡想欲絕。一日，解姥入，戚然相弔曰：
"惜乎！晚霞投江矣！"端大駭，涕下不能自止。因毀冠裂
服，藏金珠而出，意欲相從俱死。但見江水若壁，以首力
觸不得入。念欲復還，懼問冠服，罪將增重。意計窮蹙，
汗流浹踵[1]。忽睹壁下有大樹一章，乃猱攀而上，漸至端
杪；猛力躍墮，幸不沾濡，而竟已浮水上。不意之中，恍
睹人世，遂漂然泅去。移時，得岸，少坐江濱，頓思老
母，遂趁舟而去。抵里，四顧居廬，忽如隔世。次且[2]至
家，忽聞窗中有女子曰："汝子來矣。"音聲甚似晚霞。
俄，與母俱出，果霞。斯時兩人喜勝於悲；而媼則悲疑驚
喜，萬狀俱作矣。

---

1. 浹踵：濕透了腳跟。
2. 次且：磕磕絆絆，行走困難的樣子。

38   A Girl Named Wanxia (4)

Another month had passed, still thinking of Wanxia, A'duan was so grief-stricken that he wished he were dead. One day, Grandma Xie came and said sorrowfully to him, "It is such a pity. Wanxia threw herself into the river." A'duan was shocked, and tears welled up in his eyes. He broke the hair ornament and tore to shreds the clothes he had received from the monarch. That night, bringing with him the night-luminescent pearl, he escaped and wanted to kill himself. The water was like a sheer cliff. With all his strength, he tried to run his head into the water, but he could not get into it. He wanted to return to the palace but was worried that he would be punished for breaking the hair ornament and clothes. A'duan was at the end of his wits and was sweating all over in anxiety. Suddenly, he saw a big tree standing at the foot of the water cliff. He climbed the tree as quickly as a monkey. When he reached the tree top, he jumped off. To his surprise, his clothes did not get wet, and he floated out of the water and saw the world. He swam along with the river. After a while, A'duan came ashore. He took a brief rest by sitting on the bank. Then thinking of his mother, he went home by boat. On returning to his hometown, he looked around the houses of his neighbours, and felt that he was alienated from them by a whole generation. Hesitatingly he came to the door of his home. Suddenly, he heard a woman's voice from a window, "Your son is back." The voice sounded like Wanxia's. Soon he saw a woman together with his mother come out. It was indeed Wanxia, and the two were wild with joy. The mother felt all sorts of feelings well up in her heart.

初，晚霞在吳江，覺腹中震動，龍宮法禁嚴，恐旦夕身娩，橫遭撻楚；又不得一見阿端，但欲求死，遂潛投江水。身泛起，沉浮波中，有客舟拯之，問其居里。晚霞故吳名妓，溺水不得其屍。自念術院[3]不可復投，遂曰：“鎮江蔣氏，吾壻也。”客因代貰[4]扁舟，送諸其家。蔣媼疑其錯誤，女自言不誤，因以其情詳告媼。媼以其風格韻妙，頗愛悅之；第慮年太少，必非肯終寡也者。而女孝謹，顧家中貧，便脫珍飾售數萬。

---

3. 術（háng）院：妓院。
4. 代貰（shì）：代租。

It happened that while Wanxia was teaching dancing in the palace of the King of Wujiang, she suddenly found that she was pregnant. Since the laws in the dragon palace were rigid, Wanxia worried that if she gave birth to the child, she would be punished. Moreover, there was no hope for her to see A'duan, so she wanted to die. She threw herself into the water; however she did not die but emerged from the water and drifted in the current. At that time, a passenger boat was passing by, and she was saved. The passengers asked her where her home was. Wanxia was once a famous prostitute of Suzhou and she fell into the water during the performance one day, but her body had never been found. Considering her past she did not want to go back to the brothel, so she said, "The Jiang family of Zhenjiang is my husband's home." The passengers rented a boat and sent her to Jiang's home. At first, A'duan's mother thought that Wanxia had made a mistake; however, Wanxia was quite sure and told the mother everything. The mother was very fond of Wanxia for her beauty and charm, but worried that she was too young to live forever as a widow. On the other hand, Wanxia was extremely caring to her and meticulous. Seeing the family was poor, she sold her jewelry for the family.

三十九　晚霞（五）

　　媼察其志無他，良喜。然無子，恐一旦臨蓐，不見信於戚里，以謀女。女曰：「母但得真孫，何必求人知。」媼亦安之。

　　會端至，女喜不自已。媼亦疑兒不死；陰發兒冢，骸骨具存。因以此詰端。端始爽然自悟；然恐晚霞惡其非人，囑母勿復言。母然之。遂告同里，以為當日所得非兒屍，然終慮其不能生子。未幾，竟舉一男，捉之無異常兒，始悦。久之，女漸覺阿端非人，乃曰：「胡不早言！凡鬼衣龍宮衣，七七魂魄堅凝[1]，生人不殊矣。若得宮中龍角膠，可以續骨節而生肌膚，惜不早購之也。」

---

1. 七七魂魄堅凝：經過七七四十九天，飄忽不定的魂魄就會凝聚在一起。

146

39   A Girl Named Wanxia (5)

Realizing that Wanxia was sincere and loyal, the mother was very happy. However she still worried that since A'duan was dead, if Wanxia gave birth to a child, the relatives and neighbours would not believe that the child was A'duan's. So she discussed this with Wanxia and Wanxia said, "As long as you have a grandson, there is no need to let others know." Hearing this, the mother was relieved.

Now that A'duan returned, Wanxia was in ecstasy. The mother suspected that her son had not died, so she dug out her son's tomb but found that his body was still there. The mother was surprised, and she went to ask A'duan about this. It was not until now that A'duan suddenly realized that he was already a dead person. He worried that Wanxia would dislike him, therefore, he asked his mother not to talk about this. His mother agreed. Later, the mother told the neighbours that her son had not died and that the body they had retrieved from the water was not her son's. However, the mother still worried that the couple were unable to have children. Soon Wanxia gave birth to a son. Upon seeing that he was a normal baby, the mother was very happy. As time passed, Wanxia gradually realized that A'duan was non-human. She said, "Why didn't you tell me this earlier? If a ghost puts on the clothes of the dragon palace, after forty-nine days, its soul will condense and the ghost will look like a normal human; or if the ghost gets the glue of a dragon horn, its bones will be connected, and flesh and skin will grow again. It is a pity that we haven't bought the glue sooner."

端貨其珠，有賈胡出資百萬，家由此巨富。值母壽。夫妻歌舞稱觴[2]，遂傳聞王邸。王欲強奪晚霞。端懼，見王自陳：“夫婦皆鬼。”驗之無影而信，遂不之奪。但遣宮人就別院傳其技。女以龜溺[3]毀容，而後見之。教三月，終不能盡其技而去。

---

2. 稱觴：敬酒。這裏是祝壽的意思。
3. 龜溺：龜尿。傳說龜尿一旦沾在皮膚上，就不易洗掉。

Later, A'duan sold his night-luminescent pearl to a merchant from the Western Regions[1] for millions of dollars. The family became rich. One day, the couple danced and sang to celebrate their mother's birthday. A prince heard about this, and he wanted to snatch Wanxia. A'duan was scared, so he went to see the prince and said, "Both Wanxia and I are ghosts." Seeing that they did not have shadows, the prince believed it and gave up the thought. Later, the prince wanted Wanxia to teach some maids of honour to dance in a palace. Before going there, Wanxia smeared turtle urine on the face and disfigured herself. The maids of honour could not learn all of Wanxia's dancing skills. Three months later, Wanxia returned home.

---

1. the Western Regions: A Han Dynasty term for the area west of Yumen Pass, including what is now Xinjiang Province and parts of Central Asia.

四十　陸判（一）

　　陵陽[1]朱爾旦，字小明。性豪放。然素鈍，學雖篤，尚未知名。一日，文社[2]眾飲。或戲之云："君有豪名，能深夜赴十王殿，負得左廊判官來，眾當醵[3]作筵。"

　　蓋陵陽有十王殿，神鬼皆以木雕，妝飾如生。東廡有立判，綠面赤鬚，貌尤獰惡。或夜聞兩廊拷訊聲。入者，毛皆森豎。故眾以此難朱。朱笑起，徑去。居無何，門外大呼曰："我請髯宗師至矣！"眾皆起。俄負判入，置几上，奉觴，酹之三。眾睹之，瑟縮不安於座，仍請負去。

---

1. 陵陽：舊縣名，在安徽省青陽縣。
2. 文社：科舉時代，學子們為研習詩文而結的社。
3. 醵：大家一起湊錢飲酒。

40   Judge Lu (1)

In Lingyang, there was a man named Zhu Erdan, alias Xiaoming. He was bold and uninhibited but slow-witted. Though he studied very hard, he was still a nobody. One day, some scholars of a scholars' society were drinking together. One of the scholars decided to make fun of Zhu and said, "You are known to be brave. If you dare to go to the Temple of Ten Kings[1] at midnight and bring back the statue of Judge Lu from the left corridor, we will stand you a dinner."

In Lingyang, there was the Temple of Ten Kings in which statues of ghosts and gods were carved vividly in wood. In the eastern corridor stood Judge Lu, the most ferocious statue of all, with a green face and a red beard. Some people said that they had even heard the sound of torturing from the two corridors during the night. Whenever people entered the temple, their hair would stand on end. The scholars therefore thought they had put Zhu in an awkward situation by daring him to enter the temple. However Zhu stood up with a smile and left. It was not long before they heard him shouting outside, "I have invited the long-bearded master, Judge Lu, to join us!" All the people stood up. They saw Zhu come in, carrying Judge Lu on his back. Zhu put the statue on a table and poured three libations to it on the ground. Seeing this, the scholars were

---

1. the Temple of Ten Kings: It was believed that there were ten kings in charge of the Ten Courts of Justice of the nether world respectively. When people died, they will be sent to the different courts to receive the punishment they deserve according to their sins.

朱又把酒灌地，祝曰："門生狂率不文，大宗師諒不為怪。荒舍匪遙，合乘興來覓飲，幸勿為畛畦[4]。"乃負之去。次日，眾果招飲。抵暮，半醉而歸，興未闌，挑燈獨酌。

---

4. 畛畦：界限。這裏指不要在意人鬼之間的界限。

too scared to sit, and they begged Zhu to take Lu away. Zhu took another cup of wine, poured it on the ground, and prayed to Lu, "Please forgive me for my rudeness and ignorance. My humble home is not far from here. Whenever you feel good, come and take a couple of drinks with me. Please do not worry about the division between man and ghost." After this prayer, he carried the statue back to the temple. As expected, the scholars entertained Zhu at their expenses the next day. When Zhu returned home in the evening half drunk, he felt that he had not had enough, so he lit a candle and drank some more.

四十一　陸判（二）

　　忽有人搴簾入，視之，則判官也。朱起曰："意¹吾殆將死矣！前夕冒瀆，今來加斧鑕²耶？"判啟濃髯，微笑曰："非也。昨蒙高義相訂，夜偶暇，敬踐達人之約。"朱大悅，牽衣促坐，自起滌器爇火³。判曰："天道溫和，可以冷飲。"朱如命，置瓶案上，奔告家人治肴果。妻聞，大駭，戒勿出。朱不聽，立俟治具以出。易盞交酬，始詢姓氏。曰："我陸姓，無名字。"與談古典，應答如響。問："知制藝⁴否？"曰："妍媸⁵亦頗辨之。陰司誦讀，

---

1. 意：料想。
2. 斧鑕（fǔ zhì）：古代殺人的刑具，這裏有索命、傷害之意。
3. 爇火：燒火。
4. 制藝：科舉八股文。
5. 妍媸：美與醜，這裏指文章的好壞。

41　Judge Lu (2)

Suddenly, someone lifted the door curtain and came in. Looking closely, Zhu recognized that it was Judge Lu. Zhu rose and said, "I know that today will be the end of my life. Last night, I offended you, so you are here to take my life." Judge Lu smiled in his thick beard and said, "No, I am here because you kindly invited me last night. I am free tonight, so I come for the invitation." Zhu was very happy and took Judge Lu to his seat. He himself stood up, washed the cups and lit the fire. Judge Lu said, "It is warm today, so cold wine will do[1]." Zhu agreed, and placed the wine bottle on the table. He then went out to tell his servants to prepare some dishes. When Zhu's wife heard about Lu's visit, she was terrified and warned him not to go back to Lu. Zhu did not listen. When the dishes were ready, he brought them to Judge Lu. They started to drink to each other and asked each other's name. Judge Lu said, "My family name is Lu, and I do not have a given name." They talked about the classics. It seemed that Judge Lu knew the classics very well. "Do you know how to write the essays for the imperial examination[2]?" Zhu asked. "I can tell a good essay from a bad one. Reading essays in the underworld is about the

---

1. cold wine will do: In China, people like to drink hot wine, especially in winter.
2. essays for the imperial examination: The essay prescribed for the imperial examinations in the Ming and Qing Dynasties was called the *bagu wen*　(eight-part essay), which had a rigid form.

與陽世略同。"陸豪飲，一舉十觥。朱因竟日飲，遂不覺玉山[6]傾頹，伏几醺睡。比[7]醒，則殘燭昏黃，鬼客已去。

　　自是三兩日輒一來，情益洽，時抵足臥。朱獻窗稿，陸輒紅勒之，都言不佳。

---

6. 玉山：軀體，指文雅人儀表美好之體。
7. 比：等到。

same as in the world." Judge Lu was a heavy drinker. He drank up ten cups of wine without a break. Since Zhu had been drinking all day long, he was drunk and gradually fell asleep with his forehead leaning on the tabletop. When he woke up, the candle was burning out, and his ghostly guest had left.

From then on, Judge Lu would come every two or three days. They were getting closer and friendlier. Sometimes, Lu would spend the whole night there. Zhu showed his essays, and Lu always corrected them in red, saying that they were not good.

四十二　陸判（三）

　　一夜，朱醉，先寢，陸猶自酌。忽醉夢中，覺臟腹微
痛；醒而視之，則陸危坐牀前，破腔出腸胃，條條整理。
愕曰：「夙無仇怨，何以見殺？」陸笑云：「勿懼，我為君
易慧心[1]耳。」從容納腸已，復合之，末以裹足布束朱腰。
作用[2]畢，視榻上亦無血跡。腹間覺少麻木。見陸置肉塊几
上。問之，曰：「此君心也。作文不快，知君之毛竅塞
耳。適在冥間，於千萬心中，揀得佳者一枚，為君易之，
留此以補闕數。」乃起，掩扉去。

　　天明解視，則創縫已合，有綫而赤者存焉。自是文思
大進，過眼不忘。數日，又出文示陸。陸曰：「可矣。但
君福薄，不能大顯貴，鄉、科而已。」問：「何時？」曰：
「今歲必魁。」未幾，科試冠軍，秋闈果中經元。

---

1. 慧心：聰慧的心。
2. 作用：整治。

42   Judge Lu (3)

One night, Zhu was drunk and went to bed first, leaving Lu to drink by himself. Suddenly, he in his sleep felt a pain in his stomach. He woke up and saw that Lu, who was sitting on the bed beside him, had opened up his belly and was arranging his entrails. Zhu was shocked and said, "We have never been enemies. Why would you kill me?" Lu laughed and said, "Don't worry, I am now exchanging your heart for a more intelligent one. Lu put his entrails back in a leisurely manner, closed his belly, and then bandaged his waist. When all was done, there was no blood stain on the bed, and Zhu only felt a little numbness in his belly. Seeing Lu placed a lump of flesh on the table, Zhu asked what it was. Lu said, "This is your heart, the reason why you could not write good essays was that the apertures of your heart were blocked. A moment ago, I found and exchanged for you a better heart from thousands of hearts in the nether world, and I will put your heart back in its place." After saying this, Lu left, closing the door behind him.

Next morning, Zhu untied the bandage and saw that the wound had quite healed up, leaving only a red seam-like scar. From then on, his literary talents greatly improved and he had a tenacious memory. A few days later, he showed Lu an essay and Lu said, "Good! However, you are not destined to have the fortune of big success, so you can't achieve any more than passing the examination at the county and provincial levels." Zhu asked, "When will that be?" Lu replied, "This year you will be the top candidate of the imperial examination at the county level." As expected, Zhu came first in the county examination, and was among the top five who took the provincial examination that autumn.

四十三 陸判（四）

　　同社生素揶揄之；及見闈墨[1]，相視而驚，細詢始知其異。共求朱先容[2]，願納交陸。陸諾之。眾大設以待之。更初，陸至，赤鬚生動，目炯炯如電。眾茫乎無色，齒欲相擊；漸引去。

　　朱乃攜陸歸飲，既醺，朱曰：“渝腸伐胃[3]，受賜已多。尚有一事欲相煩，不知可否？”陸便請命。朱曰：“心腸可易，面目想亦可更。山荊[4]，予結髮人，下體頗亦不惡，但頭面不甚佳麗。尚欲煩君刀斧，如何？”陸笑曰：“諾，容徐圖之。”過數日，半夜來叩關。朱急起延入。燭之，見襟裏一物。詰之，曰：“君曩所囑，向艱物色。適

---

1. 闈墨：清代科舉考試結束後，主考官選取考中學子的試卷編輯成冊，叫做“闈墨”。
2. 先容：作引見人。
3. 渝腸伐胃：清洗腸胃。
4. 山荊：妻子。

43 Judge Lu (4)

When those scholars, who used to ridicule his dull-wittedness, learned of his success and read his published examination essays, they were all surprised. By asking Zhu, they learned about his fortuitous adventure. They begged Zhu to introduce them to Lu. When Lu agreed to meet them, the scholars prepared a big feast to receive Lu. Lu arrived in the first night watch[1]. Seeing his flowing red beard and flashing eyes, the group of scholars were so awestruck that their faces turned pale and teeth chattered. One by one, they all withdrew and left.

Zhu then took Lu home with him to have a drink together. When Zhu was half drunk, he said to Lu, "You have done me the kindness of cleaning and changing my innards. Now I have another thing to bother you with and wonder if you could do me another favour." Lu asked what it was. Zhu said, "If you can change one's heart, I suppose you can also change one's appearance. My wife's figure is not bad, but her face is rather ugly. Could you change it for a better one with your knife?" Lu laughed and said, "All right, but give me some time." Several days later, Lu came at midnight and knocked on the door. Zhu rose quickly and invited him in. When he lit the candle, he noticed something wrapped under Lu's garment. He asked Lu what it was. Lu answered, "It's what you asked for a few days ago. It is hard to find a beautiful head; however, I have one for

---

1. night watch: In old China, the night was divided into five two-hour periods which were called night watches.

得一美人首，敬報君命。”朱撥視，頸血猶濕。陸立促急入，勿驚禽犬。朱慮門戶夜扃。陸至，一手推扉，扉自闢。引至臥室，見夫人側身眠。陸以頭授朱抱之；自於靴中出白刃如匕首，按夫人項，著力如切腐狀，迎刃而解，首落枕畔；急於生懷，取美人首合項上，詳審端正，而後按捺。已而移枕塞肩際，命朱瘞[5]首靜所，乃去。

　　朱妻醒，覺頸間微麻，面頰甲錯[6]；搓之，得血片，甚駭。呼婢汲盥；婢見面血狼藉，驚絕，濯之，盆水盡赤。舉首則面目全非，又駭極。夫人引鏡自照，錯愕不能自解。朱入告之；因反覆細視，則長眉掩鬢，笑靨承顴，畫中人也。解領驗之，有紅綫一周，上下肉色，判然而異。

---

5. 瘞（yì）：埋。
6. 甲錯：像鱗甲一樣。

you now." Zhu lifted the wrapping and found the blood on the neck of the head still wet. Lu hastened Zhu to enter his wife's bedroom without disturbing the dogs and fowls. Zhu was afraid the door to his wife's bedroom was locked, but when Lu pushed it, it opened by itself. Zhu led him to his wife's bed where she lay sleeping on her side. Lu handed Zhu the head and took out a dagger-like sword from his boot. He then pressed the sword against the neck of the woman and cut off her head easily as if it had been a piece of beancurd. The head fell off beside the pillow. Lu then took the beautiful head from Zhu quickly and fitted it to the wife's neck. Making sure that it was correctly in place, Lu pressed it down firmly. After that, Lu inserted a pillow between her shoulders to prop her up. He told Zhu to bury his wife's head in a quiet place, and left.

When Zhu's wife woke up, she felt a little numb on her neck and something rough on her face. Rubbing the face with her hand, she got some flakes of dried blood. Extremely terrified, she called her maid to bring her a basin of water. The maid was struck with horror when she saw that her mistress's face was smeared with blood. When the face was washed, the water in the basin was reddened. The maid was scared to death when she looked up and found her lady's face entirely different. Zhu's wife looked at herself in the mirror, and was stunned, not knowing what had happened. Zhu came in and told her everything. On examining her more closely, he saw a very beautiful lady with long eyebrows reaching her temples, and dimples on her cheeks, a beauty found only in pictures. Around her neck was a red line and the colour of the skin above was different from that below.

四十四　陸判（五）

　　先是，吳侍御有女甚美，未嫁而喪二夫，故十九猶未醮[1]也。上元游十王殿，時游人甚雜，內有無賴賊窺而艷之，遂陰訪居里，乘夜梯入，穴寢門，殺一婢於牀下，逼女與淫；女力拒聲喊，賊怒。亦殺之。吳夫人微聞鬧聲，呼婢往視，見屍駭絕。舉家盡起，停屍堂上，置首項側，一門啼號，紛騰[2]終夜。

　　詰旦啟衾，則身在而失其首。遍撻侍女，謂所守不恪[3]，致葬犬腹。侍御告郡。郡嚴限捕賊，三月而罪人弗

---

1. 醮（jiào）：原為婚禮的意思，元明以後指女子再嫁。
2. 紛騰：折騰，鬧騰。
3. 不恪：恪，謹慎。不恪，不慎。

44 Judge Lu (5)

Now there was an official named Wu who had a very beautiful daughter. Since the two men who were engaged to her both died before the wedding, she was still unmarried when she was nineteen[1]. At the Lantern Festival[2], she went to visit the Temple of Ten Kings. At that time, the place was thronged with visitors of all kinds. Among the crowd was a rascal who was attracted by her beauty. He found her address after making secret enquires. That night, the rascal climbed into her house by means of a ladder and entered her room after making a hole in the bedroom door. He killed a maid first, and then forced the young lady to submit. With all her strength, the lady refused to give in, and screamed for help. The rascal was enraged and killed her by cutting off her head. Lady Wu, her mother, heard the noise and sent a maid to find out what had happened. Seeing the two dead bodies, she was in extreme terror. The whole family was woken. They placed the girl's body in the hall and put her head beside the body and cried for the whole night.

The next morning, when the family lifted the shroud, they found the body still there, but the head was gone. They lashed all the maids for their carelessness because they believed that the head was eaten by a dog. Official Wu brought the case to the prefecture authorities, and the prefect set a deadline for capturing the culprit. Three months passed, but they found no

---

1. when she was nineteen: In old China, a girl normally got married at the age of fifteen or sixteen.
2. Lantern Festival: see Passage 22, Note 2.

得。漸有以朱家換頭之異聞吳公者。吳疑之，遣媼探諸其家；入見夫人，駭走以告吳公。公視女屍故存，驚疑無以自決。猜朱以左道殺女，往詰朱。朱曰："室人夢易其首，實不解其何故；謂僕殺之，則冤也。"吳不信，訟之。收家人鞫[4]之，一如朱言。郡守不能決。

朱歸，求計於陸。陸曰："不難，當使伊女自言之。"吳夜夢女曰："兒為蘇溪楊大年所賊，無與朱孝廉[5]。彼不艷於其妻，陸判官取兒頭與之易之，是兒身死而頭生也。願勿相仇。"醒告夫人，所夢同。乃言於官。問之，果有楊大年；執而械之，遂伏其罪。吳乃詣朱，請見夫人，由此為翁婿。乃以朱妻首合女屍而葬焉。

---

4. 鞫（jū）：審訊。
5. 無與朱孝廉：與，關聯。與朱孝廉無關。

trace of the culprit. Gradually, Official Wu heard about the weird story of head-changing that happened in Zhu's family. Wu became suspicious, so he sent an old lady to check it. On seeing Zhu's wife, the old lady was shocked and rushed back to Wu. Wu felt puzzled. Since his daughter's body was still there, how could someone else have had her head? Finally, he guessed that Zhu had killed her daughter by magic, so he went to question Zhu. Zhu said, "My wife's head was changed in a dream. I don't know how it happened. It is unjust to say that I killed your daughter." Wu did not believe him, and he filed a lawsuit against him. The prefect questioned Zhu's servants and all of them told the same story. Hence, the prefect could not convict Zhu.

Zhu returned home and asked Lu how to deal with this. Lu said, "It is easy, and I will let his daughter speak for herself." That night, Wu had a dream in which her daughter said, "I was killed by Yang Danian of Suxi, and it had nothing to do with the scholar Zhu. Since Zhu did not like his wife's appearance, Judge Lu put my head in place of hers. This is why my body is dead and my head is still alive. Please don't breed enmity with Zhu." Wu woke up and told his wife, who said she had the same dream. So they told this to the prefect. After investigation, there was truly a man named Yang Danian. They arrested Yang who finally confessed his crime. Wu went off to Zhu's house and asked to be allowed to see his wife. Since then, Wu regarded Zhu as his son-in-law. He buried his daughter's body together with Zhu's wife's former head.

四十五 綠衣女（一）

　　于生名璟，字小宋，益都人。讀書醴泉寺。夜方披[1]誦，忽一女子在窗外讚曰：「于相公勤讀哉！」因念：深山何處得女子？方凝思間，女已推扉笑入，曰：「勤讀哉！」于驚起，視之，綠衣長裙，婉妙無比。于知非人，固詰里居。女曰：「君視妾當非能咋噬[2]者，何勞窮問？」于心好之，遂與寢處。羅襦既解，腰細殆不盈掬。更籌方盡，翩然遂去。由此無夕不至。

　　一夕共酌，談吐間妙解音律。于曰：「卿聲嬌細，倘度一曲，必能消魂。」女笑曰：「不敢度曲，恐消君魂耳。」于固請之。曰：「妾非吝惜，恐他人所聞。君必欲之，請便獻醜；但只微聲示意可耳。」遂以蓮鉤輕點足

---

1. 披：翻開。
2. 咋噬：吃人。

45   A Girl in a Green Dress (1)

Once there was a man whose family name was Yu. His given name was Jing and his alias was Xiaosong. He was a native of Yidu[1]. He studied at Liquan Temple. One night, while he was reading a book, he suddenly heard a girl's voice outside the window praising him saying, "Mr. Yu is diligent in his studies." While Yu was wondering how a girl had come to this remote mountain, the girl had opened the door and come in smiling. "Studying so hard!" The girl said. Yu was surprised. He stood up and saw an exceedingly beautiful girl in a long green dress. Though he knew that she was not human, he still asked her where she came from. The girl said, "You should know that I am not a man-eater. Why do you keep on asking?" Yu was very fond of her, so they went to bed together. The girl took off her dress, revealing a waist so slim that Yu could hold it in one arm. The next morning, the girl left lightly. From that time on, the girl came every night.

One night, when they were drinking together, through conversation, the girl expressed her great knowledge about music. Yu said to her, "Your voice is very delicate. If you could sing for me, I would be transported." The girl laughed and said, "I dare not sing for fear of carrying you away." However, Yu insisted on hearing her sing. The girl said, "It is not that I am unwilling to sing, but that I am afraid someone else would overhear me. Since you insist, I will try. But I will sing in a low voice, only to show you what it sounds like." Tapping out

---

1. Yidu: see Passage 13, Note 1.

牀，歌云：“樹上烏臼鳥[3]，賺[4]奴中夜散。不怨繡鞋濕，只恐郎無伴。”聲細如蠅，裁可辨認。而靜聽之，宛轉滑烈，動耳搖心。歌已，啟門窺曰：“防窗外有人。”繞屋周視，乃入。

---

3. 烏臼鳥：鴉舅鳥，天明時鳴叫。
4. 賺：哄騙。

the beats on a stool with the tip of her toe, the girl started to sing. "The bird's singing in the tree fools me into leaving you, my love, in the middle of the night; I am not complaining that my embroidered shoes are wet with dew, I am only worried that you will be alone."

Though her voice was barely audible as the buzz of a fly, yet listening carefully, Yu felt that it was mellifluous and touched his heartstrings. Having finished singing, the girl opened the door, peeped outside and said, "Beware of any stranger." She went out, walked around the house and then came back.

四十六 綠衣女（二）

　　生曰：“卿何疑懼之深？”笑曰：“諺云：‘偷生鬼子常畏人。’妾之謂矣。”既而就寢。惕然[1]不喜，曰：“生平之分，殆止此乎？”于急問之，女曰：“妾心動，妾祿盡矣。”于慰之曰：“心動眼瞤[2]，蓋是常也，何遽此云？”女稍懌，復相綢繆[3]。更漏既歇，披衣下榻。方將啟關，徘徊復返，曰：“不知何故，惶悽[4]心怯。乞送我出門。”于果起，送諸門外。女曰：“君佇望我；我逾垣去，君方歸。”于曰：“諾。”視女轉過房廊，寂不復見。

　　方欲歸寢，聞女號救甚急。于奔往，四顧無跡，聲在簷間。舉首細視，則一蛛大如彈，搏捉一物，哀鳴聲嘶。于破網挑下，去其縛纏，則一綠蜂，奄然將斃矣。捉歸室中，置案頭。停蘇移時，始能行步。徐登硯池，自以身投

---

1. 惕然：惴惴不安。
2. 眼瞤（shùn）：眼跳。
3. 綢繆：情意綿綿。
4. 惶悽（tí xī）：害怕。

46   A Girl in a Green Dress (2)

Yu asked her, "Why are you so scared?" The girl laughed and said, "The saying goes 'A ghost often behaves prudently'. This is about me." After that, they went to bed; but the girl seemed worried and unhappy. She said, "Is this day going to be the end of our relationship?" Hurriedly Yu asked why she had such feelings. The girl said, "My heart is beating fast and I have the feeling that I will die soon." In order to comfort her, Yu said, "It is common to find the heart throbbing and the eyelids twitching. Why should you be afraid of that?" The girl felt a little better. They went back to sleep. At dawn, they woke up. The girl got out of bed, dressed up and was going to leave. When she was about to open the door, she hesitated and came back to the room, saying, "I don't know why I still feel nervous. Would you please see me to the door?" Yu rose from the bed and walked her to the door. The girl said, "Please stay here and watch me. Don't go back until I have climbed over the wall. Yu said, "I will." Yu saw the girl turn off from the corridor and disappear.

Yu was about to return to his room to sleep again, when suddenly he heard the girl's desperate cry for help. Yu ran to her rescue; but looking around, he could not find her. It seemed that the cry came from the eaves. Looking up, Yu saw a spider the size of a pellet seizing something. It was this thing that cried piteously and hoarsely. Yu broke the spider's web, stripped off the tangled threads, and found a green bee which was on the verge of death. Yu carried it back to his room and put it on the desk. Motionless for a while, the green bee began to move. It crawled into an inkwell, soaked its body with black ink, and

墨汁，出伏几上，走作"謝"字。頻展雙翼，已乃穿窗而去。自此遂絕。

then crawled out and wrote the word "Thanks" by moving on the desk. Finally, it spread its wings and flew away through the window. Since then, the girl never came back again.

四十七 阿霞（一）

　　文登景星者，少有重名。與陳生比鄰而居，齋隔一短垣。一日，陳暮過荒落之墟，聞女子啼松柏間；近臨，則樹橫枝有懸帶，若將自經。陳詰之，揮涕而對曰：“母遠去，託妾於外兄。不圖狼子野心，畜我不卒[1]。伶仃如此，不如死！”言已，復泣。陳解帶，勸令適人。女慮無可託者。陳請暫寄其家，女從之。

　　既歸，挑燈審視，丰韻殊絕。大悅，欲亂之。女厲聲抗拒，紛紜之聲，達於間壁。景生逾垣來窺，陳乃釋女。女見景，凝目停睇，久乃奔去。二人共逐之，不知去向。

　　景歸，闔戶欲寢，則女子盈盈自房中出。驚問之，答曰：“彼德薄福淺，不可終託。”景大喜，詰其姓氏。曰：

---

1. 不卒：不終。

47　A Girl Named A'xia (1)

In Wendeng County, there was a talented man named Jing Xing who had been very famous since he was young. He had a neighbor named Chen whose house was separated from his by a low wall. One evening, when Chen was passing by a desolate place, he heard a girl weeping among the pines. He went over and saw a rope hung on a branch. Chen realized that the girl was going to hang herself. Chen asked her the reason and the girl wept and said, "My mother went on a long journey. She entrusted me to my cousin. But I had never thought that my cousin would be so cruel and heartless as to drive me out. A helpless girl like me would rather die." And the girl wept again. Chen untied the rope and advised the girl to marry someone. However, the girl said that she had no one she could trust here. Chen asked the girl to live in his house for the time being and the girl agreed.

Coming back home, Chen lit the lamp and found that the girl was a matchless beauty. Being wild with joy, he wanted to seduce her. The girl resisted him, speaking sternly. The noise came to his neighbour Jing who climbed over the wall to see what was going on. Chen released the girl. The girl fixed her eyes on Jing for quite some time, and then ran out of the house. Both Chen and Jing ran after the girl, but she vanished.

When Jing returned home, he locked the door and was about to go to bed. Suddenly, he saw the girl coming out of his room, appearing in all her grace. Amazed by the sight, Jing asked the girl why she was there. The girl said, "Chen does not have the fortune and virtue, so he is not the right person to marry." Jing was very happy and asked her name. The girl

"妾祖居於齊。為齊姓，小字阿霞。"入以游詞，笑不甚
拒，遂與寢處。

replied, "I came from Shandong Province. My family name is Qi, and my given name is A'xia." After entering the bedroom, Jing spoke obscene words, and the girl laughed without stopping him. So they went to bed together.

四十八　阿霞（二）

　　齋中多友人來往，女恆隱閉深房。過數日，曰：“妾姑去。此處煩雜，困人甚。繼今，請以夜卜[1]。”問：“家何所？”曰：“正不遠耳。”遂早去。夜果復來，歡愛綦篤。又數日，謂景曰：“我兩人情好雖佳，終屬苟合，家君宦游西疆，明日將從母去，容即乘間稟命[2]，而相從以終焉。”問：“幾日別？”約以旬終。

　　既去，景思齋居不可常；移諸內，又慮妻妒。計不如出妻。志既決，妻至輒詬詈。妻不堪其辱，涕欲死。景曰：“死恐見累，請蚤歸。”遂促妻行。妻啼曰：“從子十

---

1. 夜卜：在晚上。
2. 稟命：徵得父母的同意。

48   A Girl Named A'xia (2)

Since friends of Jing came to his study very often, A'xia continued to hide in an inner room. A few days later, A'xia said to Jing, "I have to leave because it is too noisy here and I am getting tired of it. From now on, I will come here only at night." Jing asked, "Where is your home?" "Not far from here," she answered. A'xia left in the morning. That night, as expected, A'xia came back. They were deeply attached to each other. A few more days later, A'xia said to Jing, "Though we love each other very much, our relationship is after all illegal. My father is now an official on the western frontier. My mother and I are going to visit him tomorrow. When I see him, I will tell him about our relationship and ask his approval of our marriage, so that we can live together till death." Jing asked, "How long shall we be separate?" A'xia said that it would be about ten days.

After A'xia left, Jing thought that his study was not a permanent place to live in with A'xia, so he wanted to move to the inner chambers, but worried that his wife would be jealous. So he decided to get rid of his wife. Thus decided, he would abuse her whenever he had the chance. His wife could not bear the insults. She wept, saying that she would rather die. However, Jing said to her, "I am afraid if you died here, you would get me into trouble. You'd better go back to your father[1] as soon

---

1. go back to your father: According to Chinese tradition, if a married woman was sent back to her father's home by her husband, it meant she had done something wrong and her husband had divorced her, which was a humiliation to the family of the woman's parents.

年，未嘗有失德，何決絕如此！"景不聽，逐愈急。妻乃出門去。自是堊壁[3]清塵，引領翹待；不意信杳青鸞，如石沉海。妻大歸[4]後，數浼知交，請復[5]於景，景不納；遂適夏侯氏。夏侯里居與景接壤，以田畔之故，世有郤。景聞之，益大恚恨，然猶冀阿霞復來，差足自慰。越年餘，並無蹤緒。

　　……[6]

---

3. 堊壁：用白灰粉刷牆壁。
4. 大歸：古代習俗。已婚婦女被丈夫遣送回家後，不再回丈夫家。
5. 復：復婚。
6. 一年多過去了，阿霞始終沒有音訊。一天，景星遇到了阿霞，質問她為甚麼違約。阿霞回答說因為他背棄了自己的妻子。同時，冥王也因此除去了他在科舉考試中獲取功名的機會。

as possible." Jing urged his wife to go home. His wife wept and said, "I have been married to you for ten years and have never done anything wrong. Why are you so heartless?" Jing did not listen and pressed her to leave. His wife then left. Jing dusted the house, whitewashed the walls and eagerly looked forward to meeting A'xia. However, it seemed that A'xia had disappeared forever, like a stone dropped into the sea.

After being sent back to her father's home, Jing's wife asked some friends to try to persuade Jing to take her back, but Jing refused. So she remarried a person named Xiahou whose field was contiguous to Jing's. Because of boundary dispute, the two families had been enemies for generations. Learning that his wife remarried the man, Jing was very angry, but when he thought that A'xia would come back some day, he was able to console himself. Over a year passed, and there had been no news whatsoever about A'xia.

...²

---

2. Later Jing learned that since he betrayed his wife, A'xia did not come back to him and married another man. Since he betrayed his wife, the king of the nether world deleted his name from the list of successful candidates of the imperial examination.

四十九　畫皮（一）

　　太原王生，早行，遇一女郎，抱襆獨奔，甚艱於步。急走趁[1]之，乃二八姝麗。心相愛樂，問："何夙夜[2]踽踽[3]獨行？"女曰："行道之人，不能解愁憂，何勞相問。"生曰："卿何愁憂？或可效力，不辭也。"

　　女黯然曰："父母貪賂，鬻妾朱門。嫡妒甚，朝詈而夕楚[4]辱之，所弗堪也，將遠遁耳。"問："何之？"曰："在亡之人，烏有定所。"生言："敝廬不遠，即煩枉顧[5]。"女喜，從之。生代攜襆物，導與同歸。女顧室無人，問："君何無家口？"答云："齋[6]耳。"女曰："此所良佳。如憐妾而活之，須秘密勿洩。"生諾之。乃與寢合。使匿密室，過數日而人不知也。生微告妻。妻陳，疑為大家媵妾，勸遣之。生不聽。

---

1. 趁：趕上，追上。
2. 夙夜：早上太陽還沒有出來的時候。
3. 踽踽：孤獨的樣子。
4. 朝詈而夕楚：詈，罵；楚，棒打。一天到晚不是打就是罵。
5. 即煩枉顧：枉，委屈；這裏是客套語。就請委屈一下，到我家暫避一時。
6. 齋：書房。

49   A Painted Skin (1)

In Taiyuan, there was a man named Wang. One morning,
Wang went out and happened upon a girl carrying a bundle,
hurrying along with difficulty. Wang caught up with her and
found that she was about sixteen years old and very beautiful.
He liked her very much and asked, "Why are you travelling
alone at dawn and in such a hurry?" The girl said, "A passerby
cannot possibly share my cares and burdens, so why bother to
ask?" Wang answered, "Tell me your troubles, and if I can
help, I will do my best."

The girl said sadly, "My parents were covetous of money
and sold me to a rich man to be a concubine. His wife was
jealous and treated me badly, often beating and scolding me. I
could not stand it anymore, so I am fleeing from here." Wang
asked, "Where are you going?" The girl answered. "I just left
home and I am not sure where to go." Wang said, "My home
is not far from here. You can come with me." The girl was
happy and went with him. Wang helped the girl with her luggage
and led her to his house. Seeing no one else in the house, the
girl asked, "Don't you have a family?" Wang answered, "This
is my study." The girl said, "It is nice here. If you pity me and
want me to live, please don't tell others I am here." Wang
consented to her request and slept with her that night. The next
day, Wang hid her in a secret room. Several days passed without
anyone knowing she was there. Wang only hinted at the girl's
presence to his wife Chen, who suspected that the girl was the
concubine of a large family. So she persuaded Wang to send
her away, but he would not listen.

偶適市，遇一道士，顧生而愕。問：“何所遇？”答言：“無之。”

One day, Wang went to the market and happened to meet a Taoist priest. As soon as he saw Wang, the priest was startled, and he asked, "Have you met anyone recently?" Wang answered, "No, I haven't."

五十　畫皮（二）

　　道士曰："君身邪氣縈繞，何言無？"生又力白。道士乃去，曰："惑哉！世固有死將臨而不悟者。"生以其言異，頗疑女；轉思明明麗人，何至為妖，疑道士借厭禳以獵食者。無何，至齋門，門內杜，不得入。心疑所作，乃逾垝垣。則室門亦閉。

　　躡跡而窗窺之，見一獰鬼，面翠色，齒巉巉[1]如鋸。鋪人皮於榻上，執彩筆而繪之；已而擲筆，舉皮，如振衣狀，披於身，遂化為女子。睹此狀，大懼，獸伏[2]而出。急追道士，不知所往。遍跡之，遇於野，長跪乞救。道士

---

1. 巉巉：山勢險峻，這裏用來形容女妖牙齒長而尖利。
2. 獸伏：像野獸一樣爬着。

50 A Painted Skin (2)

The priest said, "You are encompassed by evil influences, why did you say that you were not?" Wang did his utmost to defend himself. Seeing this, the priest left, saying, "Strange indeed, there are people who never come to realize that they are dying." Wang felt that the priest's words were cryptic, causing him to develop suspicions about the girl, but he reconsidered and gave up the thought. "How could a beautiful girl be a goblin?" he thought to himself. "The priest must be lying, since he makes a living by exorcizing evil spirits." Soon Wang returned to his study and found that the door was locked. Filled with doubt, he climbed over the wall and went to the secret room, and the door of that room was locked too.

Wang walked gingerly over and peeped through the window. He saw a hideous ghost with a green face and sharp teeth like a saw. The ghost laid a human skin on the bed and painted it with a brush. When she finished, the ghost threw away the brush, picked up the skin, shook it just like shaking a dress, and draped it over her body. Immediately, she was transformed into a beautiful girl. Wang, terrified at this sight, crouched and crawled away. He swiftly chased after the Taoist priest, but did not know where the priest had gone. So he had to search everywhere for him and finally found him in the wilderness. He threw himself at the priest's feet and asked for

曰："請遣除之。此物亦良苦³，甫能覓代者⁴，予亦不忍傷其生。"乃以蠅拂⁵授生，令掛寢門。臨別，約會於青帝廟。

3. 良苦：煞費苦心。
4. 甫能覓代者：剛剛找到可以代替它的人。
5. 蠅拂：又稱"拂塵"、"拂子"，用馬尾做成的驅趕蚊蠅的東西，道士喜歡帶在身邊。

help. The priest said, "I will drive her away. Since she cudgeled her brains to find you as a substitute[1], I cannot bear to kill her." Therefore, the priest gave Wang his horsetail whisk[2] and told him to hang it on the door of the bedroom. Before separating, they agreed to meet at Qingdi Temple the next day.

---

1. a substitute: According to Chinese superstition, certain spirits and ghosts seek substitutes to release them from their animal forms so that they can be reincarnated as human beings. Since it would take hundreds of years of practice before an evil spirit could acquire the ability of transfiguration, the Taoist priest cannot bear to kill the girl.
2. horsetail whisk: a kind of religious article which Taoists like to carry with them. Sometimes the article symbolizes the priest. Since Taoist priests have the ability of exorcizing evil spirits, evil spirits seeing the article will be scared away.

五十一 畫皮（三）

　　生歸，不敢入齋，乃寢室內，懸拂焉。一更許，聞門外戩戩[1]有聲，自不敢窺也，使妻窺之。但見女子來，望拂子不敢進；立而切齒，良久乃去。少時復來，罵曰："道士嚇我。終不然寧入口而吐之耶[2]！"取拂碎之，壞寢門而入。徑登生牀，裂生腹，掬生心而去。

　　妻號。婢入燭之，生已死，腔血狼藉。陳駭涕不敢聲。明日，使弟二郎奔告道士。道士怒曰："我固憐之，鬼子乃敢爾。"即從生弟來。女子已失所在。既而仰首四望，曰："幸遁未遠。"問："南院誰家？"二郎曰："小生所舍也。"道士曰："現在君所。"二郎愕然，以為未有。道士問曰："曾否有不識者一人來？"答曰："僕早赴

---

1. 戩戩：形容鬼走路的響聲。
2. 終不然寧入口而吐之耶：終不然，絕對不會。絕對不會把已經吃到嘴裏的東西再吐出來。

51   A Painted Skin (3)

On returning home, Wang did not dare to enter the study, but instead went to his bedroom where he hung the horsetail whisk on the door. It was around midnight when he heard some approaching footsteps. He dared not look, but asked his wife to take a peep. His wife saw that the girl came near, but was afraid to enter upon seeing the horsetail whisk. The girl stood there, gnashing her teeth for a good while before leaving. After a while, the girl returned and cursed, "The priest wants to scare me, but surely it does not mean that I will have to spit out the thing I have swallowed!" After this, she tore the horsetail whisk into pieces, broke the door down, and entered the bedroom. She then went over to the bed, lacerated Wang's belly, removed his heart, and left.

Wang's wife Chen screamed out, and the maidservant came in and lit the lamp. Wang was found dead and the centre of his stomach smeared with blood. Chen was frightened, and she sobbed silently, not daring to cry loudly. The next morning, Chen sent her younger brother to report what had happened to the Taoist priest. The priest was very angry, "I had pity on her; how dare she do this to me!" The priest followed Wang's brother to Wang's home. The girl was nowhere to be found, so the priest raised his head and looked around, saying, "Fortunately, she is not far from here." He then asked, "Who lives in the southern house?" Wang's brother said, "That's my house." The priest said, "She is now in your house." The brother was astonished, thinking this was impossible. The priest asked again, "Did any stranger visit your house this morning?" The brother replied, "I don't know because I went to meet you at Qingdi

青帝廟，良不知³。當歸問之。"去少頃而返，曰："果有
之。晨間一嫗來，欲傭為僕家操作，室人⁴止之，尚在
也。"

---

3. 良不知：實在不知道。
4. 室人：妻子。

Temple. Let me go home and check the situation." After a while, the brother returned and said, "Just as you said, there is a stranger in my house. This morning, an old woman came to my house and asked to be a servant. My wife allowed her to stay and she is still in my house."

五十二　畫皮（四）

　　道士曰：“即是物矣。”遂與俱往。仗木劍，立庭心，呼曰：“孽魅！償我拂子來！”嫗在室，惶遽無色，出門欲遁。道士逐擊之。嫗仆，人皮劃然而脱，化為厲鬼，臥嗥如豬。道士以木劍梟其首；身變作濃煙，匝地作堆[1]。道士出一葫蘆，拔其塞，置煙中，颼颼[2]然如口吸氣，瞬息煙盡。道士塞口入囊。共視人皮，眉目手足，無不備具。道士卷之，如卷畫軸聲，亦囊之，乃別欲去。

　　陳氏拜迎於門，苦求回生之法。道士謝不能。陳益

---

1. 匝地作堆：匝，環繞。在地上旋繞成一堆。
2. 颼颼：風的響聲。

52　A Painted Skin (4)

The priest said, "That is the ghost." Then, the group went to Wang's brother's home. Holding a wooden sword[1], the priest stood in the middle of the courtyard and shouted, "You evil creature, give back my horsetail whisk!" The old woman in the house was in great panic. Her face turned pale as she rushed out, trying to escape, but the priest quickly attacked her with his wooden sword. The old woman fell down, and her human skin dropped off as she turned into a hideous ghost squealing like a pig on the ground. The priest cut off her head, and her body turned into a thick cloud of smoke whirling on the ground. The priest took out a calabash[2], pulled out the plug, and put the calabash in the smoke. With a wheeze like somebody drawing breath, the smoke was drawn into the calabash in no time. The priest then plugged the calabash and put it in his bag. People around looked at the human skin which was complete with eyebrows, eyes, hands, and feet. The priest rolled up the skin, as if he were rolling up a painted scroll, and then put it in his bag and was about to leave.

Chen stopped him at the door. She knelt on the ground crying and begging for a way of resurrecting Wang. The priest told her that he could do nothing about it, and Chen was deeply

---

1. wooden sword: usually made from peach wood which was a kind of magic weapon. Chinese people believed that peach wood had the magic power of exorcizing evil spirits.
2. calabash: or gourd, a kind of magic article to lock up evil spirits.

悲，伏地不起。道士沉思曰："我術淺，誠不能起死。我
指一人，或能之，往求必合有效。"問："何人？"曰："市
上有瘋者，時臥糞土中。試叩而哀之。倘狂辱夫人，夫人
勿怒也。"二郎亦習知之。乃別道士，與嫂俱往。

grieved to hear this. She prostrated herself on the ground and refused to stand up. The priest thought for a moment and said, "My magic is limited; I do not know how to bring the dead back to life. But I can introduce you to someone who might be able to help you, only if you would beg him." "Who is this person?" Chen asked. "In the city, there is a madman who often lies on the ground in the dung and dirt. Find him and throw yourself at his feet and beg him. However, do not be angry if he brings some sort of humiliation upon you." Her brother-in-law was familiar with the location of this person in the city, so they took their leave and went to look for the madman.

五十三　畫皮（五）

　　見乞人顛歌道上，鼻涕三尺，穢不可近。陳膝行而前。乞人笑曰：“佳人愛我乎？”陳告之故。又大笑曰：“人盡夫也[1]，活之何為？”陳固哀之。乃曰：“異哉！人死而乞活於我。我閻摩耶？”怒以杖擊陳。陳忍痛受之。

　　市人漸集如堵。乞人咯痰唾盈把，舉向陳吻曰：“食之！”陳紅漲於面，有難色；既思道士之囑，遂強啖焉。覺入喉中，硬如團絮，格格[2]而下，停結胸間。乞人大笑曰：“佳人愛我哉！”遂起，行已不顧。尾之，入於廟中。追而求之，不知所在；前後冥搜，殊無端兆，慚恨而歸。既悼夫亡之慘，又悔食唾之羞，俯仰哀啼，但願即死。

---

1. 人盡夫也：人人都可以做你的丈夫。
2. 格格：難以下咽。

200

53   A Painted Skin (5)

On the way, they saw a mad beggar singing on the road. Mucus flowed profusely from his running nose, and he was too filthy to approach. Chen crawled on her knees over to the madman. The beggar laughed and said, "Are you falling in love with me, beautiful lady?" Chen told him why she had come. The beggar laughed again and said, "Any man can be your husband, so why do you want him to return to life?" Chen repeatedly implored the beggar to save her husband. The beggar said, "Strange! Your husband is dead, and you ask me to bring him back to life. Am I king of the nether world?" He angrily beat Chen with his staff, but she endured the pain.

Gradually people gathered in a crowd around them. The beggar spat out some sputum on his palm and brought it to Chen's mouth and said, "Swallow it!" Chen's face turned red and showed signs of embarrassment, but after considering the priest's exhortation, she forced herself to swallow the sputum. It stuck in her throat like cotton wadding. She exerted herself to swallow it, and it stopped in the pit of her stomach. The beggar burst out laughing and said, "She really loves me!" After this, he walked away. Chen followed him into a temple, but he disappeared. She looked for him everywhere, but there was no trace of him. Filled with shame and regret, she returned home. Chen not only mourned her husband's death, but also regretted having swallowed the beggar's sputum. She wept her heart out and even wished for death.

方欲展血斂屍[3]，家人佇望，無敢近者。陳抱屍收腸，且理且哭。哭極聲嘶，頓欲嘔。覺鬲中[4]結物，突奔而出，不及回首，已落腔中。驚而視之，乃人心也。在腔中突突猶躍，熱氣騰蒸如煙然。大異之。急以兩手合腔，極力抱擠。少懈，則氣氤氳[5]自縫中出。乃裂繒帛急束之。以手撫屍，漸溫。覆以衾裯。中夜啟視，有鼻息矣。天明，竟活。為言："恍惚若夢，但覺腹隱痛耳。"視破處，痂結如錢，尋愈。

---

3. 展血斂屍：擦乾血跡，收斂屍體。
4. 鬲中：胸間。
5. 氤氳：熱氣升騰的樣子。

As Chen cleaned her husband's body and laid it in the coffin, the other family members just stood watching her, not daring to go near her. Chen wept bitterly as she was holding her husband's body and putting his entrails back into his belly. She cried louder and louder until her voice was hoarse. At this time, she suddenly felt as if she was going to throw up. The lump that was stuck in her stomach popped out, and in the blink of an eye, it fell into her husband's chest. As she was gazing in a state of shock, she saw a steaming warm heart palpitating in his chest. She was astounded and hurriedly used all of her strength to close the wound on Wang's chest tightly with her hands. When she slackened her grip slightly, steam came out from the seam, So she quickly tore off a piece of silk to tie up the body. Touching the body, she felt that it was getting warmer, and she covered it with a quilt. In the middle of the night, Chen saw that Wang was breathing. By the next morning, Wang had revived completely and he said, "I seemed to be in a dream and felt a little pain in my heart." Looking at the spot where he was wounded, he found a scab about the size of a coin, which soon healed.

五十四　潞令

　　宋國英,東平人,以教習[1]授潞城令。貪暴不仁,催科[2]尤酷,斃杖下者,狼藉於庭。余鄉徐白山適過之,見其橫,諷曰:“為民父母,威焰固至此乎?”宋揚揚作得意之詞曰:“諾!不敢!官雖小,蒞任百日,誅五十八人矣。”後半年,方據案視事,忽瞪目而起,手足撓亂,似與人撐拒狀。自言曰:“我罪當死!我罪當死!”扶入署中,逾時尋卒。

---

1. 教習:明清時的學官,通常由進士擔任。
2. 催科:徵斂賦稅。

54   The Prefect of Lu City

Being an instructor[1], Song Guoying, a native of Dongping, was appointed as the prefect of Lu City. He was greedy, brutal and heartless. He was particularly ruthless when pressing for tax collection. His court was scattered with the corpses of people who were beaten to death by him. When Xu Baishan, a fellow villager of mine, was passing by and saw Song's ferocious behavior, he satirized him, "As an official who is supposed to be like people's parents how come that you wield your power by terrorizing people?" Song replied triumphantly, "I am flattered. Though I am only a petty official, I have killed fifty-eight people within a hundred days since I have taken up this post." Half a year later, while he was working in his office one day, Song suddenly opened his eyes wide and stood up, punching and kicking, as if he was fighting with someone. Later, he kept saying, "I am guilty. I deserve death!" Someone helped him go back to his room where he soon died.

---

1. instructor: a kind of official position in the Ming and Qing Dynasties. Generally, only a *jinshi* (one who had passed the imperial examination at the national level) could hold this position.

五十五　放蝶

　　長山王進士岵生為令時，每聽訟，按罪之輕重，罰令納蝶自贖；堂上千百齊放，如風飄碎錦，王乃拍案大笑。一夜，夢一女子，衣裳華好，從容而入，曰：“遭君虐政，姊妹多物故[1]。當使君先受風流之小譴耳。”言已，化為蝶，回翔而去。明日，方獨酌署中，忽報直指使[2]至，皇遽而出，閨中戲以素花簪冠上，忘除之。直指見之，以為不恭，大受詬罵而返。由是罰蝶令遂止。

---

1. 物故：死亡。
2. 直指使：官名。朝廷派出巡視地方的官員。

55 The Butterfly's Revenge

Wang Dousheng, a *jinshi*[1], was a native of Changshan. When he was a county magistrate, whenever he gave punishments to criminals, he would make them catch a number of butterflies as their penalty according to the seriousness of their crime. Then he would release those butterflies all at once in the court. The scene of hundreds and thousands of butterflies fluttering hither and thither looked like many pieces of brocade dancing in the wind. Wang then would thump the table and laugh heartily. One night, Wang had a dream in which a girl wearing a beautiful dress walked leisurely into his room and said to him, "Many of my sisters died because of your brutality. Now I will make you suffer reproach for your indiscreet behaviour." Having said that, the girl turned into a butterfly and flew away. The next day, when Wang was drinking alone in his office, suddenly a messenger reported to him that the censor was at the door. Wang came out hastily to receive the censor, but forgot to take down the white flowers stuck on his official hat by his wife in jest previously at home. The censor saw this and reproached him severely for his disrespect. From then on, Wang abolished the penalty of catching butterflies.

---

1. *jinshi* : a successful candidate in the imperial examination at the national level.

五十六　鳥語

　　中州境有道士，募食鄉村。食已，聞鸚鳴；因告主人使慎火。問故，答曰："鳥云：'大火難救，可怕！'"眾笑之，竟不備。明日，果火，延燒數家，始驚其神。好事者追及之，稱為仙。道士曰："我不過知鳥語耳，何仙也！"適有皂花雀鳴樹上，眾問何語。曰："雀言：'初六養之，初六養之；十四、十六殤之。'想此家雙生矣。今日為初十，不出五六日，當俱死也"。詢之，果生二子；無何，並死，其日悉符。

　　邑令聞其奇，招之，延為客。時群鴨過，因問之。對曰："明公內室，必相爭也。鴨云：'罷罷！偏向他！偏向

56   The Message of Birds

In Zhongzhou[1] area, there was once a Taoist priest who went to a village to beg food. When he finished eating, he heard an oriole sing, so he told the host to be careful in using fire. The host asked about the reason, and the priest replied, "The bird said, 'A big inextinguishable fire! Terrible!'" People around scoffed at it, and took no precaution. The next day, as the priest said, there was a big fire which burned several houses. People now realized that the priest was infinitely resourceful. Some busybodies caught up with the priest and called him an immortal. The priest said, "I am not an immortal. I merely understand the language of birds." At that time, there was a black bird singing on a tree. People asked him what it said. The priest replied, "The bird said, 'Born on the sixth. Born on the sixth. Will die on the fourteenth and sixteenth.' There must be a twin in this area. Today is the tenth, and the twins will die five or six days later." Afterwards, people found there was a pair of twins, and soon they both died exactly on the dates the priest predicted.

The official of the place heard about the miracle, and he invited the priest to his office and treated him as a guest. It happened that a flock of ducks was passing by, so the official asked the priest what they said. The priest replied, "Your wives must have had a quarrel with each other because the ducks said, 'Okay! Okay! You are partial to her! You are partial to

---

1. Zhongzhou: It is now in Henan Province.

他！'"令大服，蓋妻妾反脣，令適被喧聒而出也。因留居署中，優禮之。時辨鳥言，多奇中。而道士樸野，肆言輒無所忌。

令最貪，一切供用諸物，皆折為錢以入之。一日，方坐，群鴨復來，令又詰之。答曰：「今日所言，不與前同，乃為明公會計耳。」問：「何計？」曰：「彼云：『蠟燭一百八，銀朱[1]一千八。』」令慚，疑其相譏。道士求去，令不許。逾數日，宴客，忽聞杜宇。客問之，答曰：「鳥云：『丟官而去。』」眾愕然失色。令大怒，立逐而出。未幾，令果以墨敗[2]。嗚呼！此仙人儆戒之，惜乎危厲燻心者，不之悟也！

---

1. 銀朱：一種粉末狀紅色礦物質，可作顏料，供官府朱批用。
2. 墨敗：墨，貪污受賄。因貪污受賄而被罷官。

her!'" The official was convinced because he just came out to avoid the quarrel between his wives. The official let the priest stay in his place and gave him preferential treatment. During his stay, the priest often interpreted birds' messages, most of which turned out to be true. However, the priest was simple and straightforward, and he always said everything bluntly without reservation.

The official was greedy. He often lined his own pockets by selling office supplies. One day, when they were sitting together, the ducks came again. The official asked the priest what they said. The priest answered, "What they say today is different from the other day. This time, they are calculating for you." The official asked, "What are they calculating?" The priest answered, "They said, 'Get one hundred and eighty taels of silver by selling the office candles; get eighteen hundred taels of silver by selling office vermillion." The official was embarrassed. He thought that the priest was holding him up to ridicule. The priest asked to leave, but the official would not let him go. A few days later, when the official was entertaining guests, suddenly they heard a cuckoo singing. The guests asked what the bird said. The priest answered, "The bird said, 'Dismissed from office!'" People were shocked. The official was very angry. He immediately drove the priest out. Soon the official was dismissed from office for embezzlement. Alas, this is a warning from the immortals. It is too bad that people who are blinded by greed cannot come to see the truth!

五十七　席方平（一）

　　席方平，東安人。其父名廉，性戇拙。因與里中富室羊姓有郤，羊先死；數年，廉病垂危，謂人曰：“羊某今賄囑冥使搒[1]我矣。”俄而身赤腫，號呼遂死。席慘怛不食，曰：“我父樸訥，今見陵於強鬼，我將赴地下，代伸冤氣耳。”自此不復言，時坐時立，狀類癡，蓋魂已離舍矣。

　　席覺初出門，莫知所往，但見路有行人，便問城邑。少選[2]，入城。其父已收獄中。至獄門，遙見父臥簷下，似甚狼狽。舉目見子，潸然流涕，便謂：“獄吏悉受賕囑[3]，日夜搒掠，脛股摧殘甚矣！”席怒，大罵獄吏：“父如有罪，自有王章，豈汝等死魅所能操耶！”遂出，抽筆為

---

1. 搒（bǎng）：鞭打。
2. 少選：一會兒。
3. 賕（qiú）囑：賄賂。

57 Xi Fangping (1)

Xi Fangping was a native of Dongan[1]. His father, Xi Lian, was blunt and straightforward in character and had ill feelings with a rich man named Yang in the village. Yang died earlier. Several years later when Lian was critically ill, he said to his family, "Yang is bribing the runners of the nether world to flog me." Soon his body turned red and swollen. Lian shrieked horribly and died. Xi was deeply grieved by his father's death and refused to eat. He said, "My father is simple and taciturn. Now he is subject to bullying by powerful ghosts. I will go to the nether world to redress the injustice done to him." After that, he did not speak a word, but stood up one moment and sat down the next as if demented, for his soul had left his body.

Xi felt that he was walking out of the door, but did not know where to go. He asked the people on the road the way to town, and soon, he came to the place. His father had been taken to prison. When he came near the prison gate, he found from a distance his father lying under the eaves in an awkward position. Seeing his son, the father burst into tears and said, "All the warders here have been bribed. They flog me day and night and my legs have been mauled!" Xi was very angry. He cursed the warders saying, "If my father is guilty, he will be punished by law. How dare you take the law into your own hands?" He then went out of the prison and wrote an indictment. It was

---

1. Dongan: Anci County, Hebei Province

詞。值城隍早衙，喊冤以投。羊懼，內外賄通，始出質理[4]。城隍以所告無據，頗不直席[5]。

---

4. 質理：審理。
5. 不直席：認為席方平無理。

about the time of the morning session of the town god, so he cried out his grievances and submitted his indictment to him. Yang was scared. After giving bribes to all the people in and out of court, he was brought to the court to confront Xi. The town god dismissed Xi's indictment for lack of evidence.

五十八　席方平（二）

席忿氣無所復伸，冥行百餘里，至郡，以官役私狀，告之郡司。遲之半月，始得質理。郡司扑席，仍批城隍復案。席至邑，備受械梏，慘冤不能自舒。城隍恐其再訟，遣役押送歸家。役至門辭去。席不肯入，遁赴冥府，訴郡邑之酷貪。冥王立拘質對。二官密遣腹心與席關說，許以千金。席不聽。

過數日，逆旅主人告曰：「君負氣已甚，官府求和而執不從，今聞於王前各有函進，恐事殆矣。」席以道路之口，猶未深信。俄有皂衣人喚入。升堂，見冥王有怒色，不容置詞，命笞二十。席厲聲問：「小人何罪？」冥王漠若不聞。席受笞，喊曰：「受笞允當，誰教我無錢也！」

58 Xi Fangping (2)

Xi was resentful but could do nothing. After walking miles and miles at night, he came to the prefectural city and sued the town god for taking graft. However it was until two weeks later that the prefectural god opened the court session. The result was that Xi was severely flogged, and the case was referred back to the town god. Xi was taken back to the town and was tortured again and again. He had no way to redress his wrongs and suffering. The town god worried that he might appeal again, so he sent him back home under escort. The runners left Xi at the door of his house and went away. However Xi did not go in but turned back secretly to see the king of the nether world to accuse both the town and prefectural gods of taking bribes and bending the law. The king immediately arrested the two gods to face the charge. The two gods secretly sent a trusted runner to persuade Xi to withdraw the accusation by offering him one thousand taels of silver. Xi refused.

Several days later, the keeper of the inn where Xi stayed told him, "You are going too far to refuse the two gods. They seek a peaceful settlement with you and yet you are adamant. I hear that they both have sent something to the king today. I am afraid that things are against you." Xi thought that it was only hearsay, so he did not quite believe it. After a while, two runners in black uniform came and summoned him to court. In the court, the king looked very angry. Without even allowing Xi to say a word, he gave the order to cane him twenty times. Xi questioned the king in a stern voice, "What's my crime?" The king pretended that he heard nothing. While he was beaten, Xi cried out, "I deserve the punishment only because I don't have money!"

五十九　席方平（三）

　　冥王益怒，命置火牀。兩鬼捽[1]席下，見東墀有鐵牀，熾火其下，牀面通赤。鬼脫席衣，掬置其上，反復揉捺之。痛極，骨肉焦黑，苦不得死。約一時許，鬼曰：「可矣。」遂扶起，促使下牀著衣，猶幸跛而能行。

　　復至堂上，冥王問：「敢再訟乎？」席曰：「大冤未伸，寸心不死，若言不訟，是欺王也。必訟！」王曰：「訟何詞？」席曰：「身所受者，皆言之耳。」冥王又怒，命以鋸解其體。二鬼拉去，見立木高八九尺許，有木板二，仰置其下，上下凝血模糊。方將就縛，忽堂上大呼「席某」，二鬼即復押回。冥王又問：「尚敢訟否？」答曰：「必訟！」冥王命捉去速解。既下，鬼乃以二板夾席，縛木上。鋸方下，覺頂腦漸闢，痛不可禁，顧亦忍而不號。聞鬼曰：「壯哉此漢！」鋸隆隆然尋至胸下。又聞一鬼云：「此人大孝無辜，鋸令稍偏，勿損其心。」

---

1. 捽（zuó）：揪。

59   Xi Fangping (3)

The king was all the more angry and ordered to put Xi on a fire-bed. Two demons dragged him down to the east steps where there was an iron bed with a roaring fire underneath. The surface of the bed was red hot. Two demons stripped Xi, pressed him on the bed and rolled him until his flesh and bones were charred. It was so painful that Xi wished he could die at once. About two hours later, one of the demons said, "It's enough." So they helped him rise from the bed and put his clothes on. Fortunately, Xi was able to walk with a limp.

He was taken to court again. The king asked him, "Dare you still appeal?" Xi said, "My great wrong is not redressed, so I won't give up. If I tell you that I won't appeal again, that would be a lie. Of course I will appeal." The king asked, "What is your appeal?" Xi answered, "Everything I suffered tells what my appeal is." The king was angry. He gave the order to saw Xi in two. Two demons dragged Xi out to a wooden stake about eight or nine feet high with two wooden boards smeared with blood. While the two demons were tying him to the boards, the king ordered them to bring Xi back. The King asked Xi again, "Dare you still want to appeal?" Xi replied, "Definitely!" The king told the two demons to saw Xi immediately. They thrust Xi in between the two wooden boards and bound him to the stake. As the saw descended on him, Xi felt that his head was splitting gradually. Though he was experiencing the agony he never had, he tried his best to bear the pain without crying. He heard one demon say, "He is surely a man of iron!" Xi felt that the saw went down heavily to his chest. Then the other demon said, "This man is extremely filial and innocent. We should slant the saw a little, so that it won't injure his heart."

六十　席方平（四）

　　遂覺鋸鋒曲折而下，其痛倍苦。俄頃，半身闢矣。板解，兩身俱仆。鬼上堂大聲以報。堂上傳呼，令合身來見。二鬼即推令復合，曳使行。席覺鋸縫一道，痛欲復裂，半步而踣。一鬼於腰間出絲帶一條授之，曰：“贈此以報汝孝。”受而束之，一身頓健，殊無少苦。遂升堂而伏。冥王復問如前；席恐再罹酷毒，便答：“不訟矣。”冥王立命送還陽界。

　　隸率出北門，指示歸途，反身遂去。席念陰曹之暗昧尤甚於陽間，奈無路可達帝聽。世傳灌口二郎[1]為帝勳戚[2]，其神聰明正直，訴之當有靈異。竊喜兩隸已去，遂轉

---

1. 灌口二郎：二郎，古代神話傳說中的二郎神楊戩。灌口：在四川灌縣。
2. 勳戚：有功勳的親戚。傳說二郎神是玉皇大帝的外甥，且功勳卓著。

60 Xi Fangping (4)

Xi felt that the saw blade went zigzag down and the agony redoubled. In no time, his body was severed in two. They untied the boards, and the two parts of his body fell down. The demons returned to the court and reported loudly to the king and the king ordered them to put the two parts of Xi together and bring him to the court again. Two demons did accordingly and dragged him along. Xi felt so painful that it seemed the seam was about to split again. He fell down after walking only half a step. One of the ghosts took out a silk belt from his waist and gave it to Xi, saying, "I am giving you this as a reward for your filial piety." Xi took over the belt and wore it round his waist. All of a sudden, there was no pain at all, and he felt very strong. Coming back to the court, Xi knelt down. The king asked him the same question again. For fear of suffering more cruel tortures, Xi replied, "I won't appeal anymore." The king gave the order to send Xi back to the world immediately.

Two runners led him out of the north gate and showed him the way back to the world. They then turned and went away. Xi now realized that the nether world was even more corrupt than the world. Unfortunately there was no way for him to report this to the Jade Emperor[1]. Suddenly he recalled that it was said that the Erlang god[2] of Guankou was a relative of the Jade Emperor, and he was intelligent and upright. Appealing to him would yield unexpected results. Xi was happy that the runners

---

1. the Jade Emperor: the Supreme Deity of Taoism.
2. the Erlang god: in Chinese myths, the Erlang god has three eyes.
   He is a nephew of the Jade Emperor.

身南向。奔馳間，有二人追至，曰："王疑汝不歸，今果然矣。"捽回復見冥王。竊意冥王益怒，禍必更慘。

had left, so he turned around and went towards the south. While he was hurrying along, two runners caught up with him and said, "Just as the king expected, you won't give up and return home." They dragged him back to see the king of the nether world. Xi thought that the king must be very angry and he would have to suffer more misery.

六十一　席方平（五）

　　而王殊無慍容，謂席曰："汝志誠孝。但汝父冤，我已為若雪之矣。今已往生富貴家，何用汝鳴呼為？今送汝歸，予以千金之產、期頤之壽，於願足乎？"乃注籍中，嵌以巨印，使親視之。席謝而下。鬼與俱出，至途，驅而罵曰："奸猾賊！頻頻翻復，使人奔波欲死！再犯，當捉入大磨中，細細研之！"席張目叱曰："鬼子胡為者！我性耐刀鋸，不耐撻楚。請反見王，王如令我自歸，亦復何勞相送？"乃返奔。

　　二鬼懼，溫語勸回。席故蹇緩，行數步，輒憩路側。鬼含怒不敢復言。約半日，至一村，一門半闢，鬼引與共

61   Xi Fangping (5)

Contrary to his expectation, the king showed no sign of anger. He said, "You are indeed a filial son. I have redressed your father's wrong and he has been reincarnated into a rich family. There is no need for you to complain and call for redress here. Now I will send you back. Meanwhile, I will give you a thousand taels of silver, as well as one hundred years of life. Are you satisfied?" The king wrote it down on the life-and-death register[1] and stamped it. Then he showed it to Xi. Xi thanked the king, and came out with two demons. On their way back to the world, the demons hurried him up and cursed him, "You sly cur! Your endless appeal caused us to travel around. We almost worked ourselves to death! If you appeal again, we will put you in the mill and grind you into powder!" Xi angrily retorted, "How dare you! I can bear the saw and the knife but not the abuse. Bring me back to the king. If the king allows me to return by myself, there is no need for you two to escort me home." After that, Xi turned back.

The two demons were afraid. They persuaded Xi to go home with some kind words. Xi walked very slowly on purpose, taking a rest by the roadside after walking several steps. The two demons were angry but dared not say a word. After walking for half a day, they came to a village. When they passed by a house with its door half open, the demons asked Xi to have a

---

1. life-and-death register: see Passage 3, Note 1.

坐；席便據門閾[1]。二鬼乘其不備，推入門中。驚定自視，身已生為嬰兒。憤啼不乳，三日遂殤。魂搖搖不忘灌口，約奔數十里，忽見羽葆[2]來，旛戟橫路。越道避之，因犯鹵簿[3]，為前馬所執，縶送車前。

仰見車中一少年，丰儀瑰瑋[4]。問席："何人？"席冤憤正無所出，且意是必巨官，或當能作威福[5]，因縷訴毒痛。車中人命釋其縛，使隨車行。俄至一處，官府十餘員，迎謁道左，車中人各有問訊。已而指席謂一官曰："此下方人，正欲往愬，宜即為之剖決[6]。'"席詢之從者，始知車中即上帝殿下九王，所囑即二郎也。席視二郎，修軀多髯，不類世間所傳。

九王既去，席從二郎至一官廨，則其父與羊姓並衙隸俱在。少頃，檻車中有囚人出，則冥王及郡司、城隍也。

---

1. 門閾（yú）：門檻。
2. 羽葆：用鳥羽裝飾的儀仗隊。
3. 鹵簿：古代帝王或貴族出行時的儀仗隊。
4. 丰儀瑰瑋：丰采儀表奇偉不凡。
5. 作威福：具有賞罰大權。
6. 剖決：判決。

rest. Xi sat on the threshold. Catching Xi off guard, the two demons pushed him into the door. Before Xi realized what had happened, he had become a new-born baby. Xi was so angry that he kept on crying and refused to eat. Three days later, he died. His soul did not forget to go to Guankou. After travelling for dozens of miles, he suddenly saw a guard of honour decorated with plumes and feathers. The road was full of banners, flags and halberds. Xi wanted to dodge the guard by crossing the road. Unexpectedly he offended the guard and was caught by the outriders. They tied him and took him to a carriage.

Looking up, Xi saw a young man who was extraordinarily dignified and impressive in appearance sitting in the carriage. He asked Xi, "Who are you?" Xi was looking for someone to vent his grievances, and seeing the man, he thought that he must be a high official who had the power to redress his wrong. So he related to him all his suffering. The young man gave the order to untie Xi and let him follow the carriage.

Soon they came to a place where a dozen or so officials were standing by the roadside to welcome the young man. The young man talked to each of them. Then pointing out Xi, he said to one of them, "This man of the mortal world is going to lodge an appeal with you. You should settle the case for him immediately." Through asking the young man's followers, Xi learned that he was the ninth prince of the Jade Emperor; the one to whose care the Erlang god was entrusted. Looking carefully, Xi noticed that, unlike what the people of the mortal world said, Erlang was tall and had a thick beard.

When the ninth prince had left, Xi followed the Erlang god to an office, where his father, Yang and some runners were present. Soon there came a prisoner's carriage from which the nether world king, the prefect god and the town god got off.

當堂對勘，席所言皆不妄。三官戰慄，狀若伏鼠。

......7

---

7. 二郎神作出了如下的判決：冥王罰受火牀之刑；城隍、郡司在陰間處
   以死刑，後罰脫生為牲畜；羊某家產被抄；席廉被賜轉回人世，再添
   三十六年陽壽。席方平與其父一同返回人間，日子一天比一天富裕，
   三年以後，羊家的田產全部歸於席家。

228

After interrogation and confrontation in court, the Erlang god learned that Xi spoke the truth. The three nether world officials trembled all over like three mice curled up on the ground.

...²

---

2. Later the Erlang god announced his judgement : the king of the nether world was sentenced to be put on the bed of fire. The prefect god and the town god were sentenced to death in the nether world and then reincarnated as animals. Yang was sentenced to give all his money to Xi for Xi's filial piety. Xi's father (Lian) was allowed to return to the world to live for another thirty-six years. Finally, Xi and his father both returned to life again and grew very rich, appropriating all the property of the Yang family.

六十二　王者（一）

　　湖南巡撫某公，遣州佐押解餉金六十萬赴京。途中被雨，日暮愆程[1]，無所投宿，遠見古刹，因詣棲止。天明，視所解金，蕩然無存。眾駭怪，莫可取咎[2]。回白撫公，公以為妄，將置之法，及詰眾役，並無異詞。公責令仍反故處，緝察端緒。

　　至廟前，見一瞽者，形貌奇異，自榜云：“能知心事。”因求卜筮。瞽曰：“是為失金者。”州佐曰：“然。”因訴前苦。瞽者便索肩輿[3]，云：“但從我去，當自知。”遂如其言，官役皆從之。瞽曰：“東。”東之。瞽曰：“北。”北之。凡五日，入深山，忽睹城郭，居人輻輳[4]。入城，走移時，瞽曰：“止。”因下輿，以手南指：“見有

---

1. 愆（qiān）程：延誤了行程。
2. 莫可取咎：沒有人可以歸罪。找不到餉金丟失的原因。
3. 肩輿：轎子。
4. 輻輳：喻人煙稠密。輻：車輪的輻條。輳：車輪的軸心。像輻條都集聚於軸心一樣。

62　The King of Judgement (1)

An imperial inspector of Hunan sent an official to escort army pay of 600,000 taels of silver to the capital. On their way, the escorts were delayed by heavy rain. It was getting dark, but they still had not found a place to spend the night. Suddenly, they saw an ancient temple in the distance, so they decided to stay there. The next morning, they discovered that the army pay was gone. The escorts were both surprised and frightened. They did not know who was responsible for this. They went back and told the inspector about the situation. The inspector thought that it was sheer nonsense. He wanted to punish the official according to the law. Later, after interrogating the runners for the official, the inspector did not get any conflicting statement. Therefore, he ordered the official and his runners to return to the temple for an investigation.

At the temple, the official saw an old queer-looking blind man who claimed, "I know what is on your mind." The official asked him to tell his fortune. The blind man said, "You are here for the stolen army pay." The official said "That's right" and told the blind man his difficulty. The blind man asked for a sedan chair to carry him. Then he said to the official, "Come with me, and you will find out by yourself." The official acted accordingly, and he and the runners followed the blind man. The blind man said, "Go east." and all of them went east. Later the blind man said, "Go north," and all of them went north. Five days passed, and the group was deep in the mountains. Suddenly, they saw a city and found that it was densely populated. They entered the city and went on for a while before the blind man said, "Stop." Then he got off the sedan chair and

高門西向，可款關自問之。"拱手自去。

州佐如其教，果見高門，漸入之。一人出，衣冠漢制，不言姓名。州佐述所自來。其人云："請留數日，當與君謁當事者。"遂導去，令獨居一所。給以食飲。暇時閑步，至第後，見一園亭，入涉之。老松翳日，細草如氈。

pointed to the south and said, "There is a tall gate facing west. You go there, knock on the gate and ask for yourself." After these words, the old blind man gave them a cupped-hand salute and left.

Following in the direction to which the blind man had pointed, the official discovered a tall gate facing west, so he walked in. A man in Han Dynasty costume came out, but he did not reveal his name. The official told him their purpose of coming. The man said, "Please stay for several days, and I will introduce you to the man in charge." After that, the official was taken to a room and left there alone. Some people brought him food and drinks regularly. When he was at leisure, the official went out for a walk. Behind the house was a garden. He walked in and saw many sturdy old pines, so dense that they blocked out the sun. The lush grass resembled a soft carpet.

六十三 王者(二)

　　數轉廊榭,又一高亭,歷階而入,見壁上掛人皮數
張,五官俱備,腥氣流燻。不覺毛骨森豎,疾退歸舍。自
分留鞹[1]異域,已無生望,因念進退一死,亦姑聽之。

　　明日,衣冠者召之去,曰:"今日可見矣。"州佐唯
唯。衣冠者乘怒馬甚駛[2],州佐步馳從之。俄,至一轅門,
儼如制府衙署,皂衣人羅列左右,規模凜肅。衣冠者下
馬,導入。又一重門,見有王者,珠冠繡紱,南面坐。州
佐趨上,伏謁。王者問:"汝湖南解官耶?"州佐諾。王者
曰:"銀俱在此。是區區者,汝撫軍即慨然見贈,未為不
可。"州佐泣訴:"限期已滿,歸必就刑,稟白何所申

---

1. 鞹(kuò):人皮。
2. 甚駛:速度很快。

234

63   The King of Judgement (2)

Walking through several corridors and pavilions, the official
saw a tall pavilion. Ascending the steps, he climbed the pavilion
and saw several human skins, with all their facial features,
hanging on the wall. The stench was overpowering. This
gruesome scene made his hair stand on end. He hastily walked
out of the pavilion and returned to his room. He worried that
his skin would be peeled off sooner or later in an alien place,
and there was no way of escape and no hope of life. Considering
that he would meet death whether he escaped or stayed, he had
no alternative but stay put.

The next day, the man who wore Han Dynasty costume
came to him, saying, "You may see the master now." The official
followed him gingerly. The man was riding on a fine horse
which galloped very fast, and the official ran behind the horse.
After some time, they arrived at an outer gate which looked
like the gate of a government office. Runners wearing black
lined up on two sides of the gate. The scene looked grand and
solemn. The man jumped off the horse and led the official
through the gate. Passing through another gate, the official saw
a king, wearing a crown inlaid with pearls and embroidered
official costume, seated facing south. The official walked over,
knelt down, and performed the kowtow. The king asked, "Are
you the official who escorted the army pay of Hunan?" The
official said, "Yes, I am." The king said, "The silver is here. It
is not a large amount. After all, it is nothing to the inspector
even if he generously gives it to us." The official wept and
said, "The deadline is approaching. I will be punished when I
go back. How can I tell the inspector and demonstrate that I

證³？”王者曰：“此即不難。”遂付以巨函云：“以此復之，可保無恙。”又遣力士送之。州佐懾息⁴，不敢辯，受函而返。山川道路，悉非來時所經。既出山，送者乃去。

---

3. 申證：自我辯解的憑證。
4. 懾息：嚇得大氣不敢喘。

am innocent?" The king said, "It is easy." He gave the official a big envelope and said, "Show this to the inspector, and you will be all right." The king sent a guard to escort the official out. The official held his breath in fear, and did not dare to say anymore. He took the envelope and left the city. The mountains and roads did not seem to be the same ones he passed by when he came. When he and his retinue were away from the mountains, the guard left them.

六十四 王者（三）

　　數日，抵長沙，敬白撫公。公益妄之，怒不容辯，命左右者飛索以緤[1]。州佐解襆出函，公拆視未竟，面如灰土。命釋其縛，但云：「銀亦細事，汝姑出。」於是急檄[2]屬官，設法補解訖。數日，公疾，尋卒。

　　先是，公與愛姬共寢，既醒，而姬髮盡失。闔署驚怪，莫測其由。蓋函中即其髮也。外有書云：「汝自起家守令，位極人臣。賕賂貪婪，不可悉數。前銀六十萬，業已驗收在庫。當自發貪囊，補充舊額。解官無罪，不得加譴責。前取姬髮，略示微警。如復不遵教令，旦晚取汝首

---

1. 飛索以緤（tā）：馬上用繩索捆綁。緤，捆綁。
2. 急檄：緊急公文。

64 The King of Judgement (3)

Several days later, the official returned to Changsha. He reported his experience to the inspector. The inspector now believed even more that the official was talking nonsense. He was enraged and rejected any explanation, and ordered that the official be tied up immediately. The official opened a bundle, took out the envelope and offered it to the inspector. The inspector opened the envelope, and hardly had he finished reading the letter, when his face turned pale like ash. He hastily ordered that the official be untied and said to him, "It is nothing to lose the army pay. You may leave now." The inspector hurriedly dispatched an official document and notified other officials to replace the lost money. A few days later, the inspector fell ill, and soon died.

Prior to his death, the inspector went to sleep with his favourite concubine. When they awoke, the concubine's hair had been cut off. People in the government were shocked. No one knew how it happened. It was said that his concubine's hair was in the envelope, and besides, there was also a letter which had the following words: "From a county magistrate you have risen to this high position. Throughout, you have taken countless bribes and done countless evil. We have received your army pay of six hundred thousand taels of silver and put it in the treasury. You should pay out of your own pocket to make up the shortfall. The official who escorts the army pay is innocent, and you should not punish him. Last time, we cut off your concubine's hair. That was only a warning. If you do not follow our order, we will chop off your head sooner or later.

領。姬髮附還，以作明信。"公卒後，家人始傳其書。後
屬員遣人尋其處，則皆重巖絕壑，更無徑路矣。

We return your concubine's hair as a proof of our words." It was not until the inspector died that the letter was shown to the public. Later, an official sent some people to the mountains to look for the king's palace, but all they saw were sheer precipices, overhanging rocks and bottomless chasms. There were no roads at all.

六十五 商三官 (一)

　　故諸葛城,有商士禹者,士人也。以醉謔忤邑豪。豪嗾家奴亂捶之,舁[1]歸而死。禹二子,長曰臣,次曰禮,一女曰三官。三官年十六,出閣有期,以父故不果。兩兄出訟,終歲不得結。

　　壻家遣人參母,請從權[2]畢姻事。母將許之。女進曰:"焉有父屍未寒而行吉禮者?彼獨無父母乎?"壻家聞之,慚而止。無何,兩兄訟不得直,負屈歸。舉家悲憤。兄弟謀留父屍,張再訟之本。三官曰:"人被殺而不理,時事可知

---

1. 舁:抬。
2. 從權:根據情況變通行事。按照傳統,父喪未滿三年,不能成婚。

242

65 A Brave Girl Named Shang Sanguan (1)

In the ancient city of Zhuge, there was a scholar named
Shang Shiyu. One day, he was drunk and said something which
infuriated a local tyrant. The local tyrant incited his servants to
give him a good thrashing. After being carried home, Shang
died. Shang had two sons; the elder was named Chen, and the
younger Li. He also had a daughter named Sanguan who was
then sixteen. Originally, her family had fixed her wedding day,
but it was given up at her father's death. Her two brothers went
to court against the local tyrant. However, a year passed and
there was no result.

One day, Sanguan's fiancé sent someone to see the mother
and asked her to make an exception[1] and let them get married.
The mother was about to say yes. At this time, Sanguan came
out and said, "Don't you have parents? How can you ask me to
marry you while my father's body is still warm?" On hearing
this, her fiancé felt ashamed, and gave up the thought. It did
not take long that the two brothers lost their case and returned
resentfully. The whole family was filled with grief and
indignation. The two brothers planned to keep their father's
body unburied for later appeal, but Sanguan said, "The
authorities don't even want to pay attention to a murder case.
We can well imagine what the society is like. Do you really

---

1. an exception: According to Chinese tradition, children should
   observe three years of mourning for their deceased parents. During
   this period, they could not get married.

矣。天將為汝兄弟專生一閻羅包老耶？骨骸暴露，於心何忍矣。"二兄服其言，乃葬父。葬已，三官夜遁，不知所往。母慚怍，惟恐壻家知，不敢告族黨，但囑二子冥冥偵察之。幾半年，杳不可尋。

believe heaven will bring you an impartial and incorruptible Justice Bao[2] for your case? How can you bear to let our father's body be exposed?" Her two brothers complied with her and buried their father. That very night, Sanguan left home. No one knew where she had gone. Her mother felt embarrassed. She was afraid that her daughter's fiancé would know this, so she dare not tell her relatives. She sent her two sons to inquire about Sanguan's whereabouts secretly. Half a year passed and there had been no news whatsoever about her.

---

2. Justice Bao: Bao Zheng (999-1062), an upright official known for his upholding justice and the dignity of law. He was so much venerated that he became deified.

六十六　商三官（二）

　　會豪誕辰，招優為戲。優人孫淳，攜二弟子往執役。其一王成，姿容平等，而音詞清徹，群贊賞焉。其一李玉，貌韶秀如好女。呼令歌，辭以不稔；強之，所度曲半雜兒女俚謠，合座為之鼓掌。孫大慚，白主人：「此子從學未久，只解行觴耳。幸勿罪責。」即命行酒。玉往來給奉，善覰主人意向。豪悅之。酒闌人散，留與同寢。玉代豪拂榻解履，殷勤周至。醉語狎之，但有展笑。豪惑益甚。盡遣諸僕去，獨留玉。

　　玉伺諸僕去，闔扉下楗[1]焉。諸僕就別室飲。移時，聞廳事中格格有聲。一僕往覘之，見室內冥黑，寂不聞聲。行將旋踵[2]，忽有響聲甚厲，如懸重物而斷其索。亟問之，

---

1. 楗：門閂。
2. 旋踵：轉身。

66　A Brave Girl Named Shang Sanguan (2)

It was now about the time when the local tyrant celebrated his birthday. He called together many entertainers to perform for him. A performer named Sun Chun and his two disciples came to join the performance. One of his disciples called Wang Cheng, was ordinary-looking, but as he sang pleasantly, he won the admiration of the guests. The other called Li Yu was extremely handsome, like a beautiful girl. The guests asked him to sing but he refused, saying that he was not familiar with those songs. Later, being obliged, he sang some rustic and children's songs. All the guests applauded. Sun explained to the master in embarrassment, "Li just came to me, and he only knows how to wait at table. I hope you do not mind." Sun told Li to pour wine for the guests. At table, Li was good at pleasing the local tyrant by attending to his moods and thoughts, so the local tyrant was very fond of him. When the banquet was over, the guests all left. The local tyrant allowed Li to stay overnight. Li waited upon him attentively, helped him make the bed and undress. When the local tyrant took liberties with him, he just smiled. The local tyrant was even more fascinated by him, so he dismissed the servants and kept Li with him.

When all the servants left, Li closed and locked the door. The servants went to another room to have a drink. After a while, they heard some noise in their master's bedroom. One servant walked over and peeped into the room. It was pitch dark and soundless. When he turned and walked away, suddenly, he heard a loud thud as if a rope had snapped and a heavy object had dropped. He cried out and asked what happened,

並無應者。呼眾排闥入，則主人身首兩斷；玉自經死，繩絕墮地上，梁間頸際，殘綆儼然。

but no one answered from inside. He called the other people and broke into the room. They found that their master's head was cut off, and Li Yu had hanged himself. As the rope was broken, Li's body had fallen on the ground. People could clearly see part of the broken rope on the beam, and the other part around Li's neck.

六十七　商三官（三）

　　眾大駭，傳告內闈，群集莫解。眾移玉屍於庭，覺其襪履虛若無足；解之，則素烏[1]如鉤，蓋女子也。益駭。呼孫淳詰之，淳駭極，不知所對。但云：“玉月前投作弟子，願從壽主人，實不知從來。”

　　以其服凶，疑是商家刺客。暫以二人邏守之。女貌如生；撫之，肢體溫奭。二人竊謀淫之。一人抱屍轉側，方將緩其結束[2]，忽腦如物擊，口血暴注，頃刻已死。其一大

---

1. 素烏：白色的鞋子。
2. 緩其結束：解開衣服上的帶扣。

67　A Brave Girl Named Shang Sanguan (3)

People were aghast, and hastily they woke up the local tyrant's family members. The whole family gathered together, but nobody knew what all this was about. People moved Li's body to the courtyard. His shoes seemed empty as if no feet were wearing them. Taking off the shoes, they saw a pair of bound feet[1] in another pair of white shoes[2]. They then realized Li Yu was a girl. People were shocked again. They called Sun over and questioned him. Sun was scared to death. He did not know how to respond. Later he said, "A month ago, Li came to me and asked to learn from me. He said that he was willing to come to celebrate the birthday of the master. I really do not know who he or she was."

Since Li was dressed in deep mourning, people suspected that she was an assassin from the Shang family. Two men were assigned to guard the body temporarily. The girl looked as if she were still alive. Her body was still warm to the touch. The two men privately colluded to rape her. One man held the body and turned it over. While he was about to unbutton her clothes, suddenly, it seemed that his head was hit by something, and blood gushed out from his mouth. In the blink of an eye, he was dead. The other man turned pale with fright, and he hurried

---

1. bound feet: In ancient China, girls of wealthier families had their feet bound into a dainty shape.
2. white shoes: White is the colour of mourning apparel in China.

驚，告眾。眾敬若神明焉。且以告郡。郡官問臣及禮，並
言：「不知。但妹亡去，已半載矣。」俾往驗視，果三官。
官奇之，判二兄領葬，敕豪家勿仇。

to tell the other people. From then on, people treated her body respectfully as if she were an immortal. They also reported this to the authorities. A magistrate questioned the two sons of the Shang family, and they said, "We don't know anything about this. But our sister has left home for half a year." The magistrate sent them to see Li's body. They recognized that was their sister, Shang Sanguan. The magistrate was amazed, and he let the two brothers carry their sister's body home for burial. He also told the family of the local tyrant never to attempt revenge.

六十八 胭脂（一）

　　東昌卞氏，業牛醫者，有女小字胭脂，才姿惠麗。父寶愛之，欲佔鳳於清門[1]，而世族鄙其寒賤，不屑締盟，以故及笄未字。對戶龔姓之妻王氏，佻脫[2]善謔，女閨中談友也。

　　一日，送至門，見一少年過，白服裙帽，丰采甚都[3]。女意似動，秋波縈轉之。少年俯其首趨而去。去既遠，女猶凝眺。王窺其意，戲之曰：“以娘子才貌，得配若人，庶無可恨。”女暈紅上頰，脈脈不作一語。王問：“識得此郎否？”女曰：“不識。”王曰：“此南巷鄂秀才秋隼，故孝廉之子。妾向與同里，故識之。世間男子無其溫婉，今

---

1. 佔鳳於清門：佔鳳，擇婿。清門，無官爵的文人或不以賤業為生的家庭。
2. 佻脫：輕薄。
3. 都：美好。

68 A Girl Called Rouge (1)

In Dongchang of Shandong Province, there was a veterinarian named Bian who specialized in cows. He had a daughter called Rouge who was beautiful and bright. He was very fond of her and wanted to marry her into a scholar's family. However since Bian's family status was low, none of the scholars' families wanted to take his daughter. So his daughter was not engaged until she was fifteen. Wang, the wife of Gong who lived opposite to Bian's house, was a frivolous person who liked to play jokes on people. She often went to Rouge's chamber to chat with her and they were good friends.

One day, Rouge walked Wang to the door and saw a young man passing by. The man wore white clothes and a hat. He was handsome and elegant. Seeing him, Rouge was attracted, and her bright eyes stared at him. The young man, however, lowered his head and hurried away. Rouge kept looking at him until he disappeared in the distance. Wang made out Rouge's mind, and teased her saying, "What a wonderful match it would be if a beautiful and talented girl like you could marry a man like him." Rouge blushed and said nothing. Wang asked her, "Do you know him?" Rouge answered, "No." Wang said, "This is scholar E Qiusun, living in South Lane, the son of the late *xiaolian*[1]. I used to live in the same lane with him, so I know him well. No man in this world is as kind and gentle as he. He

---

1. *xiaolian* : a successful candidate in the imperial examination at the provincial level in the Ming and Qing Dynasties.

衣素，以妻服未闋[4]也。娘子如有意，當寄語使委冰[5]焉。"
女無言，王笑而去。

　　數日無耗，心疑王氏未暇即往，又疑宦裔不肯俯拾。
邑邑徘徊，縈念頗苦，漸廢飲食，寢疾惙頓。王氏適來省
視，研詰病因，答言："自亦不知。但爾日別後，即覺忽
忽不快，延命假息，朝暮人也。"王小語曰："我家男子，
負販未歸，尚無人致聲鄂郎。芳體違和，非為此否？"女
赬顏良久。王戲之曰："果為此者，病已至是，尚何顧
忌？先令其夜來一聚，彼豈不肯可？"女嘆息曰："事至
此，已不能羞。若渠不嫌寒賤，即遣媒來，疾當愈；若私
約，則斷斷不可！"王領之，遂去。

　　王幼時與鄰生宿介通，既嫁，宿偵夫他出，輒尋舊
好。是夜宿適來，因述女言為笑，戲囑致意鄂生。宿久知
女美，聞之竊喜，幸其有機之可乘也。將與婦謀，又恐其

---

4. 妻服未闋 (què)：未闋：期未滿。為死去的妻子服喪，還沒有期滿。
5. 委冰：託媒。

is wearing mourning apparel for the death of his wife. If you like him, I will tell him and let him find a matchmaker to make a marriage proposal." Rouge said nothing, and Wang left with a smile.

Several days passed and no news came from Wang. Rouge thought that Wang was perhaps too busy to visit E; or maybe E from a good family was unwilling to take her because of her family's low status. Pacing gloomily up and down the room, she thought about it over and over and became extremely anxious. Gradually, she lost her appetite and fell ill. Wang came to visit her and asked about her illness. Rouge answered, "I don't know. Since you left several days ago, I have been feeling restless. I know I am dying." Wang spoke in a low voice, "My husband hasn't come back from business, so we haven't told E about you. Does that make you ill?" Rouge blushed. Wang said to Rouge teasingly, "If that is the reason and you are already in this state of illness, what misgivings do you still have? Why don't you call him in tonight? There is no reason for him to refuse, I suppose?" Rouge said with a sigh, "There is no room for shyness when matters have reached this stage. If he does not belittle the status of my family, he should send a matchmaker immediately and I will recover. If he asks me to have a tryst with him, that's absolutely impossible!" Wang nodded and left.

When she was young, Wang had a lover named Su Jie who used to be her neighbour. After Wang got married, whenever her husband went out, Su would come to meet her to revive their old love. That night, Su happened to come again. Wang told him Rouge's words for fun and jokingly asked Su to tell E. Su had long heard that Rouge was a beautiful girl. On hearing this story, he was secretly very happy at the opportunity to take advantage of the situation. He was about to discuss this with Wang, but worried that Wang would feel jealous. So he

妒，乃假無心之詞，問女家閨閫甚悉。

pretended that he had no other motives and asked casually about the details concerning Rouge's bedroom.

六十九　胭脂（二）

　　次夜，逾垣入，直達女所，以指叩窗。內問：“誰何？”答以“鄂生”。女曰：“妾所以念君者，為百年，不為一夕。郎果愛妾，但宜速倩冰人；若言私合，不敢從命。”宿姑諾之，苦求一握纖腕為信。女不忍過拒，力疾[1]啟扉。

　　宿遽入，即抱求歡。女無力撐拒，仆地上，氣息不續。宿急曳之。女曰：“何來惡少，必非鄂郎；果是鄂郎，其人溫馴，知妾病由，當相憐恤，何遽狂暴如此！若復爾爾[2]，便當鳴呼，品行虧損，兩無所益！”宿恐假跡敗露，不敢復強，但請後會。女以親迎為期。宿以為遠，又請。女厭糾纏，約待病愈。宿求信物，女不許。宿捉足解繡履而出。女呼之返，曰：“身已許君，復何吝惜？但恐‘畫虎

---

1. 力疾：勉強支撐着病體。
2. 爾爾：如此。

69 A Girl Called Rouge (2)

The next evening, Su climbed over the wall and went straight to Rouge's room. He knocked on the window, and someone inside asked, "Who is it?" Su answered, "This is E." Rouge said, "I am longing for you because I want to live with you forever, not for one night's happiness. If you really love me, send a matchmaker quickly. I am afraid I can't have relations with you in private." Su pretended that he agreed with her, and implored to shake her hand as a sign of promise. Rouge did not want to be too hard on him, so she propped herself up and opened the door with some effort.

Su entered the room, held Rouge in his arms and asked to make love to her. Rouge did not have the strength to resist him, and she fell on the ground and was out of breath. Su hastily tried to pick her up and Rouge said, "Who are you, ruffian? You can't be E. I know E is kind and gentle. If he knows the cause of my sickness, he will give every care to me and won't treat me so rudely. If you keep pushing me, I will cry out. That will bring disgrace to both of us." Su was afraid that the thing would be brought to light, so he stopped pressing her. Su asked to meet her again. The girl said that they would meet again on the day of their wedding. Su said that was too long to wait, and asked for another time. Worried that he would pester her endlessly, Rouge said she would meet him after she had recovered. Su asked for a token, but Rouge refused. Su took off one shoe from her foot by force and left. Rouge called him back and said to him, "As I have entrusted myself to your care, and what else can I not spare you? I am only worried that while

成狗’，致貽污謗。今褻物[3]已入君手，料不可反，君如負心，但有一死！”

宿既出，又投王所。既臥，心不忘履，陰揣衣袂，竟已烏有。急起篝燈，振衣冥索。詰之，不應。疑婦藏匿，婦故笑以疑之。宿不能隱，實以情告。言已，遍燭門外，竟不可得。懊恨歸寢，猶意深夜無人，遺落當猶在途也。早起尋之，亦復杳然。

先是，巷中有毛大者，游手無籍[4]。嘗挑王氏不得，知宿與洽，思掩執以脅之。是夜，過其門，推之未扃，潛入。方至窗外，踏一物，耎若絮帛。拾視，則巾裹女舄。伏聽之，聞宿自述甚悉，喜極，抽息而出。

---

3. 褻物：貼身之物。
4. 無籍：沒有職業。

trying to draw a tiger, one ends up drawing a dog[1]. Then I will become the target of slander and ridicule. Now you have my shoe, and I know I can't get it back. If you change your mind, I will have to die."

Su left Rouge and went to spend the night with Wang. Lying on the bed, Su was still thinking about the shoe. He felt in his sleeve[2], but the shoe was not there. He jumped out of bed at once, lit the lamp, shook his clothes and searched about. Wang asked what he was looking for and he said nothing, suspecting that she hid the shoe. Wang deliberately laughed as if she had figured it out, which increased his suspicion. At last, unable to keep it secret, Su told Wang the truth. Afterwards, he lit the candle and went out looking for the shoe; however, he found nothing. Filled with disappointment, he went back to bed, thinking that the shoe should be somewhere on the road and nobody would have seen it late at night. The next morning, he looked for the shoe again, but still could not find it.

In this lane lived another idler named Mao Da who was jobless. He once tried to seduce Wang but failed. Knowing that Su was Wang's lover, he was looking for the opportunity to catch the two adulterers and threaten Wang with it. That night, Mao passed by Wang's house. He pushed the door, and it was unlocked. He tiptoed into the courtyard. When he came near the window, he felt that he stepped on something soft like cotton wool. He picked it up and found a woman's shoe wrapped in a scarf. After eavesdropping on Su and Wang's conversation, he was overjoyed to hear the details of Su's story and sneaked out of the courtyard.

---

1. trying to draw a tiger, one ends up drawing a dog: a Chinese proverb which means to attempt something over-ambitious and end in failure.
2. in his sleeve: The sleeves of tradition Chinese clothes were wide. They functioned as pockets for carrying things such as handkerchiefs, folding fans and other small objects.

七十　胭脂（三）

　　逾數夕，越牆入女家，門戶不悉，誤詣翁舍。翁窺窗，見男子，察其音跡，知為女來者。心忿怒，操刀直出。毛大駭，反走。方欲攀垣，而卜追已近，急無所逃，反身奪刀；媼起大呼，毛不得脫，因而殺之。女稍痊，聞喧始起。共燭之，翁腦裂不能言，俄頃已絕。於牆下得繡履，媼視之，胭脂物也。逼女，女哭而實告之；但不忍貽累王氏，言鄂生之自至而已。

　　天明，訟於邑。邑宰拘鄂。鄂為人謹訥，年十九歲，見客羞澀如童子。被執，駭絕。上堂不知置詞，惟有戰

70 A Girl Called Rouge (3)

A few days later, Mao climbed over the wall and entered Bian's courtyard. As he was unfamiliar with the layout of the house, he walked to the room of Rouge's father Bian by mistake. Bian peeped through the window and saw a man. From his manner, Bian realized that the man was here for his daughter. Flying into a rage, he grabbed a cleaver and rushed out. Mao was frightened, and took to his heels. When he was about to climb over the wall, Bian had already caught up with him. Having no escape, Mao turned back and wrested the cleaver from Bian. Meanwhile, woken by the noise, the mother cried loudly for help. Mao had no way to flee, so he killed Bian. Rouge was recovering a little those days. Hearing the noise, she got out of bed and came out. She and her mother lit the lamp and found her father's head cut open and he could hardly say a word. A moment later, he died. At the foot of the wall, they found the embroidered shoe. The mother recognized that it was Rouge's. Immediately, she closely questioned Rouge. Rouge burst into tears and told her the truth. As she could not bear to get Wang into trouble, she only said that it was E who came to meet her.

In the morning, they brought a lawsuit against E with the county magistrate. The magistrate arrested E. E was a reticent person, and though he was then nineteen years old, he was still as shy as a child in front of people. When they came to arrest him, he was scared to death. In court, he did not know what to say to defend himself but kept on trembling with fear. Seeing

慄。宰益信其情真,橫加桎械。生不堪痛楚,以是誣服[1]。既解郡,敲撲如邑。生冤氣填塞,每欲與女面相質;及相遭,女輒詬詈,遂結舌不能自伸,由是論死。往來復訊,經數官無異詞。

　　後委濟南府復案。時吳公南岱守濟南,一見鄂生,疑其不類殺人者,陰使人從容私問之,俾得盡其詞。公以是益知鄂生冤。籌思數日,始鞫[2]之。先問胭脂:"訂約後,有知者否?"答:"無之。""遇鄂生時,別有人否?"亦答:"無之。"乃喚生上,溫語慰之。生自言:"曾過其門,但見舊鄰婦王氏與一少女出,某即趨避,過此並無一言。"吳公叱女曰:"適言側無他人,何以有鄰婦也?"欲刑之。女懼曰:"雖有王氏,與彼實無關涉。"公罷質,命拘王氏。

---

1. 誣服:誣,冤枉。受冤枉,被迫服罪。
2. 鞫(jú):審問。

this, the magistrate was even more convinced that E was the killer, so he subjected E to severe torture. E was a frail scholar who could not stand the cruel torture, so he pleaded guilty to the false charges. When he was sent to the prefecture, the governor tortured him again. Filled with pent-up indignation, E wanted to confront Rouge, but whenever they met in court, Rouge would scold him severely, which made him tongue-tied. So he was sentenced to death. Several officials tried him again and again, and none of them put forward any conflicting opinion.

Finally, the case was brought to the court of Jinan Province. The governor of the province was Wu Nandai. The first time he saw E, Wu felt that E did not look like a killer, so he sent someone to talk to him gently in order to let him speak his mind freely. After hearing his words, Wu was even more convinced that E had been wronged. He turned the case over in his mind for several days before he opened the court. Wu interrogated Rouge first: "Did anyone know that you had a secret engagement with E?" Rouge answered, "No one." Wu asked again, "Was there anyone with you when you met E the first time?" Rouge said, "No one." Wu called E to court and said something to comfort him. E then said, "I once passed by her house. I saw my ex-neighbour Wang and a girl come out. I evaded them at once. After that I never talked to her." Wu rebuked Rouge saying, "You claimed that no one knew it. Why was there a neighbour with you?" Wu was going to torture her. Rouge was scared, and said immediately, "Though Wang was there, she had nothing to do with the case." Wu adjourned the hearings and ordered that Wang be arrested.

七十一　胭脂（四）

　　數日已至，又禁不與女通，立刻出審，便問王：“殺人者誰？”王對：“不知。”公詐之曰：“胭脂供言，殺卞某汝悉知之，胡得隱匿？”婦呼曰：“冤哉！淫婢自思男子，我雖有媒合之言，特戲之耳。彼自引奸夫入院，我何知焉！”公細詰之，始述其前後相戲之詞。公呼女上，怒曰：“汝言彼不知情，今何以自供撮合哉？”女流涕曰：“自己不肖，致父慘死，訟結不知何年，又累他人，誠不忍耳。”公問王氏：“既戲後，曾語何人？”王供：“無之。”公怒曰：“夫妻在牀，應無不言者，何得云無？”王供：“丈夫久客未歸。”公曰：“雖然，凡戲人者，皆笑人之愚，以炫己之慧，更不向一人言，將誰欺？”命梏十指。婦不得已，實供：“曾與宿言。”公於是釋鄂拘宿至。

71   A Girl Called Rouge (4)

Several days later, Wang was taken to court. Wu did not allow her to see Rouge and interrogated her immediately, saying, "Who is the murderer?" Wang replied, "I don't know." In order to draw Wang out, Wu said, "Rouge has confessed that you know everything about the death of Bian. How dare you conceal the truth?" Wang cried out, "Lies! That tart yearns for the company of a man. I indeed told her that I would like to be her matchmaker, but that's only a joke. She herself seduced the adulterer to come to her room. How do I know?" Wu interrogated her carefully and she told the ins and outs of the matter. Wu called Rouge in and asked her angrily, "You said Wang knew nothing. Why did she tell us she was going to be your matchmaker?" Rouge wept and said, "I am an unworthy girl. I caused the death of my father. I don't know when this case will be over, and I can't bear to involve others in this trouble." Wu asked Wang, "After making fun of Rouge, did you tell anyone about it?" Wang replied, "No." Wu said angrily, "Husband and wife share the same bed and there are no secrets between them. How can you say that you didn't tell him?" Wang replied, "My husband has gone for a long time and hasn't come back yet." Wu said, "Whoever makes fun of others likes to laugh at their stupidity in order to show off his own intelligence. Don't you fool us when you say you didn't tell anyone about it!" Wu then gave the order to pinch her fingers[1]. Wang had no alternative but to confess, saying "I told this to Su." So Wu released E and arrested Su.

---

1. pinch her fingers: Pinching a person's fingers between sticks was a kind of torture in old China.

宿至，自供：「不知。」公曰：「宿妓者必非良士！」嚴械之。宿供：「賺[1]女是真。自失履後，未敢復往，殺人實不知情。」公怒曰：「逾牆者何所不至！」又械之。宿不任凌藉[2]，遂以自承。招成報上，無不稱吳公之神。鐵案如山，宿遂延頸以待秋決矣。

然宿雖放縱無行，故東國名士。聞學使施公愚山賢能稱最，又有憐才恤士之德，因以一詞控其冤枉，語言愴惻。公討其招供，反復凝思之，拍案曰：「此生冤也！」遂請於院、司，移案再鞫。問宿生：「鞋遺何所？」供言：「忘之。但叩婦門時，猶在袖中。」轉詰王氏：「宿介之外，姦夫有幾？」供言：「無有。」公曰：「淫亂之人豈得專私一個？」

---

1. 賺：哄騙。
2. 凌藉：折磨。

Soon Su was brought to court and he declared, "I know nothing." Wu said, "A person who goes whoring can't be a good person." Su was tortured severely until he confessed. "It was I who pretended to be E to deceive Rouge, but because I lost the shoe, I dared not go back again. I really don't know anything about the death of Bian." Wu said in anger, "If you dare to climb over the wall at midnight, you would stop at nothing." And Wu tortured him again. Su could not stand the agony and admitted to the murder. Based on Su's confession, Wu made a report to his superior. All the people without exception expressed great admiration for his intelligence in settling the case. With the mass of ironclad evidence, Su craned his neck, waiting for execution in autumn.

However, though he was a dissolute person, Su was quite famous as a talented scholar in Shandong Province. He heard that an official named Shi Yushan was a virtuous and talented person who treasured men of talent most, so he wrote him a complaint in which he appealed for redress of the wrong in elegant and touching diction. Shi called for the documents and thought over the case repeatedly. At last he struck his desk and said, "This scholar was wronged!" He asked for the case to be transferred to him for a retrial. Shi asked Su, "Where did you lose the shoe?" Su answered, "I've forgotten, but I remember when I knocked on Wang's door, it was still in my sleeve." Shi asked Wang, "How many lovers do you have besides Su?" Wang answered, "None." Shi asked, "How can a licentious woman have only one lover?"

七十二　胭脂（五）

供言：“身與宿介，稚齒交合，故未能謝絕；後非無見挑者，身實未敢相從。”因使指其人以實之，供云：“同里毛大，屢挑而屢拒之矣。”公曰：“何忽貞白如此？”命搒之。婦頓首出血，力辯無有，乃釋之。又詰：“汝夫遠出，寧無有託故而來者？”曰：“有之。某甲、某乙，皆以借貸餽贈，曾一二次入小人家。”蓋甲、乙皆巷中游蕩子，有心於婦而未發者也。公悉籍其名，並拘之。

既集，公赴城隍廟，使盡伏案前。便謂：“曩夢神人相告，殺人者不出汝等四五人中。今對神明，不得有妄言。如肯自首，尚可原宥；虛者，廉得[1]無赦！”同聲言無殺人之事。公以三木[2]置地，將並加之；括髮裸身[3]，齊鳴冤苦。公命釋之，謂曰：“既不自招，當使鬼神指之。”使人以氈

---

1. 廉得：查出。
2. 三木：指古代木制的枷、銬、鐐三種刑具。
3. 括髮裸身：把頭髮束起來，衣服剝下來，準備動刑。

72 A Girl Called Rouge (5)

Wang replied, "Su and I got to know each other while we were young, So I can't refuse. Later there were some people who tried to seduce me, but I rejected all of them." Shi ordered her to give some examples to prove her words. Wang said, "My neighbour Mao Da tried to seduce me repeatedly, but I refused him again and again." Shi said, "How come you suddenly become a woman of chastity?" Shi ordered her to be flogged. Wang kept on kowtowing until her forehead was bleeding, saying that she really had no other adulterers. Shi spared her, but asked again, "When your husband was away, did anyone find an excuse to come to your house?" Wang answered, "Yes, there were some who came to my home once or twice either to borrow money or send me gifts." Those people were loafers in the neighbourhood who tried to seduce Wang but failed. Shi wrote down their names and arrested them.

After all the suspects were gathered, Shi took them to the Temple of the town god and made them kneel down in front of the god and said, "A few days ago, the god came into my dream and told me that the murderer is among you. Now in front of the god, no one can tell a lie. If the murderer can confess his crime, he will be treated leniently; otherwise, if he is proved guilty, there will be no forgiveness." All the suspects simultaneously said that they were not the murderer. Shi gave the order to lay out the instruments of torture and tortured them all. The suspects had their hair tied up and clothes stripped, ready for torture. They all cried out that they were wronged. Shi untied them and said, "If you don't confess yourself, the god will point you out." He ordered that the windows of the

褥悉障殿窗，令無少隙；祖諸囚背，驅入暗中，始授盆水，一一命自盥訖；繫諸壁下，戒令"面壁勿動，殺人者，當有神書其背。"少間，喚出驗視，指毛曰："此真殺人賊也！"蓋公先使人以灰塗壁，又以煙煤濯其手：殺人者恐神來書，故匿背於壁而有灰色；臨出，以手護背，而有煙色也。公固疑是毛，至此益信。施以毒刑，盡吐其實。

temple be covered completely with blankets to shut out light. The suspects, stripped to the waist, were told to walk in and wash their hands in a basin of water. Then they were tied to a wall. Shi said to them, "Face the wall and stand still, and the god will write on the back of the killer." After a while, the suspects were called out to be examined. Shi pointed at Mao and said, "He is the murderer!" It turned out that Shi had lime applied on the wall in advance and let the suspects wash their hands with water blended with soot. The murderer was afraid that the god would write on his back, so he stood with his back against the wall, and his back was stained with lime. On his way out, the murderer shielded his back with his hands and so his back was stained black also. Shi suspected that Mao was the murderer in the first place. Now he was fully convinced. After having been tortured severely, Mao confessed to his crime.

七十三　盜戶

順治間，滕、嶧之區，十人而七盜，官不敢捕。後受撫[1]，邑宰別之為"盜戶"。凡值與良民爭，則曲意左袒之，蓋恐其復叛也。後訟者輒冒稱盜戶，而怨家則力攻其偽；每兩造[2]具陳，曲直且置不辨，而先以盜之真偽，反復相苦，煩有司稽籍焉。

適官署多狐，宰有女為所惑，聘術士來，符捉入瓶，將熾以火。狐在瓶內大呼曰："我盜戶也！"聞者無不匿笑。

---

1. 受撫：歸順官府。
2. 兩造：訴訟雙方。

276

73　Legal Thieves

During the years of Shunzhi[1], in the Teng and Yi[2] regions, seven in ten of the people were thieves. The officials dared not arrest them. Later the thieves pledged allegiance to the government and were granted amnesty, and they were named "legal thieves". Whenever they were in dispute with law-abiding citizens, the officials would be partial to these "legal thieves" because they were afraid that the "legal thieves" would rise in rebellion again. Gradually, whenever an accuser went to court, he would claim himself to be a "legal thief", while the accused would attack the accuser as being fake. It very often happened that both the accuser and accused would accuse each other as a fake. So before telling the right from the wrong, the magistrate had to investigate, over and over again, who was the real "legal thief". Sometimes they had to ask the magistrate to check the inhabitants' register.

It happened that the officials' premises were haunted by fox fairies. Once an official's daughter was obsessed by a fox fairy. The official invited a Taoist priest to cast a spell and catch the fox. The priest seized it and put it into a bottle. While he was casting the bottle into the fire, the fox cried out from inside, "I am a legal thief!" Whenever people heard the story, they all laughed in secret.

---

1. Shunzhi: A designation for the years (1644-1661) when Emperor Fulin of the Qing Dynasty was on the throne.
2. Teng and Yi: They are now Teng and Yi Counties of Shandong Province.

七十四　蘇仙（一）

　　高公明圖知郴州時，有民女蘇氏，浣衣於河。河中有巨石，女踞其上。有苔一縷，綠滑可愛，浮水漾動，繞石三匝。女視之，心動。既歸而娠，腹漸大。母私詰之，女以情告。母不能解。數月，竟舉一子。欲置隘巷，女不忍也，藏諸櫝而養之。遂矢志不嫁，以明其不二也。然不夫而孕，終以為羞。兒至七歲，未嘗出以見人。

　　兒忽謂母曰：“兒漸長，幽禁何可長也？去之，不為母累。”問所之。曰：“我非人種，行將騰霄昂壑耳。”女

278

74 Su Xian (1)

During the time when Gao Mingtu was Governor of Chenzhou, a strange thing happened there. One day, a girl named Su was kneeling on a big stone in the river washing clothes. She noticed a lovely thread of smooth green moss rippling on the water and circling the stone three times. As she was looking at it, she was overwhelmed with a strange feeling. On returning home, she was pregnant and her belly grew bigger and bigger. Her mother privately asked her what had happened. Su told her about the incident which her mother could not understand. Several months later, Su surprisingly gave birth to a baby boy. She wanted to throw the boy away in a narrow alley, but could not bear to do so. Finally, she decided to raise the boy by hiding him in a cabinet. She swore not to marry anyone to show that she was faithful to one man[1]. After all, it was considered shameful for an unmarried girl to give birth to a child, so the boy never went out of the house until he was seven years old.

One day, the boy suddenly said to his mother, "I am growing up, so how can you keep on hiding me in the cabinet? You had better let me go, and I will not be your burden." Su asked him where he would go. The boy replied, "I am not human. I will

---

1. faithful to one man: In old China, according to the moral code, a married woman should remain chaste and faithful to her husband or betrothed, even after his death. Since Su was made pregnant by an invisible force, she wanted to remain faithful to it as a token of her chastity.

泣詢歸期。答曰：“待母屬纊[1]，兒始來。去後，倘有所需，可啟藏兒櫝索之，必能如願。”言已，拜母竟去。出而望之，已杳矣。女告母，母大奇之。

---

1. 屬纊：將死。

soar to the skies." Su wept and asked her son when he would come back. The boy replied, "I will come back after your death. After I have left, whenever you need anything, open the cabinet in which you concealed me, and you will get what you want." After this, the boy kowtowed to his mother and left. Walking out of the house, Su found that her son had disappeared. She told her mother all about this, and her mother was amazed.

七十五　蘇仙（二）

　　女堅守舊志，與母相依，而家益落。偶缺晨炊，仰屋無計。忽憶兒言，往啟櫝，果得米，賴以舉火。由是有求輒應。逾三年，母病卒；一切葬具，皆取給於櫝。既葬，女獨居三十年，未嘗窺戶[1]。一日，鄰婦乞火者，見其兀坐[2]空閨，語移時始去。居無何，忽見彩雲繞女舍，亭亭如蓋，中有一人盛服立，審視，則蘇女也。回翔久之，漸高不見。鄰人共疑之。窺諸其室，見女靚妝凝坐，氣則已絕。

　　眾以其無歸，議為殯殮。忽一少年入，丰姿俊偉，向眾申謝。鄰人向亦竊知女有子，故不之疑。少年出金葬母，植二桃於墓，乃別而去。數步之外，足下生雲，不可復見。後

---

1. 窺戶：出戶。
2. 兀坐：靜靜地坐着。

282

75 Su Xian (2)

Since then, Su insisted on keeping her word by not getting married and lived with her mother in mutual dependence. However, they were getting poorer and poorer. One morning, they had barely anything to eat. While they were considering their options, Su suddenly recalled the words of her son. So she opened the cabinet. As expected, there was rice in it for them to cook. After that, they could get all they needed from the cabinet. Three years later, Su's mother died. All the funeral needs were provided by the cabinet. Later, Su lived alone for another thirty years without even leaving her house. One day, a woman neighbour came to ask for tinder, and she saw Su sitting quietly in her lonely room. After chatting with Su for a while, the neighbour left. It was not very long until one day, the same neighbour suddenly saw a colourful cloud shrouding Su's house like a canopy. A lady dressed in splendid attire stood in the cloud. Looking carefully, she recognized it was Su. The cloud rose higher and higher, and finally disappeared. Su's neighbours were astonished. Upon entering Su's house and taking a look, they saw Su fully dressed, sitting there stiffly, dead.

Since Su did not have any relatives, the neighbours discussed how to bury her. Suddenly an elegant handsome young man came in with a smile on his face. He expressed his thanks to the neighbours. The neighbours had all heard that Su had a son, so they had no doubt about the young man. The young man provided for the burial expenses of his mother, and then he planted two peach trees in front of his mother's tomb. After saying goodbye to the neighbours, he left. Just a few steps away, people witnessed a cloud rising from the young man's feet,

桃結實甘芳，居人謂之"蘇仙桃"，樹年年華茂，更不衰朽。官是地者，每攜實以饋親友。

and he disappeared. Later, the two peach trees bore many sweet peaches which the local people called "Su Xian peaches". Every year, these two peach trees grew luxuriantly and never withered. Whenever an official visited this place, he would pick some peaches as gifts for his friends and relatives.

七十六　姊妹易嫁（一）

　　掖縣相國毛公，家素微。其父常為人牧牛。時邑世族
張姓者，有新阡在東山之陽。或經其側，聞墓中叱咤聲
曰：“若等速避去，勿久溷[1]貴人宅！”張聞，亦未深信。
既又頻得夢，警曰：“汝家墓地，本是毛公佳城，何得久
假此？”由是家數[2]不利。客勸徙葬吉，張聽之，徙焉。

　　一日，相國父牧，出張家故墓，猝遇雨，匿身廢壙[3]
中。已而雨益傾盆，潦水奔穴，崩洶[4]灌注，遂溺以死。相
國時尚孩童。母自詣張，願丐咫尺地，掩兒父。張徵知其
姓氏，大異之。行視溺死所，儼當置棺處，又益駭。乃使

---

1. 溷（hùn）：佔據。
2. 數（shuò）：屢次發生。
3. 廢壙：廢棄的墓穴。
4. 崩洶（hōng）：激流的響聲。

286

76   Two Sisters (1)

Mao, the chief minister of state, came from a poor family in Ye County of Shandong Province. His father used to be a cowherd. While Mao was young, there was a man named Zhang from a rich family who had built a new tomb on the sunny side[1] of East Mountain. One day, someone passed by the place and heard reproaching sounds inside a tomb, "Make haste and go away. Don't occupy the place of a man of eminence!" Zhang heard about this but did not much believe it. However, he had several dreams in which he was warned, "The burial ground of your ancestors originally belongs to the Mao's. Why do you occupy another's place for such a long time?" From then on, misfortune struck his family again and again. Someone suggested that Zhang move the tomb to another place, and Zhang did so.

One day, when Mao's father was grazing his herd near the burial ground left vacant by the Zhang family, it suddenly began to rain, so he hid himself in the empty grave. It rained harder and was pouring, and water rushed into the empty grave and drowned him. Mao was then still a child. His mother went to beg Zhang to give her a small piece of land to bury her husband. When Zhang learned her family name, he was surprised. He came to the spot where Mao's father drowned and found that it was exactly the place where he had placed a coffin before.

---

1. tomb on the sunny side: In China, people believe that the location of an ancestral tomb has an impact on the fortune of a family. A person is destined to be a great success if his ancestors' tombs are located on a site of high geomantic quality.

就故壙窆[5]焉。且令攜若兒來。葬已，母偕兒詣張謝。張一見，輒喜，即留其家，教之讀，以齒子弟行。有請以長女妻兒。母駭不敢應。張妻云："既已有言，奈何中改！"卒許之。

　　然此女甚薄毛家，怨慚之意，形於言色。有人或道及，輒掩其耳；每向人曰："我死不從牧牛兒！"及親迎，新郎入宴，彩輿在門，而女掩袂向隅而哭。催之妝，不妝；勸亦不解。

---

5. 窆（biǎn）：下葬。

Zhang was even more astonished, and he agreed to bury Mao's father there. He asked the widow to bring her son to see him next time. After the interment, the widow, together with her son, came to Zhang's house to thank him and Zhang was very happy to see them. He let Mao live in his house and be educated, treating him as if he were his own son. Later Zhang said to the widow that he would betroth his eldest daughter to her son . The widow dared not accept. Zhang's wife said to her, "If we give you our word, we will never go back on it!" The widow agreed.

But Zhang's eldest sister disliked Mao and often showed her resentment and contempt explicitly. Whenever someone mentioned the marriage, she would cover her ears and cry out, "I would rather die than marry a cowherd!" On the day of their wedding, the bridegroom arrived and took his seat at the wedding banquet. The bridal sedan chair was waiting outside. However the bride kept on crying in a corner of her room, wiping her tears with her sleeves. People hurried her to dress up, but she refused and did not take any advice.

七十七　姊妹易嫁（二）

　　俄而新郎告行，鼓樂大作，女猶眼零雨而首飛蓬
也。父止壻自入勸女，女涕若罔聞。怒而逼之，益哭失
聲。父無奈之。又有家人傳白：新郎欲行。父急出，言：
"衣妝未竟，乞郎少停待。"即又奔入視女。往來者，無停
履。遷延少時，事愈急，女終無回意。父無計，周張[1]欲自
死。

　　其次女在側，頗非其姊，苦逼勸之。姊怒曰："小妮
子，亦學人喋聒！爾何不從他去？"妹曰："阿爺原不曾以
妹子屬毛郎；若以妹子屬毛郎，更何煩姊姊勸駕也？"父
以其言慷爽，因與伊母竊議，以次易長。母即向女曰：
"忤逆婢不遵父母命，今欲以兒代若姊，兒肯之否？"女慨
然曰："父母教兒往也，即乞丐不敢辭；且何以見毛家郎

---

1. 周張：不知所措。

77   Two Sisters (2)

Soon the bridegroom asked to take the bride home. Music sounded, but the bride was still tearful and her hair dishevelled. Zhang detained the bridegroom and entered his daughter's room and tried to persuade her to dress up, but she cried continuously as if she heard nothing. Her father got angry and tried to force her to dress up. But she cried even more loudly till she lost her voice. The father could do nothing about it. At this time, a servant came in and told Zhang that the bridegroom was going to leave. Zhang came out hastily and said to him, "The bride is still dressing herself. I beg you to wait a little longer." After that, he hurried back to see the bride again. Zhang went back and forth several times. With the lapse of time, Zhang got extremely worried, for the bride still refused to give in. Finally Zhang was at his wits' end and thought of ending his life.

Zhang's younger daughter was standing by. She did not like her sister's behaviour, so she tried very hard to persuade her sister to obey their father's will until finally her sister was enraged and said, "You little minx have learned to talk like the rest of them! Why don't you marry him?" The younger sister replied, "Father did not betroth me to Mao. If he did, why should I bother you to persuade me to accept him?" Zhang was delighted with her straightforwardness, so he went to consult with his wife about substituting the younger daughter for the elder. The mother said to the younger daughter, "Your defiant sister is not going to obey our will, so we want to put you in her place. Do you agree?" The younger daughter replied frankly, "If you want me to marry him, even if he were a beggar, I would not dare to refuse. Besides, how do we know that Mao will stay

便終身餓莩死乎？" 父母聞其言，大喜，即以姊妝妝女，
倉猝登車而去。

poor the rest of his life?" On hearing this, her parents were very happy. They dressed her up in her sister's wedding dress, put her in the bridal chair, and hastily sent her off.

七十八　姊妹易嫁（三）

　　入門，夫婦雅敦逑好。然女素病赤鬝[1]，稍稍介公意。久之浸知[2]易嫁之説，益以知己德女。居無何，公補博士弟子[3]，應秋闈試。道經王舍人店，店主人先一夕夢神曰："旦夕當有毛解元來，後且脱汝於厄。"以故晨起，崇伺察東來客。及得公，甚喜。供具殊豐善，不索直。特以夢兆厚自託。公亦頗自負；私以細君髮鬑鬑[4]，慮為顯者笑，富貴後念當易之。

　　已而曉榜[5]既揭，竟落孫山，咨嗟蹇步，懊惋喪志。心

---

1. 赤鬝（qiān）：頭髮稀疏。
2. 浸知：慢慢了解到。
3. 補博士弟子：考中秀才。
4. 鬑鬑（lián lián）：頭髮稀少。
5. 曉榜：正榜。

294

78 Two Sisters (3)

The newly-married couple were living together in perfect harmony. The only thing bothering Mao was his wife's thin hair. But when he learned that the two sisters had exchanged places, he respected her even more as a trustworthy and virtuous wife. Soon Mao passed the imperial examination at the county level and became a *xiucai*[1]. Later he was selected as a candidate for the imperial examination at state level. On the way he passed by an inn named Wang Sheren. The host of the inn had had a dream the night before, in which a god told him, "Tomorrow, a *jieyuan*[2] called Mao will come and stay at your inn. Some day, he will extricate you from some misfortune." The host got up early, and paid attention especially to guests coming from the east. When Mao arrived, the host of the inn was very happy and provided him with a sumptuous meal free of charge. He also told him about his dream. Mao felt flattered. But privately he worried that his wife's thin hair would be the joke of the high officials and eminent people one day. Thus, he thought of changing wives after he had become rich and powerful.

When the imperial examination results were announced, Mao's name was not on the list of successful candidates. He was extremely dejected and upset. Sighing, he staggered home.

---

1. *xiucai* : see Passage 11, Note 1.
2. *jieyuan* : the first on the list of successful candidates in the imperial examination at the state level.

椒舊主人，不敢復由王舍，以他道歸。後三年，再赴試，店主人延候如初。公曰：“爾言初不驗，殊慚祇奉。”主人曰：“秀才以陰欲易妻，故被冥司黜落，豈妖夢不足以踐？”公愕而問故。蓋別後復夢而云。公聞之，惕然悔懼，木立若偶。主人謂：“秀才宜自愛，終當作解首。”未幾，果舉賢書第一人[6]。夫人髮亦尋長，雲鬟委綠，轉更增媚。

---

6. 舉賢書第一人：考中第一名舉人。

He felt too ashamed to see the host of the inn, so that he shunned the inn and went home by another route. Three years later[3], Mao went to take the examination again. The host of the inn treated him as before. Mao said, "Your prediction did not come true last time. I am ashamed to receive your treat." The host said, "The reason why you were not successful last time was because you thought of replacing your wife, so the king of the nether world eliminated your name from the list of successful candidates. How can you say that my dream was not realized?" Mao was shocked and asked how he knew this. The host told him that he had another dream after his departure last time. Hearing this, Mao regretted deeply his thought and was awed. He stood motionless like a wooden figure. The host said to him, "You should have more self-respect. Some day, you will get the first position." Soon, as expected, Mao came off first among all the candidates who took the examination. Meanwhile, his wife's hair suddenly grew quite thick and became dark and glossy, which made her even more attractive than before.

---

3. Three years later: The imperial examination was held every three years.

七十九　姊妹易嫁（四）

　　姊適里中富室兒，意氣頗自高。夫蕩惰，家漸凌夷[1]，空舍無煙火。聞妹為孝廉婦[2]，彌增慚作。姊妹輒避路而行。又無何，良人[3]卒，家落。頃之，公又擢進士[4]。女聞，刻骨自恨，遂忿然廢身為尼。

　　及公以宰相歸，強遣女行者詣府謁問，冀有所貽。比至，夫人饋以綺縠羅絹若干疋，以金納其中，而行者不知也。攜歸見師。師失所望，恚曰：“與我金錢，尚可作薪米費；此等儀物我何須爾！”遂令將回。公及夫人疑之。啟視而金具在，方悟見卻之意。發金笑曰：“汝師百餘金尚不能任，焉有福澤從我老尚書也？”遂以五十金付尼

----

1. 凌夷：衰敗。
2. 孝廉婦：舉人的妻子。
3. 良人：丈夫。
4. 擢進士：擢，選拔。考中進士。

79   Two Sisters (4)

The elder sister had married a young man from a wealthy family, which made her very proud of herself. However, her husband was a prodigal, and it did not take too long for the family to become impoverished until the house was bare and there was not enough food to eat. When she learned that her sister had become the wife of a high-ranking official, she was overwhelmed with shame and vexation. Whenever the two sisters met on the road, they would avoid each other by going different ways. Soon the elder sister's husband died and her life was even more difficult. When she learned that Mao had become a successful candidate in the highest imperial examination, it was too late to repent. She hated herself so much that she became a nun in her bitterness.

Later, Mao returned home as the chief minister of state. Reluctantly, the elder sister sent a novice to his mansion to extend greetings to him and hoped that Mao would give a subscription to the temple. When the novice came, Mao's wife gave her several rolls of silk and inserted some silver ingots among them. The novice did not know what was inside and brought the silk to her mistress. The elder sister was very disappointed and said in anger, "If I am given some money, I can buy food and firewood. What use is it to give me things like these?" She told the novice to return the silk. Mao and his wife felt very strange. Opening the parcel, they found that the silver ingots were still there. Now they understood why she returned the silk. Taking the silver, Mao smiled and said to the novice, "Your mistress could not even take advantage of the chance of having one hundred taels of silver. How can she have

去，曰：“將去作爾師用度，多恐福薄人難承荷耳。”行者歸，具以告。師嘿然自嘆，念平生所為，輒自顛倒，美惡避就[5]，豈由人耶？後店主人以人命逮繫囹圄，公為力解釋罪。

5. 美惡避就：避美就惡。

the chance of being my wife?" After that, he gave fifty taels of silver to the novice and said, "This is for your mistress' daily expenses. I am afraid she is not destined to get more than this." The novice went back and told the elder sister everything. The elder sister was speechless. She heaved a sigh, thinking over her past deeds, how she had wilfully turned things upside down and accepted the worthless and rejected the worthy. How could man decide his own fate? As for the host of the inn, he was later put in prison on account of a murder. Mao got him out by helping him demonstrate his innocence.

八十　小官人

　　太史某公，忘其姓氏。晝臥齋中，忽有小鹵簿[1]，出自堂陬[2]。馬大如蛙，人細於指。小儀仗以數十隊；一官冠皂紗，著繡襆，乘肩輿[3]，紛紛出門而去。公心異之，竊疑睡眠之訛。

　　頓見一小人，返入舍，攜一氈包，大如拳，竟造[4]牀下。白言：「家主人有不腆之儀[5]，敬獻太史。」言已，對立，即又不陳其物。少間，又自笑曰：「戔戔微物，想太史亦無所用，不如即賜小人。」太史頷之。欣然攜之而去。後不復見。惜太史中餒[6]，不曾詰所自來。

----

1. 鹵簿：舊時王公大臣出行時的儀仗隊。
2. 堂陬：書房的一角。
3. 肩輿：轎子。
4. 造：至。
5. 不腆之儀：薄禮。
6. 中餒：害怕。

80 The Little Men

Once there was a *taishi*[1] whose name I forget. One day, while he was taking a nap in his study during the daytime, he suddenly saw a diminutive honour guard coming out from the corner of his study. The horses in the honour guard were no bigger than frogs, and the people were smaller than fingers. The little guard included teams of small men, and among them was an official wearing a black official's hat and robe and sitting in a sedan. Soon, one by one, the little men left through the open door. The *taishi* felt strange, but since he was taking a nap at the time, he thought this queer sight was only an illusion.

Suddenly, he witnessed a little man returning, carrying a bundle wrapped in felt as big as a fist. The little man came directly to his bed and said, "My master would like to present you with this small gift." Having said this, the little man just stood there without handing over the gift. After a while, he laughed and said, "This gift is only a small thing, and I doubt if it is useful for you. It would be better if you would instead bestow it to me." The *taishi* nodded in agreement, and the little man happily departed with the gift. Since then, the *taishi* had never again seen similar things, and it seemed a pity to him that he had been too scared to ask from where the little honour guard had come.

---

1. *taishi* : an official historian in ancient China.

八十一　雷公

　　亳州民王從簡，其母坐室中；值小雨冥晦，見雷公持
錘，振翼而入。大駭，急以器中便溺傾注之。雷公霑穢，
若中刀斧，返身疾逃；極力展騰，不得去。顛倒庭際，嘷
聲如牛。天上雲漸低，漸與檐齊。雲中蕭蕭如馬鳴，與雷
公相應。少時，雨暴澍，身上惡濁盡洗，乃作霹靂而去。

81　The Thunder God

In Bozhou[1], there was a resident named Wang Congjian. One day, it was gloomy and raining outside. Wang's mother was sitting in her room. Suddenly, she saw the thunder god stretching his wings and flying in with a hammer in his hand. She was terrified. Without hesitation, she splashed urine from the chamber pot over him. Being smeared with filth, the thunder god seemed to have been hit by a knife or an axe. He turned and left speedily. In the courtyard, the thunder god spread his wings and wanted to fly away. But no matter how hard he tried, he could not make it. Rolling in the courtyard, the thunder god howled like a bull. At this time, the cloud got lower and lower and almost touched the eaves. The sound of the whining like that of a horse could be heard from inside the cloud echoing the howling of the thunder god. Soon there was a heavy downpour which thoroughly cleaned the dirt from the thunder god's body. Finally, the thunder god flew away along with a thunderbolt.

---

1. Bozhou: It is now in Bo County, Anhui Province.

八十二　龍

　　北直界有墮龍入村。其行重拙，入某紳家。其戶僅可容軀，塞而入。家人盡奔。登樓嘩噪，銃炮轟然。龍乃出。門外停貯潦水[1]，淺不盈尺。龍入，轉側其中，身盡泥塗；極力騰躍，尺餘輒墮。泥蟠三日，蠅集鱗甲。忽大雨，乃霹靂拏空而去。

---

1. 潦水：積水。

82   A Dragon

One day, from the sky descended a dragon on a village of the Beizhijie area. Moving slowly with its heavy body, it entered a gentry's home. The dragon was so huge that the room it entered could accommodate no more than its body. It finally pushed itself into the room. The family members of the gentry were all running about, terrified. Some went upstairs screaming and yelling, and firing cannons to drive it away. The dragon came out, crawled into a shallow pool outside the house and rolled in it until it was covered with mud. It tried several times with all its strength to raise itself above the ground, but it dropped as soon as it was only a foot in the air. The dragon stayed in the pool for three days and the scales of its body were covered with flies. Suddenly, there was a heavy rain. Along with a thunderbolt, the dragon soared to the sky.

八十三　鏡聽

　　益都鄭氏兄弟，皆文學士。大鄭早知名，父母嘗過愛之，又因子並及其婦。二鄭落拓，不甚為父母所歡，遂惡次婦，至不齒禮[1]。冷暖相形，頗存芥蒂。次婦每謂二鄭：“等男子耳，何遂不能為妻子爭氣？”遂擯弗與同宿。於是二鄭感憤，勤心銳思，亦遂知名。父母稍稍優顧之，然終殺[2]於兄。次婦望夫縈切，是歲大比[3]，竊於除夜以鏡聽卜。有二人初起，相推為戲，云：“汝也涼涼去！”婦歸，凶吉不可解，亦置之。

---

1. 不齒禮：不同等看待。
2. 殺：不如。
3. 大比：鄉試。

83   Listen with a Mirror

At Yidu, there was a family named Zheng. Both sons of
the Zheng family were scholars. The elder one gained his
reputation early, so the parents showed him special favour, and
consequently, extended their favour to his wife. The younger
brother was, on the other hand, casual and down-and-out. So
the parents disliked him, and as a result, they disliked his wife
as well. Sometimes they even treated his wife with no respect.
Suffering from the unequal treatment, the younger brother's
wife nursed resentment. She often said to her husband, "Being
a man like your brother, why can't you defend your wife from
the slights that was put upon her?" Then she refused to share
the same bed with him. The younger brother was inspired. He
studied diligently and soon gained some reputation. The parents
changed their attitude toward him a little but he was still
treated less well than his brother. In the year when the imperial
examination was held, the younger brother's wife was anxious
about the success of her husband. On New Year's Eve, she
secretly practised "listen with a mirror" divination[1]. She saw
two men pushing each other in jest and saying, "You go off
and cool yourself too." She could not figure out what those
words meant to her, so she forgot them.

---

1. "listen with a mirror" divination: a method of divination. It was thought
   that wearing a mirror on the front on New Year's Eve or New Year
   Day and going out to listen to what other people said could tell
   one's luck.

闈後[4]，兄弟皆歸。時暑氣猶盛，兩婦在廚下炊飯餉耕[5]，其熱正苦。忽有報騎登門，報大鄭捷。母入廚喚大婦曰：「大男中式矣！汝可涼涼去。」次婦忿惻，泣且炊。俄又有報二鄭捷者。次婦力擲餅杖而起，曰：「儂也涼涼去！」此時中[6]情所激，不覺出之於口。既而思之，始知鏡聽之驗也。

---

4. 闈後：考試結束以後。
5. 餉耕：餉，送飯。給耕田的人送飯。
6. 中：內心。

After the imperial examination, the two brothers returned home. One day, the weather was extremely hot and the two wives were cooking in the kitchen, preparing food for the hired labourers in the field. They both could hardly bear the heat. Suddenly, a runner rode up to their house and announce that the elder brother was successful in the examination. The mother went into the kitchen and said to the elder brother's wife, "Your husband has passed the exam. You can go and cool yourself." The younger brother's wife was filled with rage and grief, however, she was still cooking in the kitchen with tears in her eyes. Soon, another runner arrived, saying that the younger brother had passed the examination too. Upon hearing this, the younger one's wife threw down the rolling pin and overwhelmed with excitement, she shouted, "I'll go off and cool myself too." As soon as she uttered those words, she recalled the words she had heard in the "listen with a mirror" divination practice. Now she realized that the situation turned out to be true.

八十四 四十千

　　新城王大司馬，有主計僕[1]，家稱素封。忽夢一人奔
入，曰：“汝欠四十千，今宜還矣。”問之，不答，徑入內
去。既醒，妻產男。知為夙孽，遂以四十千捆置一室，凡
兒衣食病藥，皆取給焉。

　　過三四歲，視室中錢，僅存七百。適乳姥抱兒至，調
笑於側。因呼之曰：“四十千將盡，汝宜行矣。”言已，兒
忽顏色蹙變，項折目張。再撫之，氣已絕矣。乃以餘資治

---

1. 主計僕：掌管錢糧帳目的僕人。亦可稱管家。

84   Forty Strings of Coins

In Xincheng County, there was a man named Wang who was a Minister of War. Wang had a servant accountant who was very rich. One day, the accountant had a dream in which a man rushed into his room and said to him, "You owe me forty strings of coins[1], and now you need to repay me." The accountant asked what all this was about, and the man walked directly into the inner room, without saying anymore. The accountant awoke, and at the same time his wife had just given birth to a son. The accountant realized that the son was his creditor from a previous life[2]. Therefore, he set aside forty strings of coins in a room. Whenever he paid for his son's clothes, food, or medicine, he used money from this sum.

Three or four years later, the accountant counted the money remaining in the room, and there were only seven strings of coins. At this time, the nanny was carrying the child in her arms. Hearing that there were only seven hundred coins left, she called the child's name and said to him teasingly, "Almost forty strings of coins have been spent. You can quit now." As soon as she finished the words, the child's face turned pale, his head drooped and his eyes opened wide. When they touched him, he was dead. So they bought a coffin with the remaining

---

1. forty strings of coins: one string of coins consisted of a thousand coins.
2. creditor from a previous life: Chinese people believe that their children are either their benefactors or creditors from their previous lives.

葬具而瘞之。此可為負欠者戒也。

昔有老而無子者，問諸高僧。僧曰：「汝不欠人者，人又不欠汝者，烏得子？」蓋生佳兒，所以報我之緣；生頑兒，所以取我之債。生者勿喜，死者勿悲也。

money for the child and buried him. Those who owe others debts may use this story as a caution.

Once upon a time, an old man who had no child went to ask an eminent monk the reason. The monk said, "You don't owe anyone anything, nor does anyone owe you anything, so why should you have a son?" This remark means that if one has a good son, it is because he comes to repay the lot from a previous life. However, if one has a bad son, it is because he comes to demand payment for a debt. Thus, one should not necessarily be happy if one has a son; neither should one be sad if the son dies.

八十五　張不量

　　賈人某，至直隸界，忽大雨[1]雹，伏禾中。聞空中云：
"此張不量田，勿傷其稼。"賈私意張氏既云"不良"，何
反祐護。雹止，入村，訪問其人，且問取名之義。蓋張素
封，積粟甚富。每春貧民就貸，償時多寡不校，悉內之，
未嘗執概取盈[2]，故名"不量"，非不良也。眾趨田中，見
秝穗摧折如麻，獨張氏諸田無恙。

---

1. 雨（yù）：降。
2. 執概取盈：概，古代的一種尺狀量具，量穀物時，用於刮平斗斛。仔
　　細量取。

85   A Man Named Zhang Buliang

Once there was a trader who happened to pass by a village in Hebei Province. It suddenly began to hail heavily and he took shelter among the haystacks. There he heard a voice from heaven saying, "This is Zhang Buliang's field. Don't damage his crops." The trader thought that if the person was called *"buliang"* which means a bad guy, why did the gods protect him? When the hail was over, he went to the village to ask people about the person and the meaning of his name. He learned that Zhang was an untitled wealthy man who had a lot of grain reserves. In spring, poor people often went to him to borrow grain. When they returned the grain to him, he would take whatever they repaid him, and never measured it. That was why he was named "Buliang" (do not measure) [1], and not *"buliang"* (bad). Later people went to the fields and found that all the crops had been destroyed in the hail storm except Zhang's.

---

1. "Buliang" (do not measure): Zhang does not measure the repayments of his loans of grain. In Chinese, *buliang* (do not measure) sounds exactly the same as *buliang* (bad).

八十六　僧術

　　黃生，故家子。才情頗贍，夙志高騫。村外蘭若，有居僧某，素與分深[1]。既而僧雲游，去十餘年復歸。見黃，嘆曰：“謂君騰達已久，今尚白紵[2]耶？想福命固薄耳。請為君賄冥中主者。能置十千否？”答言：“不能。”僧曰：“請勉辦其半，餘當代假之。三日為約。”黃諾之，竭力典質如數。三日，僧果以五千來付黃。

　　黃家舊有汲水井，深不竭，云通河海。僧命束置井邊，戒曰：“約我到寺，即推墮井中。候半炊時，有一錢

---

1. 分深：交情很深。
2. 尚白紵：還穿著白色的衣服。意為平民。

86   The Magic of a Monk

Huang, a son of an old family, was a gifted scholar. He was also ambitious. Outside the village where Huang lived, there was a temple. A monk lived there. The two had always been on very good terms. Later, the monk roamed around the country. After more than ten years of wandering, the monk one day came back. When he saw Huang, he said with a sigh, "I thought you had already achieved success in the world. Why are you still wearing a plain gown[1]. Presumably you do not have the fortune. So let me give a bribe to the master of the nether world for you. Can you raise ten strings of money[2]?" Huang replied, "I can't." The monk said, "Please try your best to raise half of the amount. I will raise the rest. Let's have the money ready in three days." Huang agreed. He pawned all his property and got the money he wanted. Three days later, as expected, the monk brought Huang five strings of money.

In the courtyard of Huang's house there was a deep well which never dried out. It was said that the well was connected to the river and the sea. The monk told Huang to bundle up the money and put it on the edge of the well. He then instructed Huang saying, "When you estimate that I have gone back to the temple, throw the money into the well. After about half the time for cooking a meal, a coin will emerge from the water,

---

1. plain gown: In old China, people who did not have any official rank could only wear plain gowns.
2. strings of money: one string usually equalled 1,000 coins.

泛起，當拜之。"乃去。黃不解何術，轉念效否未定，而十千可惜。乃匿其九，而以一千投之。少間，巨泡突起，鏗然而破，即有一錢泛出，大如車輪。黃大駭。既拜，又取四千投焉。落下，擊觸有聲，為大錢所隔，不得沉。日暮，僧至，譙讓[3]之曰："胡不盡投？"黃云："已盡投矣。"僧曰："冥中使者止將[4]一千去，何乃妄言？"黃實告之，僧嘆曰："鄙吝者必非大器。此子之命合以明經[5]終；不然，甲科[6]立致矣。"黃大悔，求再禳之。僧固辭而去。黃視井中錢猶浮，以綆釣上，大錢乃沉。是歲，黃以副榜准貢，卒如僧言。

---

3. 譙讓：責備。
4. 將：拿。
5. 明經：貢生。
6. 甲科：進士。

then kowtow to it." After this, the monk left. Huang did not know what kind of magic it was. He was not quite sure whether this would work, and it would be a pity to throw ten strings of money into the water. So he hid nine strings of money and threw only one string into the well. After a while, a big bubble suddenly emerged. It burst with a clang, and a coin, as big as a cart-wheel, floated up. Huang was startled. He kowtowed to the coin, and threw another four strings of money into the well. As they dropped, the strings of money clattered against the big coin which blocked them from sinking. At dusk, the monk came again. He angrily asked Huang, "Why didn't you throw all the money into the well?" Huang replied, "I did." The monk said, "The emissary of the nether world got only one string. Why are you lying to me?" Huang had no choice but to tell him the truth. The monk said with a sigh, "A stingy man will never succeed. You are doomed merely to be no more than a *gongsheng*[3] in your lifetime. Otherwise, you would probably be a *juren* or *jinshi*[4] soon." After hearing this, Huang deeply regretted. He begged the monk to do the magic again, but the monk refused and left. Huang found that the four strings of money were still floating on the water. He fished up the money with a rope, and the big coin then sank into the water. This year, Huang took the national examination and was only accepted as a *gongsheng*. Thus, his life turned out just as the monk had predicted.

---

3. *gongsheng* : In the past, some candidates who did not pass the imperial examination would be accepted as students of the Imperial College.
4. *juren* or *jinshi* : a successful candidate in the imperial examination at the provincial or the national level.

八十七 某公

陝右某公，辛丑進士，能記前身。嘗言前生為士人[1]，中年而死。死後見冥王判事，鼎鐺油鑊，一如世傳。殿東隅，設數架，上搭豬羊犬馬諸皮。簿吏呼名，或罰作馬，或罰作豬；皆裸之，於架上取皮被之。

俄至公，聞冥王曰："是宜作羊。"鬼取一白羊皮來，捺覆公體。吏白："是曾拯一人死。"王檢籍覆視，示曰：

---

1. 士人：讀書人。

87 A Man Who Remembered His Previous Life

A man, who came from Shanxi Province, was a *jinshi*[1] of the year 1661. He claimed that he could remember his previous life. He told us that in his previous life, he had been a scholar who died in middle age. His soul was taken to the nether world, where he saw how the king of the nether world sat in judgment of the dead. Just like what went round in this world, there were the *ding*, the *dang* and the *huo*[2] in the hall of the king. In the east corner of the hall, there were several rows of shelves on which skins such as those of pig, sheep, dog, horse and so on were hung. After a nether world official called the names of the dead, the king would pronounce his judgment. Some of the dead people were sentenced to reincarnation as horses or pigs. The demons would take off their clothes and cover them with appropriate animal skins.

Soon the man's name was called. He heard the king say, "He should be a sheep." After this, a demon took a white sheep skin and covered the man's body. At that moment, an official said, "He once saved a person's life." The king checked the life-and-death register[3] and said, "He can be exempted from

---

1. *jinshi* : see Passage 55, Note 1.
2. the *ding*, the *dang* and the *huo* : cooking vessels in ancient China. The *ding* was a pot with three or four legs. The *dang* was a shallow, flat pan. The *huo* or the Chinese wok is a bowl-shaped pan. In ancient China, these vessels were also instruments of cruel tortures such as frying a criminal. It is said that they were used by the king of the nether world to punish the dead who did bad things while alive.
3. life-and-death register: see Passage 3, Note 1.

"免之。惡雖多，此善可贖。"鬼又褫其毛革。革已黏體，不可復動。兩鬼捉臂按胸，力脱之，痛苦不可名狀；皮片片斷裂，不得盡淨。既脱，近肩處猶黏羊皮大如掌。公既生，背上有羊毛叢生，剪去復出。

punishment. Though he has done a lot of bad things, this good deed can atone for his crimes." The demon then started to peel off his sheep skin. However, it had stuck to his body and was difficult to remove. Two demons held his arms down, pressed his chest, and peeled off the sheep skin with all their strength. The pain he suffered was beyond description. Finally, the skin was peeled off piece by piece, but not completely. A palm-sized sheep skin was left on his shoulder. When he was born as a human again, there was a piece of sheep's wool on his back. It would come out again as soon as it was cut.

八十八　餺飥媼

韓生居別墅半載，臘盡始返。一夜，妻方臥，聞人行聲。視之，爐中煤火，熾耀甚明。見一媼，可八九十，雞皮囊背，衰髮可數。向女曰："食餺飥[1]否？"女懼，不敢應。媼遂以鐵箸撥火，加釜其上；又注以水。俄聞湯沸。媼撩襟啟腰囊，出餺飥數十枚，投湯中，歷歷有聲。自言曰："待尋箸來。"遂出門去。

女乘媼去，急起捉釜傾簀[2]後，蒙被而臥。少刻，媼至，逼問釜湯所在。女大懼而號。家人盡醒，媼始去。啟簀照視，則土鱉蟲數十，堆累其中。

---

1. 餺飥（bó tuō）：湯餅。
2. 簀：炕席。

88   The Dumpling Woman

After living in his villa for half a year, a man named Han returned to his house at the end of the year. One night, as his wife was about to sleep, she perceived that somebody was walking in her room. Taking a look, she found that the stove was burning fiercely, which made the room very bright. There was an old lady who was about eighty or ninety years old, wrinkled and hunchbacked. Her thin hair was countable. The old lady said to her, "Would you like to eat some dumplings?" Han's wife was terrified and dared not reply. The old lady poked the fire with an iron tong, put a cauldron on the stove, and added water into it. Soon the water came to a boil. The old lady lifted the lapel of her dress, took out tens of dumplings from her waist bag and threw them into the boiling water. The dumplings dropped into the water with a splash. Then the old lady said to herself, "I will have to find my chopsticks." After that, she went out.

Han's wife taking advantage of her leaving rose from her bed quickly, took the cauldron from the stove and poured the dumplings on a mat. Then she lay on the bed and covered herself with a quilt. Soon the old lady came back and closely questioned the wife about where the dumplings were. The wife was scared to death, so she screamed. All the family members were woken. Not until then did the old lady go away. When they lit a lamp and examined the mat, they saw several dozen ground beetles heaped up on it.

八十九 義鼠

　　楊天一言：見二鼠出，其一為蛇所吞；其一瞪目如
椒[1]，似甚恨怒，然遙望不敢前。蛇果腹[2]，蜿蜒入穴；方
將過半，鼠奔來，力嚼其尾。蛇怒，退身出。鼠故便捷，
欻然遁去。蛇追不及而返。及入穴，鼠又來，嚼如前狀。
蛇入則來，蛇出則往，如是者久。蛇出，吐死鼠於地上。
鼠來嗅之，啾啾如悼息[3]，銜之而去。

---

1. 瞪目如椒：眼睛瞪得圓圓的。
2. 果腹：吃飽了。
3. 悼息：悲傷嘆息。

89   A Faithful Rat

A person named Yang Tianyi told me the following story. One day, he saw two rats come out from a hole. One was swallowed by a snake. The other seemed very angry, and it opened its eyes wide and glared at the snake, but dared not go forward. The snake was full, so it crawled back into its hole. When half of the snake's body was inside the hole, the rat rushed towards it and bit its tail violently. The snake was enraged and slithered out of the hole. Since the rat was agile and alert, it immediately escaped. Seeing that it was impossible to catch the rat, the snake crawled into its hole again. At that moment, the rat came out again and bit the snake's tail as before. When the snake entered its hole, the rat came out; when the snake came out, the rat escaped. They went back and forth like this for some time; the snake finally came out and spat out the dead rat. The rat sniffed the carcass, and gave a little squeak as if it were mourning the dead. Then it held the dead rat in its mouth and went away.

九十　鹿衡草

　　關外山中多鹿。土人戴鹿首，伏草中，卷葉作聲，鹿即群至，然牡少而牝多。牡交群牝，千百必遍，既遍遂死。眾牝嗅之，知其死，分走谷中，衡異草置吻旁以燻之，頃刻復蘇。急鳴金施銃，群鹿驚走。因取其草，可以回生。

90 Deer Grass

In the mountainous regions of northeast China, wearing deer-horns, the natives often hid among weeds and made a certain sound by rolling leaves and blowing them. Soon herds of deer would come and start to mate. Since there were fewer stags than does, one stag would mate with hundreds of does. After the mating, the stag would die. The does smelled it and knew that it had died. They would disperse and go to the mountain valleys and bring back a special kind of grass in their mouths. They put the grass on the side of the stag's mouth. Immediately, the stag would come back to life. At that time, the natives would beat gongs and fire blunderbusses to startle the herd. When the deer had fled, the natives would take the grass. It was said the grass could make the dead come back to life.

九十一　義犬

　　周村有賈某，貿易蕪湖，獲重資。賃舟將歸，見堤上有屠人縛犬，倍價贖之，養豢舟上。舟人固積寇[1]也，窺客裝，蕩舟入莽[2]，操刀欲殺。賈哀賜以全屍，盜乃以氈裹置江中。犬見之，哀嗥投水，口銜裹具，與共浮沉，流蕩不知幾里，達淺擱乃止。

　　犬泅出，至有人處，猙猙哀吠。或以為異，從之而往，見氈束水中，引出，斷其繩。客固未死，始言其情。復哀舟人，載還蕪湖，將以伺盜船之歸。登舟失犬，心甚悼焉。抵關三四日，估楫[3]如林，而盜船不見。

　　適有同鄉估客將攜俱歸，忽犬自來，望客大嗥，喚之卻走。客下舟趁之。犬奔上一舟，嚙人脛股，撻之不解。

---

1. 積寇：慣寇。
2. 蕩舟入莽：把船划入蘆葦叢中。
3. 估楫：商船。

332

91　A Loyal Dog

In Zhou Village, there was a trader who went to Wuhu to do business and earned a lot of money. He rented a boat and was about to go home. At the river bank, he saw a dog tied up by a butcher. He redeemed the dog at a high price and kept it on the boat. The boatman, a hardened bandit, detected that the trader had a lot of money with him. He ran the boat into the reed marshes. Taking out a knife, he wanted to kill him. The trader implored the bandit to allow him to die with his body intact. The bandit wrapped him up in a blanket and cast him into the river. Seeing this, the dog cried piteously and jumped into the river. It seized the bundle with its teeth, and drifted along for several miles with it until they were stranded in shallow water.

The dog came out from the water and ran to some people and kept barking piteously. Some people felt strange, so they followed the dog to the river and found the bundle. They dragged the bundle out of the water and untied it. The trader was still alive, and he told them everything and asked them to take him back to Wuhu where he could seek out the bandit. When he was on board, the dog disappeared. The trader was very sad. Three or four days elapsed since he came back to Wuhu, but there was no trace of the bandit's boat he had rented before among the clusters of boats gathered there.

One day, the trader met a fellow villager and was about to go home with him. Suddenly, the dog reappeared and barked at him. When he called it to him, it ran away. He went after the dog and saw it rush onto a boat and seize a boatman by the leg. It would not let go even if it was beaten. The trader rebuked

客近呵之，則所嚙即前盜也。衣服與舟皆易，故不得而認之矣。縛而搜之，則裹金猶在。嗚呼！一犬也，而報恩如是。世無心肝者，其亦愧此犬也夫！

the dog for doing this, and when he got closer, he realized that the boatman was the bandit he was looking for. Since the bandit changed his clothes and his boat, the trader did not recognize him before. They tied the man up, and by searching his boat, they retrieved the robbed money. Even a dog knows how to repay a kindness! Those ungrateful men in the world should feel ashamed before the dog.

九十二　鴻

　　天津弋人[1]得一鴻。其雄者隨至其家，哀鳴翱翔，抵暮始去。次日，弋人早出，則鴻已至，飛號從之；既而集其足下。弋人將並捉之。見其伸頸俯仰，吐出黃金半鋌[2]。弋人悟其意，乃曰：“是將以贖婦也。”遂釋雌。兩鴻徘徊，若有悲喜，遂雙飛而去。弋人稱金，得二兩六錢強。噫！禽鳥何知，而鍾情若此！悲莫悲於生別離，物亦然耶？

---

1. 弋人：射鳥的人。
2. 鋌：同“錠”。

92 A Wild Goose

An archer of Tianjin captured a wild goose. The gander
of the wild goose followed the archer to his home. It cried
plaintively and hovered over the archer's house before it went
away at dusk. The next morning, when the archer came out,
the gander was already there, and it kept on following him,
wailing. Suddenly, the gander fell at his feet. When the archer
was about to seize it, the gander stretched its neck and spat out
half an ingot of gold. The archer now realized what the gander
wanted, so he said to it, "You did this to ransom your wife,
didn't you?" So the archer set the wild goose free. The two
wild geese tarried a little, as if with a tinge of sadness in their
happy reunion. Finally, they flew away. The archer weighed
the gold, and it was almost three taels. Birds are only animals,
and yet they love each other so much! Nothing in the world is
more sorrowful than the separation of husband and wife. Isn't
this also true of animals?

九十三　狼

　　有屠人貨肉歸，日已暮。欻[1]一狼來，瞰擔中肉，似甚涎垂，步亦步，尾行數里。屠懼，示之以刃，則稍卻；既走，又從之。屠無計，默念狼所欲者肉，不如姑懸諸樹而蚤取之。遂鈎肉，翹足掛樹間，示以空空。狼乃止。

　　屠即徑歸。昧爽往取肉，遙望樹上懸巨物，似人縊死狀，大駭。逡巡近之，則死狼也。仰首審視，見口中含肉，肉鈎刺狼齶，如魚吞餌。時狼革價昂，直十餘金，屠小裕焉。緣木求魚，狼則罹之，亦可笑已！

---

1. 欻（xū）：忽然。

93   A Wolf

After selling meat at a market, a butcher was on his way home in the evening. Suddenly, a wolf came and stared greedily at the meat left inside his basket. It followed every step of the butcher for several miles. The butcher was scared. He brandished his knife in front of the wolf which seemed to step back a little. When the butcher walked on, the wolf followed him again. The butcher could do nothing about it. He thought that the wolf wanted only the meat, so he decided to hang the meat on a tree, and fetch it back the next morning. So he hooked the meat, stood on tiptoe, and hung it on the tree. The butcher showed the wolf his empty basket and the wolf stopped following him.

The butcher walked straight home. At dawn the next morning, he went to take his meat. In a distance, he saw a large object hanging from the tree as if someone had hanged himself. He was scared to death. Walking hesitatingly near the tree, he found that it was a dead wolf. Raising his head and looking closely, he saw that the meat was inside the wolf's mouth, and the hook pierced through its upper jaw. The wolf was like a fish which had swallowed a bait. At that time, wolf skin was very expensive, worth more than ten taels of silver. The butcher sold it and earned a lot of money. To catch fish by climbing a tree[1], the wolf met its death. Such behaviour is stupid.

---

1. To catch fish by climbing a tree: "To climb up a tree to look for fish" is a Chinese idiom which means making a futile quest, quite similar to the English proverb: "You cannot get blood from a stone".

九十四 大鼠

　　萬曆間，宮中有鼠，大與貓等，為害甚劇。遍求民間佳貓捕制之，輒被噉食。適異國來貢獅貓，毛白如雪。抱投鼠屋，闔其扉，潛窺之。貓蹲良久，鼠逡巡自穴中出，見貓，怒奔之。貓避登几上，鼠亦登，貓則躍下。如此往復，不啻百次。眾咸謂貓怯，以為是無能為者。

　　既而鼠跳擲漸遲，碩腹似喘，蹲地上少休。貓即疾下，爪掬頂毛，口齕其領，輾轉爭持，貓聲嗚嗚，鼠聲啾啾。啟扉急視，則鼠首已嚼碎矣。然後知貓之避，非怯也，待其惰也。彼出則歸，彼歸則復，用此智耳。

94   A Big Rat

During the years of Wanli (1573-1619), the imperial palace was troubled by the presence of a rat the size of a cat. The rat wreaked havoc. Cats that could kill the rat were widely sought from the public. However, all the cats were eaten by the rat instead. At that time, a foreign country presented a snow-white cat to the emperor. People brought the cat to the room where the rat was, closed the door and watched stealthily from outside. The cat squatted motionlessly for a long time. The rat came out from its hole hesitantly. Seeing the cat, it rushed at it furiously. The cat jumped up on a table; the rat followed, upon which the cat jumped down. They went on up and down for a hundred times. People all said that the cat was timid and incompetent.

Soon, the rat slowed down. Its fat belly began to puff and blow, and finally, it squatted on the ground to have a rest. In the blink of an eye, the cat sprang on the rat, grabbed the fur of its head with paws, gripped its neck with teeth and grappled with the rat. People could hear the meow of the cat and the squeak of the rat. They opened the door, went in, and found that the rat's head had been smashed. Now people realized that the cat was not scared of the rat but was biding its the time waiting for the rat to tire out. The strategy is, "If you come out, I will hide away; if you hide away, I will come out."

九十五 螳螂捕蛇

張姓者，偶行溪谷，聞崖上有聲甚厲。尋途登覘，見巨蛇圍如碗，擺撲叢樹中，以尾擊柳，柳枝崩折。反側傾跌之狀，似有物捉制之。然審視殊無所見，大疑。漸近臨之，則一螳螂據頂上，以刺刀攫其首，攧[1]不可去。久之，蛇竟死。視頞[2]上革肉，已破裂云。

---

1. 攧（diān）：翻來覆去。
2. 頞（è）：眉心。

95 A Mantis Caught a Snake

One day, a person named Zhang came to a valley by chance. Suddenly, he heard a great noise from the cliff. Wondering what it was, he climbed up the cliff where he saw a big snake as thick as a bowl writhing in the thicket, breaking off willow branches with its tail. The snake kept on twisting and coiling as if it had been caught by something. But looking closely, Zhang found nothing. He felt very strange. Getting closer, he discovered a mantis standing on the head of the snake. It attacked the snake's head with its sword-like forelegs. There was no way that the snake could shake it off. With the lapse of time, the snake unexpectedly died. Later, Zhang found that the skin and flesh on the forehead of the snake was torn open.

九十六 牧豎

　　兩牧豎[1]入山至狼穴，穴有小狼二，謀分捉之。各登一樹，相去數十步。少頃，大狼至，入穴失子，意甚倉皇。豎於樹上扭小狼蹄耳故令嗥；大狼聞聲仰視，怒奔樹下，號且爬抓。其一豎又在彼樹致小狼鳴急；狼輟聲四顧，始望見之，乃舍此趨彼，跑號如前狀。前樹又鳴，又轉奔之。口無停聲，足無停趾，數十往復，奔漸遲，聲漸弱；既而奄奄僵臥，久之不動。豎下視之，氣已絕矣。

---

1. 牧豎：牧童。

96　Two Shepherd Boys

Two shepherd boys went to a mountain and found a wolf's lair in which there were two wolf cubs. Each of them took one of the cubs and climbed a tree. The two trees were dozens of steps apart. Soon, the mother wolf came back. Seeing its cubs were not in the lair, she looked very upset. One boy pinched the cub's paws and ears and made it cry out. Hearing the cry, the mother wolf raised her head, and rushed towards the tree angrily. She howled, pawed and clawed the trunk of the tree. At that time, the other boy made the other cub cry out on the other tree. When the mother wolf heard the cry, she stopped howling and looked around. Seeing the other cub, she gave up the first and rushed towards the other tree, howling and pawing as before. The first cub cried out again, the wolf rushed towards the first tree again. She ran between the two trees and kept on howling and running for scores of times until her pace slowed down and her cries weakened. Finally she was exhausted and fell down on the ground stiff. Seeing that the mother wolf had been motionless for a long time, the two shepherd boys came down from the trees and discovered that she had died.

九十七　趙城虎（一）

　　趙城嫗，年七十餘，止一子。一日入山，為虎所噬。嫗悲痛，幾不欲活，號啼而訴於宰。宰笑曰：“虎何可以官法制之乎？”嫗愈號咷，不能制之。宰叱之，亦不畏懼。又憐其老，不忍加威怒，遂諾為捉虎。嫗伏不去，必待勾牒[1]出，乃肯行。宰無奈之，即問諸役，誰能往者。一隸名李能，醺醉，詣座下，自言：“能之。”持牒下，嫗始去。

　　隸醒而悔之；猶謂宰之偽局，故以解嫗擾耳，因亦不甚為意。持牒報繳[2]，宰怒曰：“固言能之，何容復悔？”隸窘甚，請牒拘獵戶。宰從之。隸集諸獵人，日夜伏山

---

1. 勾牒：捉拿逃犯的公文。
2. 報繳：交回勾牒。指沒有完成使命。

346

97 The Tiger of Zhao City (1)

In Zhao City, there was an old lady who was more than seventy years old and had only one son. One day, her son went to the mountain and was eaten by a tiger. Overcome with deep sorrow, the old lady hardly wished to live. She went to the government office, and weeping and wailing in front of the prefect, she accused the tiger of eating her son. The prefect laughed and said, "How can the law punish a tiger?" The old lady kept on wailing, and nothing could stop her. Though reprimanded by the prefect, she showed no fear. Seeing that she was old, the prefect could not bear to punish her, so he promised to catch the tiger. However, the old lady remained kneeling on the ground and refused to leave unless the prefect gave the order to catch the tiger. The prefect had no choice, so he asked the runners who would like to go and catch the tiger. One of the runners named Li Neng was drunk at that time. He approached the prefect and said that he could do it. So the prefect gave him the official order to catch the tiger. The old lady then left.

When Li awoke from his drunkenness, he regretted. But thinking again, Li thought this was only a strategem set by the prefect to end the annoyance from the old lady, so he did not pay much attention to the case. When the deadline came, Li returned the order to the prefect. The prefect got angry with him, "You said you could do it. How can you go back on your word?" Li was embarrassed. He asked the prefect to give him another order summoning the hunters to help him catch the tiger. The prefect did so. From morning till night, Li and the hunters concealed themselves in the mountain, and hoped that

谷，冀得一虎，庶可塞責。月餘，受杖數百。

they could catch a tiger in fulfilment of their duty. However, a month passed, and Li received several hundred lashes of the cane[1] for not catching the tiger.

---

1. lashes of the cane: a corporal punishment used in court in ancient China.

九十八　趙城虎（二）

　　冤苦罔控，遂詣東郭嶽廟，跪而祝之，哭失聲。無何，一虎自外來。隸錯愕，恐被咥噬。虎入，殊不他顧，蹲立門中。隸祝曰：「如殺某子者爾也，其俯聽吾縛。」遂出縲索[1]繫虎項，虎帖耳受縛。牽達縣署，宰問虎曰：「某子爾噬之耶？」虎頷之。宰曰：「殺人者死，古之定律。且嫗止一子，而爾殺之，彼殘年垂盡，何以生活？倘爾能為若子也，我將赦之。」虎又頷之。乃釋縛令去。

　　嫗方怨宰之不殺虎以償子也，遲旦，啟扉，則有死鹿；嫗貨其肉革，用以資度。自是以為常，時銜金帛擲庭中。嫗從此致豐裕，奉養過於其子。心竊德虎。虎來，時臥簷下，竟日不去。人畜相安，各無猜忌。

---

1. 縲索：捆綁犯人的繩索。

98   The Tiger of Zhao City (2)

Feeling grievously wronged, Li came to the Mountain God Temple located in the north of the city where he knelt before the god, prayed, and cried aloud. After a while, a tiger came into the temple. Li was shocked and was afraid of being eaten. However, the tiger did not pay attention to him. It squatted down at the door. Li said his prayer to the tiger, "If you are the one who killed the old lady's son, please let me tie you up." Then he took out a rope and tried to tie up the tiger. The tiger bent its neck to allow Li to tie it up. Li led the tiger to the government office. The prefect asked, "Did you eat the old lady's son?" The tiger nodded. The prefect said again, "According to the law, anyone who kills a person should pay with his life. You killed the only son of the old lady who is now in the evening of her life. How can she live on? If you can be her son, I will let you free." The tiger nodded again. So the prefect set it free.

The old lady complained that the prefect did not kill the tiger to compensate for her son's life. The next morning, when she opened the door, she found a dead deer. The old lady sold the meat and the skin of the deer for some money to support her living. From then on, things like that happened very often. Sometimes, the tiger even held gold and silks in its mouth and threw them in the old lady's courtyard. The old lady thus got rich and the tiger treated her even better than her own son did. So she thought to herself that it was a tiger of virtue. Sometimes, the tiger would come and lay under the eaves of the lady's house for a whole day, in harmony with the livestock.

數年，嫗死，虎來吼於堂中。嫗素所積，綽可營葬，族人共瘞之。墳壘方成，虎驟奔來，賓客盡逃。虎直赴冢前。嘷鳴雷動，移時始去。土人立"義虎祠"於東郊，至今猶存。

Several years later, the old lady died. The tiger came and roared in the mourning hall. The savings of the old lady were enough for her burial. So the relatives of the lady buried her. At the moment when the tomb was completed, the tiger suddenly ran all the way to the tomb. The guests all fled. The tiger came to the tomb and roared like thunder. It did not go away until hours later. Afterwards, people built a memorial hall named "Virtuous Tiger Hall" on the east side of the city, and it is still there today.

九十九　鴝鵒

　　王汾濱言：其鄉有養八哥者，教以語言，甚狎習[1]，出游必與之俱，相將數年矣。一日，將過絳州，而資斧已罄，其人愁苦無策。鳥云：“何不售我？送我王邸，當得善價，不愁歸路無資也。”其人云：“我安忍。”鳥言：“不妨。主人得價疾行，待我城西二十里大樹下。”其人從之。攜至城，相問答，觀者漸眾。有中貴[2]見之，聞諸王。王召入，欲買之。其人曰：“小人相依為命，不願賣。”王問鳥：“汝願住否？”言：“願住。”王喜。鳥又言：“給價十金，勿多予。”王益喜，立畀[3]十金。其人故作懊恨狀而去。

---

1. 狎習：熟習。
2. 中貴：王府的宦官。
3. 畀：給。

99   A Myna

Wang Fenbin told me the following story. In his hometown, there was a man who kept a myna bird. He was very fond of it and trained it to talk. Whenever he left home, he would take the myna with him. Several years elapsed. One day, he happened to pass by Jiangzhou City. By this time, he had spent all his money. He was extremely upset and did not know what to do. The myna said to him, "Why don't you sell me? Take me to the prince, and you will get a good price; so you won't have to worry about travelling expenses." The man said, "How can I have the heart to sell you?" The myna said, "Don't worry. When you get the money, leave this place as soon as possible, and wait for me under the big tree twenty miles west of the city." The man agreed and took it into the city. In the city, the man and the myna were engaged in conversation, which attracted more and more onlookers. A eunuch of the palace saw the scene and informed the prince. The prince called the man in and wanted to buy his myna. The man said, "Me and the myna depend on each other for survival. I won't sell it." The prince asked the myna, "Do you want to live in the palace?" The myna said, "I'd love to." The prince was very happy. The myna said again, "Give him ten ounces of silver as the reward. No more than that." The prince was even more pleased. Immediately, he gave the man ten ounces of silver. The man pretended that he was sad and left.

王與鳥言，應對便捷。呼肉啖之。食已，鳥曰："臣要浴。"王命金盆貯水，開籠令浴。浴已，飛檐間，梳翎抖羽，尚與王喋喋不休。頃之，羽燥，翩躚而起，操晉聲曰："臣去呀！"顧盼已失所在。王及內侍，仰面咨嗟。急覓其人，則已渺矣。後有往秦中者，見其人攜鳥在西安市上。

The prince talked to the myna, and the myna answered fluently. The prince ordered that meat be fed to the myna. When the myna was full, it said, "I want to take a bath." The prince gave the order to open the cage and let the myna bathe in a gold basin. When it finished bathing, the myna flew to the eaves, combed its plumage, and was still talking incessantly to the prince. After a while, when its plumage was dry, it flapped its wings and said with a Shanxi accent, "I am leaving!" The prince looked around and the myna had disappeared. The prince and his servants looked up to the sky and heaved deep sighs. They tried to find the man but the man had disappeared too. Later, a traveller to Shanxi saw the man and his myna on the streets of Xi'an[1].

---

1. Xi'an: The capital city of Shanxi Province.

一百　毛大福

　　太行毛大福，瘍醫[1]也。一日，行術歸，道遇一狼，吐
裹物，蹲道左。毛拾視，則布裹金飾數事[2]。方怪異間，狼
前歡躍，略曳袍服，即去。毛行，又曳之。察其意不惡，
因從之去。未幾，至穴，見一狼病臥，視頂上有巨瘡，潰
腐生蛆。毛悟其意，撥剔淨盡，敷藥如法，乃行。日既
晚，狼遙送之。行三四里，又遇數狼，咆哮相侵，懼甚。
前狼急入其群，若相告語，眾狼悉散去。毛乃歸。

　　先是邑有銀商寧泰，被盜殺於途，莫可追詰。會毛貨
金飾，為寧氏所認，執赴公庭。毛訴所從來，官不信，械
之。毛冤極不能自伸，惟求寬釋，請問諸狼。官遣兩役押

---

1. 瘍醫：治療各種外傷的醫生。
2. 數事：數件。

358

100 Doctor Mao Dafu

Mao Dafu, a native of Taihang, was a doctor who specialized in the treatment of trauma. One day, after paying a home visit, he was on his way home when suddenly he saw a wolf. The wolf spat out a wrapped bundle and sat at the side of the road. Mao picked up the bundle, opened it, and found a few pieces of gold jewelry. While he was marvelling at this, the wolf jumped with joy and slightly pulled at his robe. After that, it walked away. Mao did not understand what that meant, so he walked on. However, the wolf pulled at his robe again. Seeing that it did not have ill intent towards him, Mao followed it. Not far away there was a lair in which another wolf was lying ill. Mao found on its head a big sore which had festered. Mao realized what the wolf wanted. He went over to the sick wolf, cleansed the festered sore, and applied some ointment on the wound. It was getting dark when he was about to leave. The wolf saw him off in the distance. After going three or four miles, Mao met several wolves. They howled and sprang on him. Mao was terrified. At that moment, the former wolf rushed into the wolf pack and seemed to be telling the other wolves something. The wolves all went away, while Mao returned home.

A few days earlier, a dealer in silver named Ning Tai was killed on the road. The murderer had not been caught. One day, when Mao was selling jewelry at a market, he was seen by Ning's wife who brought him before the court. Mao told the official how he obtained the jewelry, but the official did not believe him and tortured him. Being unjustly accused, Mao knew that he could not prove his innocence, so he asked the official to be lenient with him and allow him to see the wolves.

入山，直抵狼穴。

值狼未歸，及暮不至，三人遂反。至半途，遇二狼，其一瘡痕猶在。毛識之，向揖而祝曰：「前蒙饋贈，今遂以此被屈。君不為我昭雪，回去搒掠死矣！」狼見毛被繫，怒奔隸。隸拔刀相向。狼以喙拄地大嗥；嗥兩三聲，山中百狼群集，圍旋隸。隸大窘。狼競前齧繫索，隸悟其意，解毛縛，狼乃俱去。歸述其狀，官異之，未遽釋毛。

後數日，官出行，一狼銜敝履委道上。官過之，狼又銜履奔前置於道。官命收履，狼乃去。官歸，陰遣人訪履主。或傳某村有叢薪者，被二狼迫逐，銜其履而去。拘來認之，果其履也。遂疑殺寧者必薪，鞫之果然。蓋薪殺寧，取其巨金，衣底藏飾，未遑[3]收括，被狼銜去也。

---

3. 未遑：沒有來得及。

The official sent two officers to escort Mao to the mountains. They went straight to the lair of the wolves.

The wolves were not there when they arrived and did not come back until sunset, so they returned. Half way back, they met two wolves, and on one wolf's head, there was a scar. Mao recognized it, so he bowed to the wolves, saying, "The gifts you gave me a few days ago have become the proof of my guilt. If you don't tell the truth, I will be beaten to death!" Seeing that Mao was tied up, the wolves rushed furiously at the two officers. The officers pulled out their broadswords. One wolf howled loudly with its mouth touching the ground. Soon after it howled two or three times, hundreds of wolves from the hills came over and circled the officers who became very frightened. The two wolves went to Mao and gnawed at the rope that tied him. The two officers realized what the wolves wanted, so they untied the rope and the pack of wolves dispersed. The two officers went back and reported the incident to the official. The official also wondered about this, but did not set Mao free.

A few days later, the official went out on business. On his way, he saw a wolf holding a shoe in its mouth and putting it down on the road. The official passed over it. But the wolf picked up the shoe, ran ahead of the official, and again put it down on the road in front of him. The official ordered to pick up the shoe and the wolf left. When he returned to his office, the official secretly sent someone to look for the owner of the shoe. Several days later, he heard that a person named Cong Xin was chased by two wolves, which took away one of his shoes. He called Cong in and Cong claimed the shoe. The official suspected that he was the murderer. After interrogation, Cong admitted to his crime. It happened that Cong killed Ning and took his huge sum of money. Since Cong was flustered, he did not find the jewelry hidden inside Ning's clothes before the wolves took them.

聊齋誌異一百段＝100 passages from strange
stories of Liaozhai / 王娟編譯. --臺灣
初版. --臺北市：臺灣商務, 1999〔民88〕
　　面 ； 公分. -（一百叢書：31 ）

　　ISBN 957-05-1595-3（平裝）

857.27　　　　　　　　　　88008005

一百叢書 ㉛

聊齋誌異一百段

100 PASSAGES FROM STRANGE STORIES OF LIAOZHAI

定價新臺幣 350 元

編 譯 者　王　　娟
　責任編輯　金　　堅
出 版 者
印 刷 所　臺灣商務印書館股份有限公司
　　　　　臺北市重慶南路 1 段 37 號
　　　　　電話：(02) 23116118・23115538
　　　　　傳眞：(02) 23710274
　　　　　郵政劃撥：0000165-1 號
　　　　　出版事業：局版北市業字第 993 號
　　　　　登 記 證

• 1998 年 10 月香港初版第一次印刷
• 1999 年 7 月臺灣初版第一次印刷
本書經商務印書館(香港)有限公司授權出版

ISBN　957-05-1595-3（平裝）　　　　b 10061000

一百叢書　　100 SERIES

英漢　·　漢英對照

讀者回函卡

感謝您對本館的支持，為加強對您的服務，請填妥此卡，免付郵資寄回，可隨時收到本館最新出版訊息，及享受各種優惠。

姓名：_____　　　性別：□男 □女

出生日期：____年____月____日

職業：□學生　□公務（含軍警）　□家管　□服務　□金融　□製造

　　　□資訊　□大眾傳播　□自由業　□農漁牧　□退休　□其他

學歷：□高中以下（含高中）　□大專　□研究所（含以上）

地址：□□□_____

_____

電話：（H）_____（O）_____

購買書名：_____

您從何處得知本書？

　　　□書店　□報紙廣告　□報紙專欄　□雜誌廣告　□DM廣告

　　　□傳單　□親友介紹　□電視廣播　□其他

您對本書的意見？（A/滿意 B/尚可 C/需改進）

　　　內容_____　編輯_____　校對_____　翻譯_____

　　　封面設計_____　價格_____　其他_____

您的建議：_____

_____

_____

臺灣商務印書館

台北市重慶南路一段三十七號　電話：（02）23116118・23115538
讀者服務專線：080056196　傳真：（02）23710274
郵撥：0000165-1號　E-mail：cptw@ms12.hinet.net

100臺北市重慶南路一段37號

臺灣商務印書館 收

對摺寄回，謝謝！

傳統現代　並翼而翔

Flying with the wings of tradition and modernity.